KNIGHT'S WAR

AN ALICE SKYE NOVEL

BOOK FIVE

TAYLOR ASTON WHITE

LIQUID MIND PUBLISHING

Liquid Mind Publishing

THE ALICE SKYE SERIES

Witch's Sorrow

Druid's Storm

Rogue's Mercy

Elemental's Curse

Knight's War

Veil's Fall

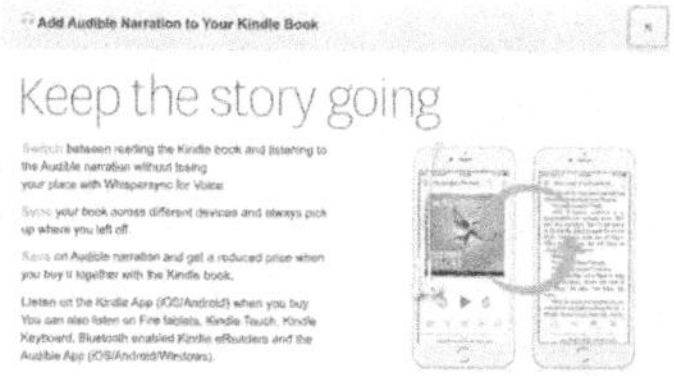

Click Here to add Audible Narration of KNIGHT'S WAR and keep the story going!

PROLOGUE

She staggered, the body she possessed physically weak, but strong in chi. She wouldn't be absorbed quickly, unlike the last one.

Her lip lifted in a snarl, her last host's body pathetically laying on the thread-bare carpet. She had been old, with wrinkles decorating her pink face and pains in joints she never knew existed.

She wouldn't have chosen her, but the old hag had been the only choice. It was either find a body, or, well, she couldn't comprehend what could have happened. In all that time alone, she didn't realise she could die.

Or could she?

It wasn't exactly something she wished to explore.

The initial feeling of terror was subsiding, her new host's soul crumbling beneath her own. It wouldn't take long before she couldn't feel the other woman anymore. Maybe a few weeks or so, depending on the tenacity of her spirit. But, for now she would be an annoying voice that begged and cried for her life. Pathetic really.

With a swift flick of the wrist she pulled off the stained fabrics, laying bare her flesh to the mirror.

It wasn't too bad, she thought as she brushed her new fingers through her auburn hair. Her skin was pale, like snow, not that she had seen snow in several millennia's. But she remembered the whiteness of it, so white it hurt her eyes. The skin would bruise easily, which meant she would need to wear long sleeves to hide the pinprick marks that tarnished the inner arms.

The ribs were visible, as was the collarbone and cheeks. At least the breasts were generous, as generous as they could be in a body so thin. It wouldn't take long to fatten the body up, to strengthen it.

Then she would begin her plan.

A plan she has had too long to prepare.

"Yes," she said aloud, enjoying the sensual purr of her own voice in a new, pretty face. "This will do nicely."

CHAPTER
ONE

Alice stared at the logo of a coffin, wondering if she should laugh or cry. It wasn't particularly sympathetic considering the reason she was there. To be fair, she would have normally found it amusing, but everything that could have gone wrong that morning, had gone wrong.

It had all started with a call to a mechanic because her beloved car had decided it wasn't interested in being a car any longer, and wanted instead to be an expensive, rusty ornament. It had resulted in her having to take public transport, which took longer than she had expected. Unfortunately her appointment wasn't close to any bus stops, which meant she had to run the rest of the way in the rain while wearing a white t-shirt and no jacket.

Her bra on full show was not exactly the attire she was expected to wear for a meeting with the officiant. She shouldn't have bothered rushing though, especially considering she had been waiting at the office of D.E.A.D. for over two hours, after waiting two months for the actual appointment. The official meeting was to deal with the Death, Estate and Assets of the true Dead. Alice didn't

realise when she lost Dread, that when a vampire died the second time around there would be so much paperwork.

You would have thought for a Breed who had technically died already, that they would have the foresight to plan better. But no, the Vamps apparently believed the grim reaper wouldn't catch up with them, and if they did everything would be dealt with through the slowest administration ever anyway.

Now when a vampire died under capital punishment, everything in their possession automatically went to their master, the vampire who originally turned them. If that person was already dust, it went to their master and so on until one of their great-grand-masters was found to be alive. Or alive as they could be being the living dead.

If there wasn't a trackable trace it went to the closest kin. It seemed pretty stupid to Alice, which was exactly what she told the receptionist when she made the appointment. Apparently it had always been that way, and it saved Bonors - the name commonly referred to vampires live-in blood donors, much to their annoyance - from making a claim against the estate.

Which meant Alice had been fighting D.E.A.D. for access to Dread's townhouse and possessions. Not only had she had to deal with mourning the man she looked to as her father, but she also had to deal with the most unhelpful Breed possible. Time apparently wasn't an issue for the almost immortals.

Vampires didn't die very often, not compared to other Breed. Which was why the selection period for new vampires was restricted to once or twice a year. If she went by the amount of young Vamps in the room she assumed the office also registered the newly turned.

A freshy to her left was still caked in mud, having spent

the evening buried somewhere to complete his transition. His eyes were dark, pupils completely dilated to cover his irises as he stared at her with a feral, hungry expression. His mouth was slightly open, new fangs peeking through while saliva dripped down to soak his shirt. Around his throat was a collar with a lead attached, the end connected to a tight fist.

"Alice Skye?" a monotone voice called from the front desk.

"Yeah," Alice replied, holding her hand up. "That's me." She ignored the growl of the newly turned beside her.

The man appraised her slowly, his face less than impressed. "Come with me."

Alice quickly followed behind, taking a seat opposite his desk in a small, windowless room. A metal name plate faced her.

"It's nice to meet you Mr Floof," Alice said with a tight smile. It wasn't a name she would have personally picked, especially as it wasn't uncommon for vampires to change their name once turned. They believed it was better to have a new name for a new life. Or death, as it were.

Mr Floof looked to be in his late fifties, with a rounded stomach and receding hairline. Fine lines cracked his pale face, wrinkles that he would have received before his turn. She assumed he was older than two-hundred in undead terms, because the age restrictions when petitioning to be transformed came into place around then. She doubted he was younger than the thirty-five cut off age, or if he was his previous life did not treat him well.

Mr Floof read from a folder on his desk, his eyes slowly moving from one side of the sheet of paper to the other.

"So..." she began.

He held up his index finger, his attention still on the paperwork.

Heat spiked in her chest, her cheeks flushing as she held her response back. Usually Tinkerbell would have popped into existence at her sudden anger, but she had been learning to control her outbursts. Her power was connected to her emotions, so she had been training with Riley and The Guardians to control it. She no longer risked burning down a building when she was outraged, but that didn't mean her patience was infinite.

"Just to confirm," Mr Floof said in his flat voice, "that you are here to discuss the assets of one Nahaliel Dread?"

Alice nodded. "That is why I'm here, yes."

"I'm sure you're aware that protocol is for everything in Mr Dread's possession to be passed onto his master. If no clan master, or master's master can be tracked it would go to next of kin. You are neither." He held up his finger once again when she began to speak. "You are not legally adopted, therefore not classed as kin. In fact, when I was writing up the paperwork I discovered you were declared dead between the ages of six to eighteen."

Alice waited for him to drop his hand. "Wow, that's weird," she replied in the same monotone voice. "Must have been an error." It wasn't, she was technically declared dead. Dread had thought it was the safest option, then when she turned eighteen she decided to correct it, wanting to use her family name as an adult rather than the fake one she went by as a child.

Mr Floof narrowed his eyes. "It was... curious."

"So, have you found his master?" Dread had never mentioned the person who turned him, and she had never asked. "Who?" she continued before he could answer.

"That's confidential information."

"But you've found them?" *Shit.* "Where does that leave me?"

He shuffled the paperwork, staring down at his notes before he replied. "Normally you would be advised there was nothing we could do. The protocols came into place for a reason to protect my kind from... vultures."

She raised an eyebrow. "Are you saying I'm a vulture?"

He immediately looked down, shuffling his papers as he cleared his throat. She was confident that if he had recently fed, his face would have flushed with embarrassment. "No, no, that wasn't what I was saying. However, you are not kin so you do not inherit any wealth or property."

She never wanted his wealth or property, but she knew there was something he would have left her to find. "There needs to be..."

He held up another finger, and she forced herself not to break it. "Let me finish, please."

Alice bit back her reply.

"It's an unusual situation, but the new owner has put forward that you be given temporary access to Mr Dread's property."

"Really?"

Why would they do that?

"Yes, but only so you can collect your personal belongings under supervision."

Alice thought his response through. "What do you mean supervision?"

"A representative for the estate will be in contact. It's not down to us here at D.E.A.D. to facilitate."

"But..."

"Our time is up, Miss Skye," Mr Floof said with a fake curve to his cheek. "I hope you take the time to fill out our survey. It helps us improve our service."

With a loud snap his hand blurred, and a red stamp marked his paperwork.

THE BELL CHIMED when she pushed the door open into the garage, the smell of oil and petrol assaulting her nose immediately. A red SUV was high on the service lift, a man hidden beneath in a hole.

"Hello?" she called as she stepped further inside and scanned the small area for her car. She found it at the back, the pale blue beetle covered in rust and a few scratches. Mostly put there on purpose to try and keep the car running with enchantments and wards. They didn't work, but the aesthetic looked interesting.

"Who's there?" the man said, popping his head up to frown at Alice. His caramel skin was darkened with smears of black, his overalls more grey than the original blue. "Can I help you?"

"I'm here to pick up my car?"

"Oh, you the bug?" he gestured to her rust bucket. "You should really stop with all that magic crap. It doesn't work, not with that much metal." He sniffed, brushing his arm across his face to wipe some of the muck away. "Those spells or runes, or whatever they're called are just crap."

She knew the metal would interfere with spells, but not wards which was what she had used. Even though they still hadn't worked.

"Is my car okay?" she asked instead of responding. His chi was lacklustre which made him human, and therefore someone who didn't understand.

The man grunted as he stepped out of the hole, wiping his hands on a dirty rag. "Define okay? I got it back up and

running again, but I would think about scrapping her. She's barely road legal and she's going to cost you some pretty pennies when she keeps breaking down."

"Shit." Alice dropped her shoulders. She loved her car, even when it was being temperamental. "It's all I can afford right now."

"It's just a suggestion," he muttered as he popped into a glass office, coming back with some paperwork in his hand. "This time it was just the battery, but another time it may be something more serious. I also had to replace the two front tyres which I've added to the invoice at the bottom."

"Great," Alice sighed as she accepted the paperwork. "Just great."

CHAPTER TWO

Her car spluttered to a stop outside Riley's, the late morning sun washing over the house on the outskirts of the city with a welcoming glow. It was the beginning of summer, the temperature cool, but comfortable as she stepped out, closing her eyes to feel the wind in her hair.

Her phone had remained silent on the drive over, no calls or texts as she waited with little patience for the representative to make contact. She had no interest in Dread's money, or even the townhouse. She wanted memories. He was her father figure for almost two decades, yet due to a ridiculous law she wasn't able to access the house she lived in from six to eighteen.

"That's one piece of crap," a voice beside her muttered.

Alice held back her flinch as she opened her eyes, settling her attention on Sythe as he judged her car with open interest. As she had spent more and more time there, she had begun to realise just how dangerous The Guardians were, especially when their speed and agility made them virtually silent.

"Yeah, well it's my piece of crap," she replied as she

tightened her fist around her keys. "Leave my car alone, she's been through enough today."

"Your exhaust sounds funny," he said, his heavy boots silent on the driveway as he walked the circumference of her car.

"It's fine, the mechanic said so."

Sythe shook his head with a frown. "You're late for training, he's already down at the clearing." Without another word he walked away, heading behind the house.

With one last look at her car she walked towards the surrounding trees, following the dirt path. As soon as the thick branches covered her in shadow she calmed. She was, and always would be an earth witch, regardless of her increasing ability in arcane. Someone who was attuned to nature in such a way that she craved the surrounding green. She wanted to sink her toes into the earth, and feel the roots beneath her feet.

It didn't take her long to find the clearing, a large flattened circle that was surrounded by trees for privacy. To the left was a handmade wooden obstacle course, while the rest of the space was used for sparring. Both Titus and Axel were running through, trying to beat each other's time in a blur too fast for her to distinguish. Riley met her eyes as soon as she appeared, a slow smile curling his lips.

"Appointment go well?" he asked, arms crossing to drop her attention down to his naked chest. Small bursts of sunlight broke through the canopy of leaves above, glittering across his skin.

"Am I interrupting something?" she replied with a smirk. "You seem to be all in various stages of undress."

"We run hot," Axel chuckled, smacking his palm over his own naked chest while Titus shook his head.

"I assume your appointment with D.E.A.D overran, so

we don't have much time," Riley began, his head subtly shifting to face his men. "You know what to do."

Alice knew he wanted to ask her how it went, but he also knew she wouldn't want to discuss it in front of Titus or Axel. Not something so personal.

With a sigh she dropped her bag to the earth before she held out her arm.

The warmth in her hand was familiar and strong. It crackled as it grew with barely any effort until her arm was completely encased in blue flames licked with green.

"Do it again," Riley said with a sensual smirk that caused her stomach to knot in excitement.

Unable to stop her tongue from darting out to lick her dry lips she released her energy, only to repeat the same motion of the fire climbing up her arm once again. Riley's eyes narrowed, following her tongue at her accidental tease.

"Do it again," he growled, voice deepening.

"This is becoming uncomfortable," Titus murmured, arms crossed against his chest. He leant against a tree, his knee bent as the wind played with his pale shoulder-length hair. "It's clear her powers are developing far quicker than we anticipated."

"No shit," Axel chuckled beside him. "She can hold onto that arcane longer than any witch I have ever seen. Fuck, I bet she can give you a run for your money, Tit."

Titus snarled. "Call me that again, pretty boy," he threatened. "Just because she has the power, doesn't mean she has the experience."

"Is there a reason they're here?" Alice asked when she flicked a glance to her right.

"You need to be trained by different styles of instructors," Riley replied. "And they need to learn patience."

"Patience?" Axel muttered. "Patience my arse."

Patience? she mentally added. *That's a bit bloody rude.*

Riley chuckled as if he knew exactly what she thought. "Axel, you ready?"

Axel stretched, then immediately jumped into the makeshift circle. "Ready to eat dirt, my little doomsday?" He grinned, holding his hands out as arcane coated his fingertips.

"Bring it on, pretty boy," she said, using the same nickname Titus had just used.

His grin tightened, his dark eyebrows coming low over deep green eyes. In a flash he threw a bolt of arcane, the purple sphere dissipating at her feet as she jumped out of the way with a gasp.

"So slow," he taunted, readying another.

Alice steadied her legs just as he threw a larger sphere, the arcane burning across her flesh before she was able to rebound it back.

"That's more like it," Riley clapped.

A high pitched hum in the distance, beating in intervals like a drum.

Bom. Bom. Bom. Bom.

"Watch out!"

Alice moved out of the way of the bolt just in time, the purple ball hitting the tree directly behind her.

"Sorry," she said, shaking her head to clear the noise. "Let's go again."

What the bloody hell was that?

She managed to dodge every bolt, returning some with her own blast of arcane. Her chi pulsated, energised as she tested its strength. Witches were restricted in their magic, their chi's only able to stretch so much before they needed to recover. Alice was different, the closest to the original

Elementals who each brandished a single element. Over time and a millennia of breeding, witches once singular powers mixed amongst the elements and diluted. Yet, Alice still held the strength from her ancestors power. It was supposed to be a gift, yet it felt like a curse.

Who really wanted to be in a prophecy for the end of the world?

Bom. Bom. Bom. Bom.

A pop of pressure forced her head to turn, the drum-beat hum increasing in pitch until her ears ached.

Fire burned across her torso before she fell against a tree, her head snapping back onto the bark with a crack.

"Alice?" Riley called as he jumped over the clearing, his hand reaching out to touch her face. "Are you..."

Wild magic woke up inside her, electric as it snapped out in a blast of lightning to send Riley flying across the circle. Riley twisted mid-air, landing in a crouch with his fist smashed into the earth.

Chest tight, Alice controlled her breathing as the wild magic wreaked havoc inside her chi, wanting her to turn, to move.

Bom. Bom. Bom. Bom.

"Superhero landing," she said, sucking in a breath. "Cool."

"What the fuck was that?" Axel asked, jaw dropped. "Was that just wild magic? How the fuck can you use wild magic?"

"Are you part Fae?" Titus added as he cautiously approached, eyes warily watching her arms that instinctively covered in blue flames.

She ignored them as Riley appeared in front of her, his mouth set in a grim line. "Are you okay?" she asked as the

wild magic teased along her fingertips until she recalled all her magic. She hadn't been able to call the wild magic since the trials, having thought it had gone dormant since she had been working with Peyton to try and remove their familiar connection.

What made it suddenly come back?

She couldn't feel Peyton, which meant he hadn't opened the bond they shared, a bond they had struggled to remove. Apparently witch, Fae pairings were supposed to be impossible. Which meant there wasn't much information on how to break the connection.

"That was... unexpected," Titus murmured.

Riley flashed her a look of concern. "How long has it been back?"

"Back?" Axel screeched. "What do you mean back? How can she have wild magic? How is it not ripping her apart?"

Alice watched their lips move with a frown, but was unable to concentrate on the words. Pressure built in her head as the hum continued.

Bom. Bom. Bom. Bom.

It eased when she turned towards the forest, even more so when she started walking forward, then running.

"Alice?" a voice shouted behind her as she ran.

Trusting her reflexes to not trip over any debris on the forest floor she vaulted past the trees, feeling Riley running smoothly beside her a minute later. He said nothing, silently following her until she saw a glint through the heavy bush.

"Shit."

She skidded to a stop, the high-pitched hum becoming increasingly uncomfortable the closer she became. In the centre of the forest was an iridescent transparent oval,

partially covered by a dead bush. Part of it burned through a tree, leaving the hole in the charred trunk.

"What's that?" she asked, able to see Riley through the oval as he carefully walked around it. It distorted his image, like a pool with ripples.

"It's a portal," he replied as Axel and Titus appeared from behind the trees. "Fae."

"What's a Fae portal doing here?" Axel asked with a frown.

"It looks broken," Titus added.

Bom. Bom. Bom. Bom.

"I can... feel it," Alice murmured, mainly to herself as the wild magic danced along with the hum.

Riley's arm wrapped around her waist, his attention on the spectrum of colours that seemed to just float in the air. Every few seconds a random rune would flash beside it, disappearing as fast as it appeared, but not before it scorched the bark further.

"Search the grounds, something may have come through."

Axel and Titus immediately followed Riley's order.

"Is the gateway not supposed to be here?"

Riley took a second to reply, his fingers entwining with hers. "No. If there's a door, it means there's a tear in the veil. And when there's a tear, there is usually something here that shouldn't be."

"Of course there is," she said, deadpan. "Because that's all we need."

Riley chuckled. "I'll have a look around, see if there's something going on that we need to be made aware about." He laid a kiss against her neck before he began to tug her back towards the house. "Am I seeing you tonight?"

Alice angled her head so he could easily claim another

kiss. They were officially dating, at least, that was what the magazines had speculated ever since The Wharf. Not that either of them had confirmed or denied it.

Their feelings were new, strange so they had decided to take it slow, the stress of both their lives making it difficult to be normal.

She craved him. Which scared her.

Yet, just being near him made her excited, her chi electric as it brushed against his.

"So, sweetheart?" he pressed when they broke out into the open.

Alice turned so her lips brushed his, just a soft contact that caused him to suck in a sharp breath, a growl rumbling his throat. "You know I'm busy."

"Mmmm." He leant down for one last kiss.

"I fixed it," a voice interrupted. "It sounds better now," Sythe said from beside her car.

Alice pulled back. "What do you mean, fixed it?"

Sythe stood, his grin growing as he attempted to rub the black substance that covered his hand down his shirt. "I've figured out why the exhaust was making weird noises and fixed it. It's only temporary though as I didn't have the right tools. To be honest, I would replace the whole thing."

Riley grunted. "Sythe, I need you to go find Axel and Titus."

Sythe's smile immediately dropped, his eyes shimmering silver as his beast peeked through. "Sire."

Alice waited for him to leave before she approached her car, unable to see any difference. "I don't know how you all live together." She could barely deal with Sam spontaneously bursting into the bathroom with gossip while she was in the shower. She couldn't imagine having to share with six others.

Riley patted the roof. "They have their own places, but choose to stay here. It calms our beasts to be close to one another," he shrugged, as if he was talking about the weather and not mystical creatures for which they shared their souls. "You get used to it."

CHAPTER THREE

Alice skimmed her finger across the handwritten letter, feeling each dent of the pen. Sam had placed it with the rest of the post in his newly handmade rack, assuming it was just another bill. To be fair, from far away it looked like a bill, the envelope nondescript with just her details printed on the front. She wouldn't have noticed if it wasn't for her icing disaster. It was when she was cleaning she noticed the envelope was thick, expensive compared to the usual bills.

Miss Skye,

The letter began.

I apologise for the delay in getting this to you. Due to the unusual circumstances of my clients death The Elders have only just released the relevant paperwork.

To confirm, Nahaliel Dread, of his own Master, has now

been registered as true dead. He advised me that in the event of his death you will be given this key.

My deepest condolences,

L.R.Spencer
Spencer & Harvey

The key was gold, heavy but thin, too thin to be used in a normal lock. The bow was in the shape of an eye, the pupil cut out and replaced with red glass.

"What's that?" Sam asked a few seconds after the front door slammed shut. "And why is there icing everywhere? Did any actually get on the cake?"

Alice held the key up further, looking through glass.

"And I ask again," he murmured as he moved closer, placing his work bag on the kitchen counter beside the mountain of washing up she had yet to do. "What's that?"

"It's from Dread. It was supposed to be sent to me when he died, but was delayed due to, well, you know."

"Overlord? Bloody hell. Why would he send you a key?" Sam scanned the letter. "No other notes?"

"No, that's it." She had checked. "Hopefully I'll know more when I visit his place."

"You got access?" Sam rested his chin on the top of her head, his arms wrapping around her shoulders. A gentle purr vibrated his chest, the immediate sensation comforting. "Wait, did you just say visit?"

"Apparently." She patted his hand, feeling him sink his nose into her hair. "I received a message when I got home

to meet a representative of the estate at his place tomorrow morning."

"Vampire laws are stupid." He pulled back, tilting his head to the side. Eyes wide he shooshed her, flicking off the light in the kitchen before he grabbed the matches from the drawer.

Alice grinned, anticipation racing through her bloodstream as she flicked off the living room lights too and held her breath, Sam following quickly behind.

If she couldn't control herself, he would hear, and then it would be ruined.

She had to time it perfectly.

Waiting, she caught Sam's attention from across the room, his eyes reflective in the freshly lit candle light.

You ready? she asked with a tilt of her head.

He sniggered and wiggled his eyebrows. *I was born ready, baby.*

Light footsteps on the path before a knock on the front door. Alice knelt down behind the sofa, muscles tensed as she waited for it to open.

Another knock, slightly louder before the handle squeaked, and Kyle pushed the front door open an inch. His emerald green eyes narrowed, sweeping across the living room to settle on Poe, who watched him with fascination from the kitchen doorway.

"Meow."

Alice waited as patiently as she could, a grin creasing her cheeks.

"HAPPY BIRTHDAY!" Alice and Sam shouted in unison, jumping up from their hiding spots.

In a blur the cake erupted from Sam's outstretched hand, hitting the ceiling with a squelch. They all stood silent, the cake sticking. A few candles had dropped to the

floor, while others were missing, probably still attached to the cake.

"Shit!" Sam began to stamp on the candles that were still alight. "Kyle, what the fuck?"

Kyle stood still, face flushed with a fist covered in blue icing. His eyes teased red, the outsides of his irises ringed with black. Shoulders tight he walked through into the kitchen, the back door slamming shut a second later.

"What's up with him?" Sam asked just as the cake fell from the ceiling. It splatted against the floor, exploding into a pile of icing and candles that decorated everything within a two foot radius, including Poe.

"Meow."

He didn't seem to mind as he began to lick at his paws, attention settling on the mountain of mush with an excited gleam in his multicoloured eyes.

"Kyle?" she called through the back door, hoping he hadn't disappeared after his outburst. "What was that about?"

Kyle stood on the grass, arms crossed with his hands digging into his skin hard enough she could see the red marks left by his nails.

Alice took a deep breath as she stepped out into the garden, the movement-sensitive light flashing on to wash over them with a pale light.

"Kyle? Are we just going to ignore what just happened?" He had only just started to regularly visit, their bond raw, but growing. "It was only a birthday cake." She had even baked it herself. It had taken her three hours and two attempts, the first she had burnt and not even two cases of ready-made icing could save it. The second she was proud of, even if it was slightly wonky. Okay, it was very wonky,

but it wasn't like it would be noticed now it decorated the entirety of her living room and cat.

"I don't celebrate my life," he said, so quietly she wasn't sure if the reply was for her.

"I wanted to celebrate your life." It was a good idea at the time, to celebrate his first birthday free and together. A new memory.

"If you knew what I've done, you wouldn't want to," he murmured, the wind playing with his dark hair. He had allowed it to grow, the length almost at his shoulders compared to his usual self-hack job. "I shouldn't celebrate my life, when I was the reason they lost theirs."

Alice hesitantly approached, her hand reaching out to touch his shoulder. His muscles were hard beneath her fingertips, but he didn't move away. She wanted more than anything to wrap her arms around him, tell him it would be okay. But she knew he didn't like to be touched, even from blood who loved him.

"Tell me."

He closed his eyes. "I've killed people, lots of people."

"Kyle..."

"I see their faces when I close my eyes, every single one." His voice tightened. "I was good at it, The Master's pet executioner." He turned, his eyes filled with unshed tears before he dropped his chin. "I don't deserve to be standing here."

"No, you don't get to do this," she snapped, forcing his attention on her. "You don't get to wallow in undeserved blame. You carry all this guilt over something that was out of your control."

"I..."

"No." She dropped her hand to move in front of him,

wary of his flinch. "It wasn't your fault. You were a child, manipulated by dark magic and abuse."

"I killed them Alice." His voice cracked. "And I didn't even hesitate."

"You're a victim just as much as they were." She made sure she kept eye contact, made sure he could see the truth in her words. "You survived him, Kyle. Instead of living with this crushing guilt, live knowing the man who forced you to do those things, who chained you like a creature isn't even dust. He's gone, and he's not coming back."

A single tear fell down his cheek.

"There is no point wallowing in the past," she quietly added. "Especially one as shit as ours."

"If I didn't know better, I would say you were the older sibling." He looked up, eyes widening before a ghost of a smile curved his lips. "What's that?"

Alice self-consciously touched her head, only just remembering the children's party hat. It was too small, and the elastic string cut into her jaw.

She couldn't stop her laugh. "I bought party poppers and a banner too."

"I'm sorry about the cake." His eyebrows drew together.

She tried to adjust the string, but it fell off her finger and snapped back. "Ow."

She heard a cackle from inside the house.

"Shut it Sam!"

"Well maybe you should have bought bigger hats," he mused. "I came over to update you on your stalkers."

"You mean the secret society that doesn't exist?" She rolled her eyes at his disapproving look. It was true, they didn't technically exist, she had looked. "Can we not just celebrate your birthday without any drama?"

All she wanted was just one night without a problem.

One night to wear a stupid hat and eat cake with no talk about training or work. One night where the end of the world wasn't a shadow that stalked her every move.

"You know we can't. It's not like they're going to have a day off. The Knights are professionals."

"Professional?" she mused. "Professional what, exactly?"

Kyle gave her a morose smile. "Assassins."

Ah, she thought. *That made sense.*

"Well, they're doing a shit job, aren't they." Alice let out a long breath. "I haven't noticed anyone, not in a while." She had been careful since her not-so-friendly encounter with The Knights last psychopath, Chester. He had made her aware that they wanted her dead, just not yet.

Having an unknown deadline regarding your own demise wasn't entirely helpful.

"Shit." With an annoyed huff she moved to sit in a wooden chair, pulling her legs up to curl beneath her.

"I've tracked them and they seem centralised down south, but I have yet to find out where."

"Then what?" she asked, turning to him. The moon bounced off his too-pale face, making him look ghostly with his dark hair and continuously changing eyes. "Ask them politely to stop?" She chuckled, putting on a high-pitched girly voice. "Oh please don't kill me, I'm a good girl, I promise!"

Lines appeared around his mouth. "No, but I can't just sit here and do nothing while they're still a threat to you."

Alice remained silent, unsure what to say. She could have had a normal life, but no, she had to be a fucking horseman of the apocalypse. That shit didn't have a walk-through.

"You found out any more about being War?" he asked,

crouching beside her. Alice picked at the armrest. "I can barely find any information on it other than the poem." She knew as much as she needed about being an Elemental, someone who was born with the power of her ancestors, the original Dracos, but knew little about being War.

"It's not a widely known thing, maybe only those who have studied the history of witches would have even heard of it. It's an ancient foretelling that's been translated so many times I doubt it's even the original poem. But that doesn't make it any less true."

The conversation irritated her. "I'm working on it, okay?"

"Hmm." Kyle moved to the seat opposite, resting his palms flat down on the table. "What about Riley?"

Alice slanted her eyes to him. "What about him?"

"Why isn't he here?"

"You wanted me to invite my boy..." she caught herself with a frown. Boyfriend wasn't the right word for him, their relationship was too intense for such a simple word.

Kyle tilted his head, deciding not to comment. "You have a bruise on your arm."

Alice automatically looked down at the small mark on her skin. "I fell into a tree." Which wasn't a lie.

He narrowed his eyes. "Anything else?"

She straightened, her arms tightening on the chair. "What's that supposed to mean?"

"Who wants cake?" Sam shouted from the doorway, three plates balanced in his hands. "Now it has been scraped from the floor, and maybe half eaten by Alice's pussy. But, it still tastes good."

"Sam!" Alice smiled, but didn't look away from Kyle. She wasn't sure where he was going with that conversation, but it wasn't good.

Sam broke into her eyeline, his amber eyes wide in warning. They said one word.

Don't.

Clenching her jaw she accepted the plate he held out, turning her attention to the blue blob in the centre. She didn't want to argue with her brother, especially not on his birthday. She knew Kyle was finding it difficult adjusting to his freedom, and she wasn't sure how she could make it easier for him. She guessed allowing him to be an overprotective big brother was a start.

"Thanks," Kyle mumbled with a frown as Sam placed his slice on the table in front of him. Careful not to accidentally touch him.

"Cheers!" Sam shouted, holding his spoon in the air. "To fucked up parties! Because nothing in this house is ever simple."

Alice smiled once again, this time genuine. "To Kyle," she said as she held up her own spoon in a salute.

Kyle shook his head, a smirk playing on his lips. "To fucked up birthdays."

CHAPTER
FOUR

"You've got to be shitting me!" Alice kicked at a stone, sending it across the driveway just as Danton pulled up. The stone hit the side of his expensive looking car, and from the narrowing of his eyes he thought it was on purpose. It wasn't, but she wasn't going to deny it. "What are you doing here D?"

Danton took his time to get out, his pale face even more ashen than usual.

"Tell me this isn't some sick joke?" she continued when he just stood there. "Tell me you're not the representative?"

"Ma petite..."

"No." Wind whipped at her hair, obscuring her vision before she tugged it behind her ears.

"I'm sorry..."

"No!" she barked once again, the word loud and harsh enough to shock even her. Heat burned across her chest and up her throat, her anger almost physical enough to breathe fire. "Don't you dare."

"I will not stand here and defend my actions," he

quipped back, his accent clear. "Not to you. But I'm the only person who can accompany you into this house."

"Why only you?" She knew she was being unreasonable, blaming him for the actions of Dread. D hadn't forced him to attack a Councilman. But she could never forget how D followed the execution without a second thought. Obeying his Mistress with zero hesitation on a man who had been his mentor, who had been his friend.

No, she couldn't forgive him.

"Parce que ma puissante sorcière, without me you wouldn't have access at all." He looked at his heavy boots with a frown, his dark hair slicked back from his face so tight that it didn't even budge at the movement. "Laisse moi faire ça. Let me do this for you." He looked up, jaw clenched.

A sharp reply caught on her tongue, but instead she snapped her mouth shut. Eyes burning, she looked away to blink, concentrating on the beautiful wisteria that crept up the front of the townhouse. She knew exactly where the hidden cameras were, expertly entwined into the foliage. The place may look like an upscale townhouse in the expensive part of the human district, but in reality it had been home to a powerful vampire ever since it was first built. Dread had also bought the neighbouring property, allowing him complete privacy in the quiet street since the early twentieth century.

"I made a deal with the new owner so you could be here, but only once. Only for today."

Alice sucked in a breath. "Why?"

"Because you deserve everything that was in his name. But, vampire laws are old, as are the Breed that created them. I may not agree with it, but it is what it is."

"Did Dread's assets go to his maker?" she asked.

Danton shook his head, his dark eyes trailing across her features. “Non.”

With that one reply she knew he wouldn’t answer anymore of her questions, and to be honest, she didn’t care who inherited it all. Not really. It was all just things. Inanimate objects to collect dust.

“What has Valentina got to say about this?”

D’s eyes hardened before he quickly looked away. “We should not speak of the Mistress, ma petite sorcière.”

“Why?” she asked, pushing him. “Isn’t her hand up your arse?”

A growl escaped his throat. “You are too young to understand the decision I’ve made to be here. The loyalties earned. I choose to stand beside her.”

Alice laughed, the sound hollow. “Sure you do.”

“Putain d'enfer, be careful Alice. She’s still a councilman, one who has more power and influence than you know. She’s fascinated, sees a lot of herself in you.”

“That’s a joke, right?”

“I would stay away from her.”

Alice heard the warning. “She doesn’t know you’re doing this, does she?” His silence was deafening. “Fine, shall we get this started?”

With a shallow nod he followed her into the large, open planned space. The air was thick with dust, the place stale, vacant. Glass crunched beneath her boots as she made her way further inside, her eyes sweeping across the chaos that was left of the once pristine living room.

“I’m sorry, I didn’t realise,” D quietly murmured.

Reaching up Alice grabbed a broken frame from the wall, smiling at the photograph of herself and Dread in front of a large red door, a quiet smile on her young face and the usual scowl on his.

"It's okay," she replied, pulling the photograph out from beneath the broken shards and into in her satchel. She knew the Officers from the Department of Magic & Mystery had been inside, had assumed that it wasn't a friendly visit.

"Is there something specific you're after?" he asked a while later.

She had wandered through the first floor, almost in a daze as she took in the smashed TV, overturned sofa and cracked walls. Blood still splattered across the dark oak flooring, assumingly from the Officer that first confronted Dread. She had the biggest urge to put everything right, to clean up the mess. She had even caught herself fluffing pillows until D shot her a confused look.

"I want to know what Dread was up to... before."

"Before?"

"He was searching for something, and I need to know what."

Danton followed tightly behind as she brushed her fingers across the large floor to ceiling bookcase that took up the whole left side. It held thousands of books, mostly foreign. Alice paused, her finger touching the familiar groove three books from the wall. She glanced behind her shoulder, wondering if D would give her privacy. When he crossed his arms across his chest, face stoic she pressed the button, watching his expression turn to surprise as the bookcase moved with a exhale of air, revealing stairs leading down.

"This isn't in the plans."

Alice smiled at his raised eyebrow. "Dread liked to keep his office private." So private that the builders who created the soundproof basement were paid generously for their secrecy.

The office below was essentially a soundproof metal

box, around a third of the size of the floor above and looked basic in comparison. It compromised of yet more shelves, a desk with a computer and a wall of screens that displayed footage from the various security cameras that surrounded the property. She had never been allowed to play down there as a child, but sometimes when Dread worked late she would sit on a pillow in the corner, reading. Her books were still on the bottom shelf of his desk, dust and grime a thick layer on the once colourful covers.

She hadn't been down there in years, not since she had moved out at eighteen. Various files piled high in the corner where she used to sit. One, placed at the top and written in perfect calligraphy stated '*War.*'

"What was the old man up to?" Danton murmured, studying the computer.

Alice ignored him, her attention on the thick plastic file that contained loose sheets of paper as well as a leather journal. She picked up the journal, opening to the first page to study Dread's handwriting.

"Hey, look at this," D said as he moved the mouse beside the computer. He clicked a button, rewinding the CCTV footage.

Alice dropped the journal back into the red file, bringing it with her to sit at the desk. Taking over from D she watched the screens flash through the past, slowing it down after Dread's arrest, watching carefully for any change. Dread seemed to stay down in his office for the majority, the one room that wasn't covered. Roughly a week before his death, a figure appeared on his drive.

"How did he get there?" she asked, trying to figure out how the man suddenly appeared. She clicked frame to frame.

"Putain d'anges déchus!"

"What?"

He shook his head, muttering to himself before he pressed his finger to the black shadow on the screen. "Fallen angel."

"Fallen angel?" She had never heard of them.

"Watch," Danton said, urging her to repeat the footage. "There." Alice paused at his shout, confused even when he pointed at the shadow behind the man that was there in one frame, and gone the next. "Wings."

Alice clicked through the frames once again, watching as the shadow behind the man disappeared into his back. They didn't look like wings, but she didn't have time to argue. The footage continued, Dread meeting the man at the front door, the first time he had left his office in days.

"Who are you?" she asked the man as he clasped Dread's elbow in a familiar greeting. "What's a fallen angel?"

"Exactly like it sounds."

"I've never heard..."

"They would have been mentioned in training, but they're not a registered Breed. They're incredibly rare and keep to themselves which would be why you wouldn't have come across any." D frowned, tapping at the screen on the top right with a fingernail. "When was this?"

Alice looked up. "That's the live feed."

"Merde, that means we're not alone."

"Shit." Alice clicked back all the live screens.

"Looks like there's three," he said with a tilt of his head.

"Friends of yours, or mine?" She didn't recognise the two men and one woman who had broken through the front door, but that didn't mean anything. They wore all black and were armed to the teeth, their weapons on clear

display. "I don't think they're mine." The Knights were usually more subtle.

"Non, they're mine," he growled, fist tightening. "We need to leave, now."

Alice watched the invaders split up, heading in different directions in the house. "Who are they?"

"They're a warning."

"A warning? A warning for what?"

Danton ignored the question. "If I don't deal with them, they could become a problem."

Alice glanced back at the screen, noting how one man, which looked to be the leader, brandished a gun while the two others held large knives. "So they're not a problem now?"

"Morceau de merde," he muttered to the figure on the screen. "Can they get down here?"

Alice checked the switch. "Unlikely." Not unless they knew how to open the door.

"They shouldn't have known I was even in the city."

Alice circled her arms around the file, holding it to her chest. "What you thinking?"

Danton's Adam's apple bobbed as he swallowed, dark eyes widening when he turned. "Level red."

"Great, just great." Alice called her chi, feeling the power thrum through to her fingertips. The traffic light system was used to determine the danger of Paladin contracts. Green was classed as the simplest, amber was classed as a higher risk while red meant possible death. Danton was warning her that his visitors weren't there for a friendly talk. "You ready?"

D tensed, his attention back on the screens. "You take the woman, I'll take the other two."

Alice hugged the file closer, her arms anchored. "Seems a bit sexist."

"They're all Vamps."

"Oh, fucking hell." She hated Vamps, they were a pain in the arse with their superior speed and strength. Even as a Paladin she wouldn't be given a Vamp contract unless she was partnered with one.

The door slipped open silently, allowing them to enter back into the living room without notice. Alice set down her file, pushing it with her foot into a safe corner. The plastic sliding across the wooden floor would have been loud enough to alert the waiting Vamps, their hearing the best of all Breed.

Danton pointed to the stairs while he turned towards the front reception room. There was no point in staying quiet, not when they could pinpoint her position with sound alone. So Alice rushed up the stairs, stopping at the top just as the female smirked from her old bedroom doorway.

"Ciao," the woman greeted with a smile full of teeth. Her fangs elongated, making it hard for her to close her red-painted lips.

Alice knew very little Italian, but she knew 'ciao' meant both hello and goodbye, and she could guess which one the woman meant. A blade glittered in her hand.

"We can talk about this," Alice said, hands held out in submission, her fingertips burning, ready.

A knife blurred, but Alice had been training with The Guardians. Able to feel the air shift, Alice moved to the side, the cold metal only just missing.

"Ventilabis!" A wall of flame pushed forward, throwing the woman with a bang against the banister. With one leg Alice kicked out, sending her down the stairs with a crash.

"Figlio di puttana!" The woman scrambled to her feet with a growl.

D appeared behind her, blood dried to his face. Without a word he grabbed her head, breaking her neck in one clean move. Alice sucked in a breath, even knowing a broken neck wouldn't kill a vampire. But it would leave her incapacitated until she healed.

"Danton," a deep voice sang, the Italian accent thick. The leader stepped into view, his gun trained towards D's chest.

"Matteo," D nodded. "It's been a long time."

Matteo's smiled tightened when he looked at the women collapsed on the floor. "Luca?"

"Your other man is gone," Danton answered, tone like steel. "You shouldn't have come here."

"You know this isn't personal."

"Seems pretty personal to me," Alice muttered, taking her place beside Danton.

Matteo shifted his attention to her, eyes narrowing. "A strega, interessante."

"What do you want, Matteo?"

Matteo snapped back to D, Alice forgotten. "Salvadore wants his rightful position as head of The Elders."

"Mistress would never allow it."

"Which is why I'm here," he grinned. "Valentina has been in reign for too long. It's time for someone else to rule Europe, but first her soldier must go." He pulled the trigger.

"ARMA!" Alice's aura pulsed, her shield forming around them a milli-second too late. The bullet pierced Danton's stomach, a sea of red growing from his centre. He collapsed to his knees, hand clutching his wound.

"Wood," he coughed, blood bubbling from his mouth.

"Shit. Shit. Shit." A normal bullet wouldn't kill a

vampire, not unless it shredded their heart. But wood could. Alice dropped to her knees beside him, pulling his hands away to look at the wound.

A laugh echoed.

"ADOLEBITQUE!" Alice flung her arm out blindly, her attention on Danton. A yelp before something smashed against the shield. But it held, her aura strong.

"You'll be seeing me again, Danton. Non è finite!" Matteo snarled.

D ignored him. "Ma petite... get it out!"

"Fuck sake." She carefully put her fingers in the bullet hole, feeling around for the bullet. "Stay calm and still."

"Tu essaies de rester calme," he replied, voice strained.

"Ah, it's only a little bullet hole," Alice smiled, trying to make him feel better. "Isn't it lucky you have no risk of infection?"

It was one of the reasons she was removing the bullet straight away, rather than in a sterile room. Vampires were resilient, once she removed the wood, Danton would heal enough that it wouldn't risk his life.

Her finger squelched, Danton tensing as she touched the bullet. "Ah, there it is."

D moaned as she cautiously pulled the bullet out, careful to not irritate the pieces she could feel inside. The bullet had hit bone, splintering on impact.

"You need to go to the hospital." The wood would no longer poison his system, but he still needed the rest removed. The bullet thudded to the floor when she dropped it, surprisingly heavy. It was a metal slug surrounded in oak, a specialised bullet.

"Hmmmm." Danton climbed to his feet, his skin wet with both perspiration and blood. "I need.."

Alice held out her wrist, looking away as his fangs

struck. It wasn't the first time she had given an emergency feed. She closed her eyes, trying to ignore the euphoric sensation that was rushing through her bloodstream. Vampire saliva released a pheromone, tricking their victim into believing their bite was pleasure rather than pain. The tingles felt good, great even, a feeling that many blood junkies craved. The idea that people were addicted to the sensation of a blood kiss made her uncomfortable.

His fangs released, a warm tongue licking across the bite a second later. "Merci."

Alice pulled her wrist back to her chest, not needing to check that D had healed the bite completely, leaving no evidence. Convenient, really.

"Matteo will be back, he needs to send my Mistress a message."

Alice checked to make sure Matteo was indeed gone when her eyes settled on the body beside her file.

Ah, she thought. *That must be Luca.*

"Killing her soldier would make a statement."

His lips tightened at the name. "Oui."

Alice stepped past the dead vampire, his body already beginning to decay as she picked up the file. She didn't care for politics, Vamp or any other. But she couldn't just leave him.

"Do you need help?"

The question caught D off guard. He bowed, a slight hiss escaping his lips as the splinters in his gut dug into flesh. "You honour me, but this is no business for a witch."

"Well then," she murmured picking up the file. "I recommend you wear a bullet-proof vest next time."

CHAPTER FIVE

Alice was greeted by Sam's distinctive chuckle, his legs draped over the side of the sofa as she rested a bag of greasy fast food on her hip, the file balanced on top.

"What are you doing?" she asked as she dropped her keys onto the side table.

Sam let out another loud giggle, the sound ending in a gentle growl. "Hey baby girl, did you know it's illegal to sing any profane, indecent, or obscene songs in public?"

"What?" She kicked at Poe's toy, the small ball flying across the living room to bounce off the wall before a black blur screeched after it. Poe slipped on the wood, colliding with the wall before he scrambled after his ball with a yowl.

Sam ignored the cat's clumsiness as he dropped the book to his chest, stretching his arms wide. "I'm reading about old British laws. It's also illegal to handle a salmon in suspicious circumstances."

Alice couldn't help her smirk. "What makes it suspicious?" Not that she would appreciate someone walking along with a smelly fish.

"And," Sam continued, wiggling his eyebrows, "it's also

against the law to shake a carpet outside before eight in the morning." He sat further up, eyes alight with humour. "But the book doesn't specify which *type* of carpet."

She watched his face, not understanding. "Oh for... bloody hell Sam!"

"Oh baby girl, one would assume that since you're receiving the magnificent dick more, you would understand the dirty jokes."

She stuck her tongue out at him, unable to give him her usual one fingered salute with her arms full.

"Very mature," he grinned, eyes flicking to the red file. "What's that? Did you find something at Overlord's?"

"That must be Little War, did she bring the food?" a deep, smoky voice bellowed from the kitchen. "Ah ha! That must be better than the insufficient crap you have in that cold wall door." Lucy strutted in, a half-eaten block of cheese in his fist.

Alice stepped back. "Lucifer?"

"Oh," Sam began as he jumped over the sofa. "Lucy's here by the way." He rolled his eyes, taking the file from her outstretched hands while Lucy snatched the fast food, a grin creasing his cheeks.

"I see my wards are working well," Alice muttered, loud enough Lucy's eyes narrowed. "Lucy, why are you here? I thought we agreed you wouldn't turn up unannounced?"

He bit into the cheese, chewing slowly while he opened the paper bag with a rustle. Light glinted from his chest, which made Alice immediately drop her eyes to the nipple rings that flashed through the strategically cut slits in his black t-shirt. Lucy's skin was a healthy pink compared to his natural ashen grey, the colour part of his 'normal' image that he tried to portray when he was Earth Side. Except, he

preferred to keep his eyes red, enjoying the alarmed looks when people got too close.

"I'm up here looking for that skinny runt you call a brother. Bastard pinned me to a wall with my own knife," Lucy snarled, his teeth sharp and pointy – also something he preferred to keep. "I'm going to stick the same knife up his fucking..."

"So yeah," Sam interrupted. "That's why Lucy's here."

"You arseholes really know how to make a guy welcome," Lucy growled, bending himself onto the sofa.

ALICE MOVED INTO THE KITCHEN, Sam following tightly behind.

"Did he literally just turn up?" she asked, closing the fridge door that had been left wide open.

"In a poof of smoke," Sam shrugged, peering inside the file with peaked curiosity. "Now tell me about this. Anything in here that explains the weird key thing I found on the counter?"

"I don't know, I didn't have time to look through it." Not when she had to deal with Danton's 'friends.' Dread was clearly up to something in the weeks before the trial, she just hoped the answer was in the box. "I'll go through the contents and see what I can find."

"Have you asked her yet?" Lucy called through. "Let's get this fucking party on the road!" He appeared in the doorway, the cheese in one hand, and a burger in the other.

Sam frowned. "Hey, you going to share?"

Lucy responded by shoving the whole thing in his mouth, a challenge in his eyes.

"Asked me what yet?" Alice asked.

"We're going to a concert!" Lucy muffled, meat and bun covering his teeth.

"We are?"

Sam placed the file on the counter. "Ash called, he's working at an event and reserved us some tickets. There's some indie bands playing tonight at The Pavilion and thought you would want to go?"

"Of course we're going!" Lucy injected, puffing his chest out.

"I've told you there are only two tickets!" Sam snapped at Lucy. "Two as in Alice and I."

"And I've already said," Lucy responded in a dark voice. "I don't need a ticket."

~

A BAND WAS in full swing on the Pavilion stage, two guitarists and a drummer hitting out a rock number much to the excitement of the crowd. Lucy vibrated with energy beside her, his scary eyes scanning the crowd of people.

"This is great!" he bellowed, louder than he needed to. "I've never seen so many humans in one room." His tone dropped an octave.

"Hey!" she shouted back, yanking his shirt to gain his attention. The fabric ripped further, exposing more of his chest through the strategically placed slits. A few women gasped at the sight. "Best behaviour or I'll send you back." She didn't actually know the spell off by heart to send him back to Hell, but from his silent snarl the threat was enough.

"Scouts honour."

"Scouts honour?" Sam parroted, his hands holding two

drinks, with a third balanced. "How do you even know what a scout is?"

Lucy ignored the question, grabbing the balanced beer and downing it in one. "I'm going to find us a table." He stalked off, the crowd parting as if an invisible shield surrounded him.

Sam watched after him. "Yeah... I don't trust him."

Alice couldn't exactly disagree with the statement. "Do you really think he knows what a scout is?"

"You mean the thousand-year-old Daemon? Fuck no," Sam snorted. "But as he magically appeared inside, even with the restrictive-magic spells, I don't think we can really stop him."

A glass dome hung high from the ceiling, filled with a deep green smoke that swirled every now and then with red. It wasn't uncommon for upscale bars, expensive restaurants and larger venues to pay for the extra protection. The glass dome absorbed spells, limiting the magic in the area.

While magic was frequently used in concerts for arcane light shows and floating instruments, it could get out of hand if any magic-bearer in the audience decided to add their own flare to the show, especially after a drink or two.

Sam lifted his arm in a wave.

Alice turned, noticing Ash towards the side of the bar, a blush colouring his cheeks.

"So, you two still a thing? He's cute."

"A thing?" Sam laughed. "We get on, have some great fun and we fit in bed. I don't see why it needs a label."

"I know, but does he know that?"

Ash smiled at their approach, the blush deepening when Sam went to kiss him on the cheek. His Paramedics uniform was so white it glowed beneath the lights, a red

cross with wings was stitched to his breast pocket, along with the slogan *'Here for your Health.'*

"I'm glad you could make it," Ash said, his hand nervously brushing the honey brown of his hair. "I wasn't sure if this was your thing."

"Thank you so much for the tickets! The band's great." The music stopped, the crowd breaking into a raucous applause before another song started up, heavy on the drums.

"You're welcome. I kinda have to work right now, but after did you guys want to grab a drink or something?" Ash aimed his question at Sam.

"We would love to," Alice answered for him, nudging her best friend.

"Yeah," Sam said. "We're going to go find a table, why don't you meet us when you finish?"

Ash nodded with a quiet smile, turning away just as a fight broke out between two men. "Excuse me."

Sam watched after Ash with a frown. "Come on." He grabbed Alice's arm, entwining it within his as he pulled her through the dancing crowd. It didn't take them long to find Lucy, a harem of curious women surrounding the table as he watched them with predatory eyes. One woman was brave enough to approach, her shiver overly dramatic when he exposed his spikey teeth in greeting. She was quickly pulled away by her friend.

The Pavilion was a large venue, with tables placed around the edge of the room and the centre kept clear. The stage was large, but crudely built with an amateur painted backdrop of the constellations amongst the stars.

Scratches and marks blemished the tacky wood beneath their feet, evidence of furniture scraping when there were

no music events on, and the place turned back into a conference centre.

"Little War, Samion, over here!" Lucy waved when he noticed them. "Look at all these well-bred females!" He smiled again, exposing his teeth and holding the expression.

Alice sat down opposite, wondering how long he could smile without his cheeks hurting. "What are you doing?"

"I think he's flirting?" Sam answered, taking the other seat.

Lucy's smile turned into a snarl, his eyes glowing. "How else am I supposed to gain their interest in sex?"

"That's not how you flirt over here." Sam laughed, slapping his knee. "Is that what female Daemons find attractive?"

The band continued their rock song, loud enough that both Alice and Lucy leaned forward. Sam turned away, his attention on something on the dance floor. Without a word he stood up, mumbling something to the table before he joined the throngs of dancers.

"There are no female Daemons," Lucy said matter of factly, curling his hand around Sam's beer and pulling it towards himself. "We're all male. True Daemons are druids that embrace the ancient magic. There are other creatures who have Daemon tendencies, but they were forced into their transformation and are not of true blood. They're known as Lessers."

Alice sipped her drink, a cocktail. "What do you mean other creatures?"

Lucy settled back in his seat, his legs stretched forward, long enough people had to step over them to pass. "Not many druids choose their birth right and transcend into Daemons, not since we're bound to The Nether. Which has

been several millennia now. " His eyes narrowed. "Except your fucking brother, his ceremony was unusual."

"Out of everyone who tried to create their own Daemons, how many succeeded?"

Lucy caught her eye. "One that I know of, Zelroth, or The Master as your brother likes to call him. Fucking fool, thinking he can create those abominations. Like he's some sort of god." Lucifer chuckled, downing Sam's drink. "I was very happy to hear of his demise."

"But, why?" Alice looked down, watching her cocktail ripple from the beats of the band. "Why even bother to try?"

"We're a Breed of about fifty. Some of the Originals believe that if we had larger numbers, even with Lessers, we could break the chains that keep us beneath." He leaned forward once again with a smirk. "I would be careful, Little War. There are brothers of mine who would love for the veil to fall, to allow my kind their freedom we have craved since the beginning of time."

"Is that a threat, Xahenort?"

His smirk turned into a grin. "Zelroth was a fool to try and kill you. He believed he would become War if he absorbed your essence. He had plans to find the horsemen, break their seals and force them to start the prophecy."

"Seals?"

Lucifer eyed the rest of her cocktail, his dark grey tongue snaking out to lick the bottom of his lip. Alice pushed the glass over, wanting him to keep speaking freely. He very rarely offered her knowledge without an exchange. She should invite him Earth Side more often.

"Your seal is the final connection to your gift."

"Curse," Alice interrupted. "It's a curse."

"Maybe to you, but to others that power is a gift."

"I'm already a Draco, that connects me to my ancestors and their magic. I don't need to be War too."

"Yet it's because of your ancestors that you *are* War, and not simply another Draco."

She had never considered that.

"It would be wise to embrace your powers. Because once your seal breaks, and it will break, you will become the true War, a warrior, a horseman who's fate is to break down the veil that separates the realms. At least, that's what the old world believed."

Old world? she thought. *Shit. Shit. Shit.*

"What side are you on?"

Lucy tightened his smile. "It's amazing what people would do for their freedom."

Alice sat straighter, the hair on the back of her neck rising. "That didn't answer my question."

"No?" he chuckled, eyes flicking behind her. "You may need to save your cat."

"What?" Alice turned, scanning the crowd until she noticed Sam in the corner with Ash, and Ash wasn't happy. "Shit!"

Alice squeezed through the crowd, fighting her way as the dancers ignored her shouts.

"Excuse me!" She pushed a man a little too hard, who was pushed back in return. Within seconds everyone that surrounded her were pushing and laughing, the mosh pit difficult to escape.

An arm appeared through the bodies, her scar pulsating as Lucy yanked her towards him. He carefully placed her to the side before joining in in the mosh pit.

"YOU READY FOR ME, HUMANS?"

Alice didn't have time to deal with that, she just hoped he kept to his word that he wouldn't hurt anybody, or kill.

"Sam?" she said when she was close enough to touch his shoulder.

"Can you not even keep it in your pants for TEN MINUTES?" Ash cried at Sam. "SERIOUSLY?"

"It was just a kiss, I don't know why you're so angry!" Sam answered with a controlled anger. "It's not like I was fucking her right on the dance floor! You know what, for a stallion you're a real fucking prude!"

Ash's mouth dropped open. "FUCK YOU SAM!"

'Immediate assistance needed outside the venue.' The radio buzzed on Ash's shoulder.

"Bennet responding," he calmly answered into the receiver. "Location?"

'Located through the emergency exit, east of the building. Police are en route.'

"Police? Shit." He clicked off the receiver. "I don't think I can keep doing this Sam," Ash said quietly. "Look, I need to work, I'll call you later... maybe."

"Hey, wait!" Sam reached out, but Ash had already made his way towards the exit. "Ash? Fuck." He turned to Alice, eyes wide. "What do I do?"

"Sam..."

"I really like him, baby girl, but I am who I am."

"Let's just go home, we can grab some food and watch that new cooking show you keep talking about?"

"No, fuck that. I'm not letting Ash ruin my night." Sam shrugged off her hand. "I need to have a drink and dance, I'll see you back at home."

"Wait, Sam!" Her phone vibrated in her back pocket. "Shit!" The caller ID flashed, one that demanded her response. "Shit. Shit. Shit."

CHAPTER SIX

"Now let's start again, who found the body?" Brady asked with a tired growl. His pen was poised, ready with his notepad as the man who found the corpse shakily told his story for the third time.

The area directly beside the Pavilion had been cordoned off, police tape and cones keeping every curious pedestrian away. Which had been difficult considering the sheer amount of crowd that left the venue to try and get a sneak peak of the wrapped man. And it was a man, for that they were certain. Alice didn't need Jones to confirm it considering the semi-transparent fabric that wrapped him from head to toe was tight, so tight you could see his crown jewels very clearly.

He was also a shifter, but what animal she had no idea. His face was stretched, a snout protruding from the centre that looked half formed with his lower jaw clearly broken. Claws had pierced through the fabric, unravelling the weave enough she noticed the nails pushing away from the skin in a way that made her clench her own fist.

"Have you ever seen anything like this before?" she

asked Peyton when he stood beside her, his usual scowl in place.

"A few pets have been found like this over the past few weeks. This was expected."

Her chi ached beside him, longing for the bond that he kept strangled, cut off.

The more they tried to break it, the stronger it became.

"Expected? You expected this?" she gestured to the body that was expertly wrapped, arms and legs bound together. He had been placed carefully onto a chair, body rigid. It reminded her of a mummification, but instead of bandages it was white woven fabric as fine as silk, and each limb was individually wrapped.

She wanted to take a closer look, but wasn't able until Jones had finished with his team.

"Well, not exactly this. The fabric is new, before they were wrapped in cord."

A tut behind them. "Someone clearly has a weird kink," Lucy chuckled.

"Excuse me, you can't be behind the..." Peyton began, his voice cutting off when he faced Lucifer.

Alice felt their bond ignite, his wild magic electric.

"Hey, hey," she snapped at Peyton. "This is Lucifer. He's with... me," she awkwardly finished.

Peyton turned to Alice, his eyes like ice. He was furious, the bond vibrating through her in waves of heat.

"I have word of your brother, so I will take my leave," Lucy said, his eyes mockingly rolling over Peyton in challenge. "Listen out for the hounds."

They blinked and Lucy was gone.

"What is he?" Peyton asked, his anger simmering before he cut off their connection once more. "Did he just say hounds?"

Alice immediately touched her thigh, her fingertips searching for the scar through the fabric of her jeans. "How easy is it to create a portal to the Far Side?"

Peyton paused, taking his time to answer. When he spoke her tongue tingled, bound with magic. She couldn't share the knowledge even if she wanted to.

"Only royalty can make portals, and even then it's difficult. High Lords are able to open the doorways already in the veil, but only for a short time. Why?"

"I... found an entrance, a Fae portal deep in the forest. But it was broken."

"An entrance? How did you know...?"

"I felt it."

"That's impossible," he whispered. "Only Fae can..." Peyton slammed his mouth shut, his eyebrows raised. "We really need to sort out this bond."

"What do you guys think?" Brady asked when he approached. Bags were heavy beneath his tired eyes and baby sick was dried to his collar, but neither Alice nor Peyton mentioned anything. He was happy being a father, well, they assumed he was happy considering he rarely smiled. But he always updated them on pictures of his baby, Alison whether they wanted to see or not.

Peyton frowned. "You've seen something like this before?"

"We think he's been skinned beneath the fabric," Jones answered instead as he removed the hood from his overalls, allowing it to sag on his shoulders. "The Pathologist will need to confirm once they unwrap him, but there's no flesh on his hands from what I can see."

"You comparing them to the pets?"

"I've already scheduled a call with the Pathologist assigned as well as the veterinary clinic that made

the call. We just have to hope they're not already cremated."

"What's your initial thought?" Peyton asked. "Other than Brady's statement we have no leads."

Alice noticed the glint of glass in the corner. "What about the CCTV?"

"Broken."

"How convenient," she muttered.

Jones played with his zipper. "He has defensive marks on his hands, but I can't confirm whether he was alive or dead when he was skinned."

"What a comforting thought," Alice cringed. "You ready for us to take a look?"

"We're going to be a while, but if you don't step on any of the markers you should be okay." With a nod he moved back to his team.

Up close, the body looked fake, as if someone had wrapped a mannequin in organza then splashed it with fake blood.

"He smells like magic," Peyton said, deadpan.

Alice raised an eyebrow. "You can smell magic?" Peyton was still shy about his Breed, barely acknowledging it since his recovery. It was no longer a secret that he was Fae, except his royalty status which he made blatantly clear would not be discussed. He even kept his hair long enough to hide his distinctive ears. At least he seemed to be embracing his natural hair colour, the pale silver suiting his complexion. "What does it smell like?" she asked, trying to coax him into telling her more.

He watched her with quiet eyes. "Fresh rain after a lightning storm."

"Wow, very specific," she smirked. She could only smell

death, the distinctive aroma growing the longer she was there. She would have preferred the fresh rain.

The body was sat awkwardly on a wooden chair, the table on its side to his right with smashed glass glittering on the floor.

Carefully kneeling, making sure she didn't move any of the markers left by the forensic team, she checked closer to the head. The fabric was tight, covering every available inch of the face. Other than the shape, which they knew was a shifter, she couldn't see anything.

"There's nothing for us here, we need him unwrapped."

"Hmmm, I'll update Brady. We can't do anything without the pathology report. Let's hope they find something interesting." Peyton moved away, stepping over the tape that kept the crowd away. A uniformed officer blocked the crowd, his lip lifting in a snarl.

"Fucking faerie," the officer murmured beneath his breath, his attention on Peyton's back.

Alice found herself beside him without even a thought. She wasn't sure if Peyton had overheard, but it didn't matter. "Officer..."

His eyes flashed with alarm when he realised she was beside him. "Officer Leary, ma'am."

"Ma'am? It's Agent Skye. But I must say, I'm surprised it wasn't bitchy witch?" She had heard that a few times when she had first started working for Spook Squad. "Or maybe just Freak? What makes Detective Peyton suddenly get the special treatment and not me?" She made sure her voice was dramatically loud.

"Ah..." His eyes grew to saucers.

"Do we have a problem, Officer Leary?"

"What's going on here?" Brady asked with a scowl, Peyton on his heel.

"No, no, no..." Leary stuttered. "Nothing, sir."

"I was just making sure there isn't anything that could distract him from his job. Because surely, if Officer Leary had a problem with another member of the team it would be reason for termination, wouldn't it, Detective Brady?"

Brady's eyes narrowed, turning his full dark stare to the Officer. "It would be reason for transfer, at least." Brady had caught one clerk back at Scotland Yard calling Peyton a name to her colleagues. She was immediately removed from her post.

"No problem here, Detective."

"Then you should probably get back to work," Peyton said with a distinctive monotone. Officer Leary stepped away with a dramatic nod before Peyton turned his attention to Alice, his expression hard.

Fuck sake, she thought. Peyton was the only person who would be pissed off at her defending him.

Brady broke the tension. "Peyton mentioned you felt a magical presence? Can you specify further?"

Alice bit the inside of her cheek. Peyton was the one who had smelt one, not her. She personally couldn't feel magic residue, not unless it was exceedingly strong. "Not really. I would suggest hiring a necromancer, they may be able to enlighten us on what the fuck happened."

"Do you have any suggestions?"

Alice shook her head. "A necromancer is a black witch, one who specialises in the darker arts of magic. The practice has been outlawed unless under supervision of The Magicka."

Black magic witches were the most powerful of all the classes, using death and blood to create spells and potions. Every spell required a sacrifice in various levels of severity,

whether it was a plant, blood, chi or death. The larger the sacrifice, the larger the return.

The class was outlawed, with only a certain amount of witches allowed to train under the watchful eyes of The Magicka. Those who practiced without their permission were hunted and executed.

"How do we find someone then?"

"We need to ask The Magicka," Peyton muttered. "Or better yet, Frederick Gallagher."

"The councilman?" Brady asked. "Alice, can you set up the meeting?"

She sighed, pinching her nose. She didn't want to, but at that moment she couldn't think of an alternative. "Yeah, sure." Which meant she would have to organise a meeting with one of the men she would happily see dead.

"Good, organise it ASAP. We know this will be breaking news in the morning, which means we're going to have everyone on our arses to get it closed quickly."

"Without the pathology report, we have nothing," Alice answered.

Brady scanned the crowd. "Let's allow Jones to finish up and re-group. I'll wait for the Coroner and organise a fast track."

CHAPTER SEVEN

It was surprisingly easy to set up a meeting with Councilman Gallagher, if the three hours on hold with The Magicka's internal switchboard before being transferred to six different people didn't count. His secretary had said he was busy until the end of the year, until Alice explained the situation... forcefully.

Her name was known, and apparently her threatening to turn up at his office to make a scene was a decent threat. Frederick was running for city mayor, as if being the corrupt head of The Magicka wasn't enough for him.

"You seem nervous," Brady murmured as they waited in the large foyer. "I don't like it when you're nervous."

Alice waited until some students passed, their eyes curious as they clutched a stack of books to their chest. "I'm not nervous," she said quietly. *Just uncomfortable,* she added mentally.

They were at the University of London Magic, the place where aspiring witches and mages came to study and develop their skills. It was where you were assigned your tier, a tier Alice never received as she didn't study

there or at any of their partnered campuses across the globe.

Genetically she was a witch, but on paper she was nothing.

The university was part of the older area of the city, the walls thick stone that created a cold draft whatever the season. The foyer was tall, the floors above busy as students lined up on the many balconies above, waiting for their classes. A stained glass dome was situated at the top, creating bursts of multi-coloured light across the drab, grey interior.

Students ranged from eighteen to twenty-one on average, their uniform emblem a black pentagram with silver accents.

In the distance Alice could hear construction work, signs explaining they were opening up part of the section for younger students, eleven to seventeen in the following spring.

"Why are we here again?" Brady asked as he crossed his thick arms, checking his watch impatiently. "Why do we need this guy's permission?"

"Because I know nothing of dark magic, and Frederick is the only person who can help us." She knew that for a fact. She had checked.

"Frederick?" Brady smirked, eyebrow raised. "You on first name basis?"

Alice just shook her head. "It's complicated," she whispered as more students walked past.

Brady sat quietly for a moment, a slight frown pinching his eyebrows. "Tell me about black magic." He made it an order. "Or is it dark magic?"

Alice played with the lint on her trousers. "They're the same, it's just different degrees of severity. The first thing

you're taught as a child is that black magic requires a greater cost than most witches could handle. Many witches don't even have the chi capacity to hold the spell. Dark magic is the same as black, but easier to balance, and the sacrifice isn't as severe." It was illegal for a reason.

"What about you?" Brady asked. "Can you do black magic?"

"I don't do black magic."

"That's not what I asked."

Alice turned, Brady's dark eyes watching her without a hint of judgment. Since Peyton came out as Fae he had been asking more questions about Breed, but that question wasn't something she wanted to answer. She had done dark magic, not black, and she still remembered the thick, oily feeling of it suffocating her aura. The idea that black magic was stronger...

"Would you ever do it?" Brady asked when she remained silent.

She didn't want to answer that question either, especially as she wasn't sure.

Heels slapped loudly against the hard wood, drawing their attention to the secretarial looking woman with a face like stone.

"Agent Skye and Detective Brady?" she asked with a clipped tone. "Could you please follow me?"

Without a backwards glance to make sure they were following she guided them past the cafeteria, down two corridors before she opened up the door labelled 'Chancellor's office.'

Frederick sat behind a large mahogany desk, a backdrop of candles floating in the air, orange flames flickering. A book lay before him, the pages turning on their own every few seconds.

He remained seated, lips curled in a tight smirk as he gestured for them to take a seat.

"Councillor Gallagher," Brady greeted with his hand held out.

"Detective," Frederick replied, his gaze dropping to the outstretched hand until Brady dropped it. "I'm very busy, you have five minutes."

"I'm sure five minutes will be sufficient enough," Brady growled, his voice deepening as his anger spiked. "I wasn't aware you were Chancellor."

"Oh, I'm not," Frederick smiled. "I just wanted a suitable space to hold this meeting." His attention changed to Alice, his head barely moving due to his high-neck, stiff collar. "This university is a beacon of superiority to our Breed, therefore it is appropriate for me to speak with... Spook Squad." He said the name with obvious distaste. "A police unit that specialises in Breed investigations, yet counts an *ungraded* witch amongst them."

Alice bit the inside of her cheek. She was working, she couldn't retaliate.

Brady shifted in his seat. "We are in need of assistance with an ongoing homicide investigation. Agent Skye enlightened me that you would be able to supply us with a witch trained in black magic."

Frederick shot out of his chair, a loud laugh erupting from his throat. The candles behind him flickered, one extinguishing with a hiss.

"And why should I give you permission for this? Black magic is the biggest immorality amongst witches, and therefore those who practice it are sentenced to immediate death." He dramatically swiped a finger across his throat, a smirk playing along his thin lips. "As are those witches who rebel against The Magicka."

"You're the only person who can point us to an approved witch," Alice said with an acidic tone, "One who could help us catch a murderer."

Frederick grunted, moving to sit at the edge of the desk, his long, velvet green cloak close enough to brush Alice.

Alice straightened, not allowing him to use his height as an intimidation.

"Why would I care about that?" he asked, bending over her.

"If you're unable to do it, we will speak to a councilman that can." Brady's chair scraped as he stood, eyes hard. "It seems your capabilities have been exaggerated."

"I am the only person who can give you permission," Frederick snapped.

"Then give it," Brady bit. "If you had accepted a call we wouldn't have had to come here to ask permission in person, but instead we have wasted hours that could have been put to better use." He paused for a breath, jaw clenched. "We appreciate you're busy, but we need a black witch to assist us in a homicide."

Frederick paused, leaning back on his arms. "The Shifter Slayer?"

"The what?" Alice replied before Frederick twisted his wrist, and the morning newspaper appeared in his hand. Alice scanned the headline, annoyance spiking.

'An unusual body was found late last night at The Pavilion according to several eyewitnesses. Described as what they believe to be a partially-transformed shifter wrapped in silk, numerous accounts of the evening depict it as a harrowing sight. Police have made no statement regarding the incident, and the cause of death has yet to be deter-

mined. Scotland Yard deny to comment, but we, the public still want to know whether The Shifter Slayer is likely to strike again.'

"Why do they always give the bad guy a cool name?" Alice muttered. "He should be called Micro-penis Maniac or something."

Brady read through the newspaper too, scrunching it up in his large fists.

"Shows incompetence to your team if you were unaware of this article, doesn't it, Detective?" Frederick asked, the calculation in his eyes cold.

"Councillor Gallagher, would you please point us in the direction of a witch who could assist us," Brady replied with a controlled anger.

Frederick grinned, sitting himself back into the chair with the backdrop of candles. The book continued to turn its pages, the small movement making the little flames sway.

"I'll let the Coven of Crones know you are to be expected. Speak to Christine Shade. She may, or may not help you."

Brady leaned forward, his large shoulders shifting beneath his black trench coat. "Thank you for your time." He moved towards the door, gesturing for Alice to follow.

"Oh, Alice I have something for you." Frederick produced a piece of paper. "This is your eviction notice."

"Eviction notice?" Alice scanned the paper. "Evicted from what?" It stated he had bought her family's house from the bank.

"I'll be nice and give you a month," he sniggered. "The protection clause ended when the benefactor passed. So it

went up for sale and I couldn't help myself. I've always wanted a house in that part of the neighbourhood."

"Of course you did." She screwed the paper up in her hand. Due to her parents passing and both her and Kyle also being declared dead, the house was returned to the bank. It was Dread who organised that the house couldn't be sold or rented out, and after several denied court applications they agreed. It sat vacant for two decades until Alice approached them, but it looked like Dread's original agreement had come to an end.

"My offer is still open, you know," Frederick said as she turned to leave.

Hand on the door, she looked back. "Why would you want to soul-bind with an *ungraded* witch?" she said, sarcasm dripping from every word.

"Careful," he warned. "Don't believe you're safe just because you bested the trials."

She clicked her fingers, the one candle without a flame bursting into life in a pop of blue.

Frederick's head jerked, his attention on the single candle.

"Blue flames burn hotter, remember that."

His face was tight when he turned back.

"It was nice to see you, Fred."

CHAPTER EIGHT

Alice couldn't control her smile, her cheeks hurting as she noticed her reflection in the glass window. "You promised it would just be burgers."

Riley squeezed her hand, a smirk tipping his lips as his eyes flashed silver. "These are burgers. It's literally called *'The Burger Joint.'*"

"*Normal* burgers!" she laughed. "This is..."

"You never specified it to be a normal burger, besides, define normal?"

Alice snapped her mouth shut.

Shit.

The restaurant was busy, with many couples without reservations being turned away at the door. Inside - from what she could see through the window - was a sea of dark oak tables alight with candles.

Riley pulled her closer, planting a warm kiss on the top of her head. "This place is new, and it's owned by someone I would call a friend. He asked for an investment to expand so I thought it would be a great place for us to try."

"Investment?" Alice waited until the waiter had sat

them down at a private table before continuing. "How many investments do you have?" The quiet murmurs of the restaurant were a welcoming ambience, every table occupied with smiling couples, friends and families.

"Enough." He moved the candle over to the side, head tilted as he stared at Alice with undying attention. "The Guardians were expected to be The Order's personal warriors. They looked to control us in every aspect. So as soon as we all came of age we refused."

"Refused? How did you refuse?"

Riley sat back, eyes dancing with humour. "A few of my brothers travelled, some stayed while I watched my father. He may have been a bastard, but he was a great businessman. I knew we couldn't run from what we are for long, from what they made us. So I studied, and decided to plan for our future."

"How long were you separated?" Alice inched forward, enthralled with his words. Riley was very reserved when he spoke of The Guardians, the men he called brothers. She was excited that he would share these memories with her.

"All in all, five years. Many people believed I created my capital using my father's money, but they were wrong. I wanted nothing from him, not when he was the one who forced me to share my soul with this beast. So I watched, waited. I knew we would never be rid of The Order, but we could be financially independent. We would never be their puppets, dogs they controlled."

"Is that why you donated all of your fathers assets to charity?"

A shallow nod. "Fitting really, giving to the children's charity that he used as a camouflage for his... other work."

Alice reached over to place her hand over his, giving it a little squeeze.

"Our beasts call for one another, which is why you'll see them around the house. Sometimes the pull is too much and they come home, as they like to call it. Everyone has a role within the group, and together we've made it work, even against the unknown."

"Are you ready to order?" The waiter interrupted, placing two glasses of water onto the table.

Alice skimmed the menu. "Two burger specials, and one of each side, please."

"Anything else?" the waiter looked expectantly at Riley.

"Add a bottle of your best red, thank you."

"Of course." With a nod the waiter moved away, returning only a minute later with a bottle of red wine and two glasses.

"So," Riley began with a raised eyebrow. "Two speciality burgers and every side?"

Alice waited for the wine to be poured, savouring the taste before replying. "You said you're looking to invest, you may as well try as much as you can."

"I've never had someone order for me before," he growled, his voice dropping low as his chi brushed hers, stroking. She felt it all across her body.

"That's because it's normally the guys doing it for the girls." She took another sip of the wine, trying not to moan at the taste. She didn't even want to dare look at the price of the bottle. "I had this date once, I must have been no older than eighteen and he ordered me a salad and water."

Riley narrowed his eyes. "Is he still alive?"

"Just." He definitely didn't get a second date.

The burgers were huge when they arrived, accompanied with more sides than the table could hold.

"Erm..."

"What?" Riley teased, taking a big bite into his double patty burger. "You want a salad?"

In retaliation she threw two chips at him, thick enough they made a noise when they hit his plate. She would have been embarrassed at her actions in a respectable restaurant if Riley didn't lean over and rub ketchup onto her nose.

Giggles to her left, loud enough Alice couldn't help but turn her head. Two young teenage girls sat at a table of four, what she assumed were their parents completely oblivious to the fact they both held their phones out, pointed at Riley.

Alice looked down at the table, trying to cover her face with as much of her hair as possible. She had been featured in a few of the city's gossip magazines, much to her frustration. She didn't need any sort of media interest, not when she was still learning about herself, learning what she could become. She didn't need the world watching, waiting for her to fail. Especially considering they were only interested in her because of who she was sleeping with. It was one of the reasons she didn't want to go to the more expensive restaurants, because they were the places Riley was expected to be.

"Shit, Alice, I'm sorry." Riley touched her hand. "Look, we can go. I'm sure we can get some takeout boxes, go back to yours and find a movie to watch."

Alice looked through her hair, noticing how once the girls got their shot they went back to bickering like siblings at the table. She knew attention was a part of Riley's life, so much so he probably didn't even notice until he saw her reaction.

Was she willing to give up her privacy for him?

"No, we're here for your friend." Alice took a large bite

of her burger, this time allowing a moan to escape. "And this is gooood," she pretty much purred.

Between them they finished both their burgers, and half of the sides. But they made sure to try everything.

"Okay, you need to invest," Alice groaned, leaning back in her chair. "This place is amazing." She already knew she would bring Sam as soon as she could make a reservation.

"I knew it would be, it's why I brought you." He caught her eye. "You fancy taking the desserts home?"

A warm lump in her gut, growing until her nerves peaked with excitement. "We better pay the bill then."

It didn't take long until Riley held two takeout boxes, the desserts a secret as they made their way out the restaurant and into the cool evening air.

Stars glittered, the full moon shining brightly as a man in chefs whites followed outside, much to the delight of the waiting line. Riley welcomed him with a familiar hug, moving to the side to chat privately.

Alice held her hand out for a passing cab, waving frantically as it passed her by.

"Fuck sake."

"Alice Skye, you always seem to pop up in the most unexpected of places," a dark voice chuckled.

Alice turned, her arm wavering as another cab zoomed past, the headlights washing over the man who had helped her gain entrance into the Troll market. "Nate," she said with a polite nod. "How..." She didn't really want to say how pleasant it was to see him, because it wasn't. "Who's your date?" She flicked her gaze to the tall, slim brunette. The woman had a cold stare, her artificially plumped lips slightly twisted into an unfriendly snarl.

"Annabelle," he said to his guest rather than Alice, "go make sure our table is ready. I'll be along shortly."

Annabelle didn't seem to enjoy being dismissed, but other than the slight flush in her caramel skin she did nothing, instead staring daggers at Alice as if it were her fault.

"Now Alice, we have business to discuss," Nate began, his attention flicking behind her before quickly returning.

"I don't think we do."

"My token, I would like it back."

"Token? What..." She remembered the token with the sigil of a jawless skull with runes and markings etched into the side. "I gave that to the guard as you said, and he allowed me access into the mausoleum."

"Yes, yes, but now I would like it back," he said with an impatient snap. "Where is it?"

"I just said I gave it to the guard."

"You get it back when you leave, and clearly you left, well, not completely unharmed, but alive." His gaze swept down her full length, lingering uncomfortably. "Now where is it?"

Her exit wasn't exactly planned from the market, she was carried out high as a kite if she remembered correctly. "I was never given it back."

"You idiot, it's not handed to you. It will reappear once you're back home, somewhere familiar. It was supposed to return to me automatically since I'm its owner, but since It hasn't you must have it."

"I don't have it." She really didn't, not that she noticed, anyway. "And if you had heard I wasn't 'completely unarmed' then you're in the wrong crowd."

His smile tightened. "It's good to have friends in many areas, Alice. It would be wise to remember that considering without me you wouldn't have had access to the market at all."

"Blackwell," Riley growled, his free arm coming around

to circle her waist. "Is there a reason your harassing my date?"

An audible click, followed by a flash.

Shit. Shit. Shit.

"Bloody cameras," she moaned.

Alice spun in Riley's arms, pulling his face down. She didn't know why Riley and Nate disliked each other, but she couldn't deal with the confrontation being in the newspaper.

"Storm," Nate replied tartly. "I was only asking Alice for something that is mine."

"I think you should leave, otherwise we may create a scene."

Alice noticed a passing cab. "HEY!" She lifted her arm, the black car slowing down to a stop on the side of the road. "It was nice seeing you Nate," she lied, tugging Riley away. "I'm sure you'll find your lost token. Maybe some of your friends could help."

WARMTH AT HER THROAT, Riley gently kissing down her neck to linger on her collarbone.

Alice groaned, trying to tug his mouth back up to her lips, but he resisted with a chuckle. "I'll find a movie while you sort out the desserts."

Alice stretched up, brushing her lips against his as he let out a reluctant groan. They didn't get to spend much alone time together, not when both of their lives were so busy with work and training. With Sam at Club X, Riley jumped at the chance to join her back at her place, to spend the evening together cuddling and watching terrible movies.

Being normal.

Just Alice and Riley.

"Behave," he growled as she climbed off the sofa and headed towards the kitchen.

Butterflies in her stomach she paused at the threshold, watching him search for the remote which he found wedged between the armrest and the cushion. With a click he turned on the TV, flicking through the channels until he paused on the new cooking show Sam had mentioned. It was a competition for witches and mages to create their best potion under stressful circumstances, using the ingredients given to them. From the pale look of the majority of contestants it wasn't going well.

Leaving him to find a film, she entered the kitchen, making sure to stroke across Poe's fur who slept on the table. He purred at her touch, eyes opening to reflect in the light.

"What do you think it is?" she asked him as she opened the first takeout box, excited to see the decadent chocolate fudge cake.

Poe climbed to his feet, nose in the air. With a yowl he attempted to jump towards the counter, but he slipped, knocking off Dread's thick file as he stumbled to the tiles. Poe landed on his feet, paperwork and the leather journal tumbling around him.

"Shit." Alice dropped the cake, kneeling to carefully pick up the loose papers that had fallen out.

Her hand brushed something soft, unexpected. Beneath some papers there was a large feather, dove grey in colour and as long as her forearm. It looked immaculate, not a barb out of place considering it must have been squished inside.

"I heard a crash, everything okay?" Riley appeared beside her, helping.

Alice brushed her hand down the feather, surprised at how strong it felt. Poe meowed, batting at a thin wooden box, about an inch thick and no wider than her open palm. It was warm when she touched it, almost hot.

"Alice..."

The concern in Riley's voice forced her attention up, his mouth set in a grim line.

"I think you should read this." He handed her the leather journal, his thumb holding open a page.

I DIDN'T BELIEVE it when Jackson came to me, but now I have no explanation for how fast his child's powers are developing. Far faster than anyone anticipated.

Even now, as I write this I can't really believe it. Not without more evidence. But that doesn't matter, because The Council believe which means I must keep her hidden until I find someone I can trust. Someone who can teach her control of her ancestral magic, otherwise if, or even when the seal breaks, she will be consumed with the force of the magic. And that, I will not let happen.

ALICE SLAMMED THE JOURNAL SHUT, not wanting to read anymore just as the box burned in her hand, hot enough she hissed out a breath.

"What is all this?" Riley murmured, frowning at the wood.

"This is all I have left of Dread." Alice shuffled the papers, placing them back into the file along with the journal and feather. She left the box out. "I haven't been through it yet."

Riley brushed his fingers through her hair, tucking

some loose strands behind her ear. Her heart, which hurt while reading Dread's notes fluttered, Riley's chi brushing over hers in a calming way. She was finding excuses not to look inside the files, whether it was work, a concert or a date with Riley.

Since when was she so weak? A coward?

The files were the last of Dread, her father, the man who brought her up strong in the only way he knew how. He knew she was different, yet he tried everything in his power to keep her safe, even until the end.

"I haven't been able to read it. I..." she began, the vulnerability hitting her hard. "You want to help me?"

Riley silently picked up the file, balancing it on the counter as he grabbed both the takeout boxes and two spoons. "Come on." He urged her into the living room, both sitting on the floor. Reaching over he muted the TV, a new horror film that Alice had wanted to see. "Cake will help."

Alice accepted the paperwork and spoon, scooping a large chunk into her mouth. "What do you have?" she tried to say, but it sounded more like 'wha do yu avve?' as the fudginess stuck to her teeth.

Riley raised an eyebrow, opening his own. "Looks like cheesecake."

"Hmmm, not as good as chocolate." She held her box closer to her chest when he tried to sneak a peek. "Mine," she growled.

Riley raised an eyebrow, a smirk lifting his lips before he lunged forward, taking them both down onto the rug. A deep kiss, his tongue brushing across her lips. "Mmmm, chocolate."

Alice lay there, laughter building as she tried to find where their desserts had gone. Riley, in his speed, had care-

fully balanced both her chocolate cake and his cheesecake on top of one another by her head.

"Meow!" Poe trotted over, his multicolour eyes staring at her only an inch away, pink tongue stuck out the side of his mouth. With a purr he headbutted her.

"Okay, okay." Alice sat up, patting Poe on the head before turning her attention to Dread's paperwork. "I think Dread was researching before he died."

"Researching what?" Riley glanced at the papers Alice brought out and placed on the floor, his spoon poised as he started on his own dessert.

Alice opened the journal, his words flowing across the pages. "Researching me."

War, the concept and ideology still unbelievable, even with all the evidence, Dread noted in his masculine script. *There are three parchments that I've been able to authenticate. I couldn't let it rest, not knowing what she was up against as War. But that's now three similar prophecies, with several more yet to validate.*

He went on to explain the poem she knew off by heart, and even highlighting several sentences, adding his own comments while referencing to other pieces, all in different languages. Except, it wasn't just the poem she knew, it was more.

The watchers, the winged gods observe from a height.
Supposed protectors of the realm, failing in their fight.
The veil was torn, destroyed, the bane allowed to grow.

Amongst the Earth Side, the magic, the elemental glow.
Once mortals, corrupted from the other world, so bound with a seal.
It gave the winged gods time, to plan, to heal.
Generations of Earthen warriors delayed in the truth of the past.
Anger, resentment, the winged gods knew wouldn't last.

The seals corrode, over time, one by one.
The bane, the poison, grows until it's won.
They were no longer mortals, their power out of control.
The Far Side darkness spreading, shading their soul.
With intensity, detestation, they mount their once preventable fate.
What once was a gift, but now a curse. The winged gods knew it too late.

With steady breaths, they ride towards the dawn.
Mortals cower in the dark, defenceless, prepare to mourn.
Shadows move across their souls, as darkness, corruption and power grows.
The four elements, magnets against mortal breath. Generations of lies, of wrath.
Power in its truest form, made physical with greed.
Are they saviours who wish to lead?
Famine destroys along the path, against Pestilence in his wrath.
Death stares and waits his turn, as War's flames turn to burn.
The apocalypse they bring to earth, destroying it for all it's worth.

The watchers, the winged gods observed from a height.
Supposed protectors of the realm, failed in their fight.

"'The watchers, the winged gods,'" she read aloud.

"Winged gods?" Riley frowned over her shoulder. "Angels?"

"Angels?" she parroted. "Don't you mean Fallen Angels?" A Breed she had only just learned even existed.

Riley chuckled, sitting back. "Those that are fallen, were once angels. Not necessarily what different lexicons described, but pompous arseholes who believed themselves better than everyone else."

"Really?" Well, wasn't she learning a lot lately.

Riley's forehead creased, his smile tight.

"How do you know about them?" she pushed. "Riley?"

He caught her eye, giving her his complete attention. "I promise that's all I've heard. But I will find out more, if I can."

Alice released a breath she didn't know she was holding. They trusted each other, but it was still difficult, a minefield of secrets that they were learning to share.

"A fallen angel met with Dread just before he died."

A raised eyebrow. "That's interesting."

"I don't even know where to begin," she laughed, the sound hollow. "Most of these papers are in another language." A language she had never even seen before. At least, she assumed it was a language, the words a mixture of runes and hieroglyphics. She wasn't sure if they were read left to right, right to left or in their panels top to bottom.

"Let me have a look..." Riley studied the sheets, taking his time until he found a total of ten pieces of paper with the same style writing. "There's a box?" He showed her a 3D diagram.

"This?" Alice looked for the small wooden box, finding it suspiciously close to Poe.

When she picked it up, it was cold. She slowly turned it in her hands, unable to figure out how it opened. It looked to be solid, with no indents or lines. Except, there was a faint rattle.

"There's something inside." She handed it to Riley, who didn't comment on the temperature of the box, which made her feel like she was crazy.

"I think these are the instructions on how to open it." With a shake of his head, he set it down. "There's also this."

Alice stared at the image on the sheet, unsure why a deep sick feeling had settled in her stomach. She went to touch it, her hand shaking until she clenched her fist.

"What's that?"

Riley watched, his attention on the tremors that rattled down her arm. "I'm not sure, but I have someone I can ask." Concern deepened his voice.

"Someone who can translate?"

Riley looked at the papers again. "Do you trust me?"

Before, Alice would have hesitated. But not now, not for him.

"Yes," she replied immediately. "I trust you."

Riley's hand gently gripped her neck, his lips soft against her own. She held him against her when he began to pull back, wanting to feel his heat, to help fight against the increasing nausea.

A dark chuckle, one that deliciously vibrated down to her thighs.

"I need to go, sweetheart."

Alice reluctantly released her grip.

"I'll get back to you as soon as I know something." Another lingering kiss. "Stay safe."

Alice smiled, but stayed on her knees as Riley left.

She stared at the remaining papers, unable to concentrate as the nausea slowly subsided. It was a drawing, only a drawing, and yet she felt something awaken inside, terrified. Or was it exhilaration? She wasn't sure.

How could a drawing of a coin, the centre cut out in a diamond shape cause such a reaction?

CHAPTER NINE

"Are we getting out of the car?" Alice asked Peyton when he made no move to exit, his hands gripping the steering wheel. "We have to meet the Pathologist at three."

The leather squeaked beneath his fists. "What should we expect?"

Alice opened the car door, stepping out to observe the large cottage situated in the shadow of the bastion. A bastion that surrounded a castle she recognised, the grounds still blackened.

She kept her eyes up, not wanting to check to see whether the blood stains still tainted the grass. "I have no idea."

The cottage was two storeys, the pale stones echoing the style of the castle perfectly. The roof was thatched, a chimney bellowing out thick smoke that darkened the sky above.

"The air is thick," Peyton murmured as he joined her. "Like oil."

Alice understood what he meant. "You want to wait in the car?"

Peyton shot her a scathing look, eyebrows crossed.

The large circular door opened as they approached, the doorway dark and empty.

"You must be Alice Skye," a voice purred from inside the house. "And Detective Brady."

"Peyton," Alice corrected. "Detective Brady had to attend another meeting."

The cottage was larger inside than anticipated, the space to the left open plan. Fire crackled in the oversized hearth, a black cauldron swinging above, the liquid bubbling away. A woman sat on a thread-bare armchair, the pattern similar to the random rugs placed sporadically on the floor. Skulls and bookshelves adorned the bare walls, thick leather grimoires and crystals carefully placed on the wood.

Alice flared her chi in greeting, the returning chi powerful.

Peyton remained by the threshold, his muscles tense as two other women entered, both taking a seat on one of the large matching sofas.

"Are you Christine Shade?" Alice asked the woman when Peyton remained silent. She was young, maybe in her early thirties with eyes so dark she could have been a vampire. Alice assumed the High Priestess would be older, or at least older than the rest of the coven. The two women that joined them watched with both curiosity and disinterest. The left was a similar age to the priestess, her brown skin glowing while the other woman, who looked to be in her fifties, had skin as white as snow.

"Frederick mentioned you were coming."

Alice knew the cottage held three other witches, their chis pulsating in the distance rather than concealed. They wanted her to know they were there, and they were close.

"I don't usually take these meetings," Christine said leaning forward in her chair, her hair pure white as it partially covered her meanly pinched face. "But I was curious to see you up close." She stood, the cat leaping off her lap to sit by the open fire. "We watched you complete your trials, and defeat that monster. Impressive."

Peyton's head snapped to Alice, ears red.

She hadn't kept her trials a secret, but she also hadn't given Peyton the details. It wasn't like he ever asked. He was aware she had been hurt, and had already begun healing when he recovered from his own ordeal.

"But I don't see how you require our services." A different cat jumped onto her legs, yellow eyes staring. She stroked the black fur, her nails long and grey.

"Has Frederick explained the circumstances?" At Christine's nod Alice continued. "I'm unfamiliar with black magic, I was hoping you or one of your coven could assist."

"You don't taste entirely of earth magic," Christine said with a smirk. "You don't require our magic, you need our knowledge."

"I'm unfamiliar with black magic," Alice repeated.

"Lie, but I'll allow it to pass." Christine stood, her long lace dress touching the floor. It tugged at the rugs as she walked forward, getting caught in the fringe. She stopped when she was nose to nose with Alice, their height similar. "You're connected," she hesitated, eyes flicking to Peyton then back again. "Connected to him. Now isn't that interesting." She lifted a single finger, the tip touching Alice's cheek before lightning struck, pushing her back.

Her skin was blackened, the finger bent at a painful angle, but she didn't comment. The two other witches stood, wands ready.

Peyton moved behind her, the wild magic electric

between them. He had opened their connection, allowing his magic to react and protect.

Christine laughed. "I will help with your investigation in exchange for the spell used to tether the..." she hesitated, her chi stretching to touch Peyton. "Hmm, what are you? You feel human, but there is clearly magic between you?"

Peyton crossed his arms and didn't correct her. He may have embraced his hair, but he still looked and felt human. The only reason she thought different was because of the wild magic that was a taunt tension between them.

"I don't know how it happened," Alice shrugged. "It was an accident. We're actually trying to remove it."

Christine narrowed her eyes. "Tell me how you did it. He feels human but clearly has magic, which must make him a weak mage at the very least. It's impossible to connect two magic bearers in a familiar link, yet there you stand... boasting it."

"I'm sorry, we don't know..."

"TELL ME!" she snapped, the hearth exploding. The cats screeched, running away as a dark substance oozed from beneath Christine's dress. "TELL ME HOW I CAN CONNECT ANOTHER MAGIC BEARER TO MY POWER!"

The dark substance grew, slowly creeping towards them.

Alice calmly stepped back, taking Peyton with her. "I don't know how it happened."

"Christine?" the older witch cautiously warned.

The Head Priestess grabbed her broken finger, bending it back into place with an audible click. "I offer you one of my witches service for one-thousand per hour, plus expenses."

"You never had any intention of helping us, did you?" Peyton finally said, anger shooting his words like bullets.

Christine chuckled. "I took this meeting as a favour to Frederick, and maybe to meet Alice." She settled back into the armchair, the black substance staining the fabric. "I wonder if our councillor knows you have a familiar?"

Peyton ignored her question. "Then you have wasted all of our time."

"It's illegal you know," she continued. "The punishment is death."

"I think it's time to leave." Alice backed away, keeping all the witches in her sight.

"Good luck finding a black magic specialist," Christine clicked her tongue. "We're the only coven in over three-hundred miles that are trained in the darker arts." She turned to the closest witch. "Kyra, escort these two out, I have to call Frederick."

"Priestess," the woman named Kyra bowed. "If you could please..." She held her arm out, gesturing towards the front door.

"Shit." The air was cold, the soil beneath Alice's feet damp. "Shit. Shit. Shit."

"She won't call him, you know," the dark witch said. "She hates Frederick, and she's too interested in learning how you did it to sabotage that."

Alice looked towards the sky, unable to see through the soot and smoke from the chimney.

"I really don't know how it happened," she murmured.

"Good, because that sort of information is forbidden for a reason." Kyra closed the door behind her, stepping down onto the earth. "What help do you need with your investigation?" she asked, eyebrows pinched.

A dark chi brushed Alice's, an uncomfortable sensation like little pinpricks across her aura.

"Are you a necromancer?" Not that Alice needed the

woman to actually confirm, she could feel the death that radiated off her, even from the short distance. It didn't necessarily mean she was bad, or even evil. But it was hard to get over such a 'go fuck yourself' atmosphere that she naturally presented.

Her chi, however, didn't match her cat-like eyes when they met, the dark amber orbs quiet, but wary. The woman tugged at her long black braid, a beautiful compliment to the bronzed brown of her flawless skin as she gave Alice a shallow nod.

"My name's Kyra Farzan."

"We need someone to assist us in the Shifter Slayer case," Peyton answered. "There was a magical residue at the scene..."

"One that I'm inexperienced with," Alice finished. "I hoped a necromancer would have better luck."

Kyra looked towards the closed door, taking her time to respond. "Do you have the body?"

Peyton jingled his keys. "We do..."

"Then I will assist you, but I can't guarantee that I will have the answers you need."

"That's great!" Alice smiled. "Will that be a problem with Christine?"

Kyra shook her head. "I'm not part of the coven, I'm registered independent with The Magicka. She doesn't make the decisions for me."

Alice moved to the car. "Brilliant, meet us at three."

* * *

She waited patiently, or as patiently as she could without bringing unwanted attention to herself. No, she only wanted one man's attention, and he was currently working behind a desk, his dark hair messy from the amount of times he had frustratedly yanked at it. He looked to be in his thirties, thirty-six to be exact. She knew he lived alone, had no pets or parents. Had no friends.

He wouldn't be missed.

Which was exactly what was needed if they were to go under the radar. It was obvious the fates were in her favour, which made a change.

The clock ticked, his lunch hour coming up just like she knew it would. On cue he slapped his pen down, thick eyebrows furrowed as he aggressively pushed himself away from his desk.

She felt excitement hum through her blood, much to the horror of her host. But that wouldn't matter, she could feel her slipping away, almost gone. Just as they all did. She should thank her, in the month she had had control of the body she had already improved it, regardless of how stubborn the voice was.

She was strong, beautiful. Not a pathetic piece of addicted flesh.

She wouldn't waste it.

She slipped off the seat, elegantly walking forward until she was just about...

"Oh, fuck," he said in strong Russian when he walked straight into her, his hand automatically reaching out to stop her fall. "I..." he paused, eyes widening. "Who are you?" he snarled, his demeanour becoming aggressive once more.

One of his colleagues coughed violently, vomit scenting the air seconds later.

He quickly reached into his pocket, placing a mask over the bottom part of his face.

She smiled, her lips painted the same shade as her hair. It was a stunning effect, she knew this from the reactions it had on the men who she had passed in the hall.

"I'm here to release you," she replied in his native tongue. "And remove the muzzle you have put upon yourself."

His hand squeezed her arm, hard enough she knew he would bruise her beautiful skin.

"Release me from what, exactly?" He tugged her closer, pulling down the mask so his breath brushed across her face. She was tall, with the heels as tall as he was, which was just shy of six-foot. Unlike the mortals around them, ones who coughed and sneezed, she wasn't effected by his anger. The emotion amplified his aura, one that made people sick.

"You know exactly what I want to release," she purred, her fingers on her free hand walking up his white shirt until she felt what called her beneath. "Now tell me Vladislav, what's going to happen if I tug on this?" She pulled the chain from beneath the shirt, the coin at the end cool to the touch.

Vlad hissed, pushing her away while quickly tugging his necklace back, hidden. "Who are you?" he growled in English.

She felt her cheeks crack into a smile. "They call me... Pandora."

CHAPTER TEN

Hospitals were always cold, their corridors painted in white. Clinical.

Needs to be pink, Alice thought to herself as she walked down yet another pale corridor. *Maybe even green.*

Surely if the paint was bright, exciting it would make the patients feel slightly better? Rather than the drab, boring pallid ice that seemed to welcome death within its walls.

Now, rainbow walls wouldn't allow such horror, she mused.

"What are you smiling about?" Peyton asked as they entered the examination room, his black trench coat a stark contrast to the bright white. It made her smile harder.

"Nothing."

"Detective Peyton and Agent Skye?" a woman in a white lab coat asked when she looked up from her folder.

"That's us." Alice smiled at the doctor, noting her name from the stitching on her breast pocket. Dr Vivian Anderson, Chief Pathologist.

"That's great, my colleague Dr Le'Sanza said you were punctual."

"Punctual?" Alice laughed, knowing her friend of many years had probably said a lot more than she was just 'punctual.' She missed him, but Miko had been working well at the Supernatural Intelligence Bureau's Tower, and the last she heard he had accepted a permanent position there.

"Apologies for the delay, the body has taken longer than usual to process." The Dr went to pull back the white sheet when Alice stopped her.

"We're waiting for a third person."

Peyton grunted, his phone beeping a second later. "We're not, we don't have long. They've found another body."

"Already?"

Dr Anderson tugged down the sheet in one swift movement, revealing a shock of red. "We will make this quick then."

Alice was prepared for the visual, but she couldn't help her flinch. The woven fabric had been removed, leaving the man naked beneath. Muscles, tendons and even a bone or two wasn't what bothered her, it was the exposed eyes that were forever open, his eyelids removed.

"Do we have an I.D.?" Alice asked with a grimace.

"No, and nothing on the missing persons register either, but that isn't surprising considering he's a shifter."

No, shifters very rarely asked for help outside their Breed as the majority were part of a group, pack, or pride. Even loners were known to the areas local Alpha.

"What about the pets?" Peyton asked.

"We can't confirm as the veterinary had already disposed of the bodies, but from what he told me over the phone the details are very similar."

Alice opened her mouth for a question, but was stopped with a hesitant knock.

Kyra pushed the door open, her large eyes open wide and framed in black. "Hello?"

"Oh, is this the third person you was waiting for?" the Dr asked. "Hello, I'm Dr Anderson."

"Miss Farzan," Peyton nodded in greeting. "It's great you could join us."

Kyra glanced at the body, then settled her attention on the floor.

Alice noticed, wondering how a necromancer, a witch that specialised in blood and death didn't like the sight of a body. "We need to get as much information as possible before we head to the new crime scene." She aimed her question at Kyra, knowing Dr Anderson would be able to give her the rundown of the report.

"Another body?" Kyra asked with a slight husky tone to her voice. "What exactly do you expect me to look for?"

Alice turned to the examination table, the body contorted mid-shift, flesh hacked and bones broken. "I don't even know where to start." The sight was grotesque, like something Hollywood would exaggerate. Yet it was real. "I know there was magic involved." Peyton had confirmed it.

Interest flashed in Kyra's eyes. "I'm going to need some space. Does he have a name?"

"No," Peyton said, watching her with both curiosity and irritation.

Dr Anderson shrugged. "Not yet," she said with disinterest. "He's John Doe on the forms until the dental records come back."

"John it is then." Mouth tight, Kyra returned her attention to the table.

"Detective Peyton, allow me to talk you through my

findings," Dr Anderson waved him over to the desk, paperwork neatly piled on top.

Alice waited, watching Kyra as she stood as still as a statue beside the body. Opening her third eye she blinked, confused with the colours that melded together before she realised what was happening. Kyra had pushed her aura out of herself, moving it slowly in a concentrated mass over the body.

"Here they are," the Dr smiled. "It's always the last place you look."

"Anything interesting?" Alice accepted the thin folder handed to her, flicking it open to begin reading the notes. She had read many autopsy reports, but she never understood all the jargon.

"What's the C.O.D?" Peyton asked as he looked over her shoulder.

Dr Anderson pointed to the right page. "Cause of death has been classed as drowning."

"Drowning?" Both Peyton and Alice echoed together.

That was unexpected.

"Yes, three millilitres of water was found in the sphenoid sinus, as well as the lungs. From the state of what's left of his flesh he wasn't in the water long, just enough to drown. There is very little evidence of haemorrhage in the remaining tissue, so I suspect he was already dead before he was skinned, at least the majority of it."

Alice frowned. "What do you mean?"

Dr Anderson flipped through the report in Alice's hands, stopping at a close up picture of the only skin left on the body, his groin. "There..." She pointed to the severed flesh. "It suggests he was alive when that was cut."

"Only there?" Alice scanned the pictures, but she couldn't tell.

"We have his time of death around eight hours before he was found. I said before his death was classed as drowning, however it's noted that around the edges of his groin there was some tissue growth."

"Growth? Then how could he have drowned?"

"It's only a theory, and we don't like to work on theories but we believe he passed out in the water, was removed before he died to start the skinning process, then when he became combative was forced to ingest valerian root."

"Valerian root?"

"Yes, a small amount. It was only flagged because his tests came back human, when, well, clearly he isn't."

"Valerian root is used as a relaxant," Peyton murmured quietly.

"You're right," Alice added. "It's supposed to help Breed sleep, but could be fatal to a human. It was probably used to calm him before he was returned to the water."

"That's the theory," Dr Anderson confirmed.

Alice hoped he had passed quickly, the drug working. The idea of fighting for his last breath while being skinned...

Peyton frowned. "Where's the stuff he was wrapped in?"

Dr Anderson moved to the second table, careful not to interrupt Kyra. Beneath the white sheet was the fabric, left in the same position they were cut. It created a slight cocoon shape, the top sagging into the centre. Up close they were pale, almost white yet not as the silver table beneath gave them a slight metallic sheen.

Kyra turned to join them, tears staining her cheeks before she wiped them away with the sleeve of her jumper. "You were right, there's this dark signature, but it's buried beneath something I have never seen before."

"What do you feel about these?" Peyton carefully reached out, touching the fabric with his bare hands.

"Excuse me!" Dr Anderson shouted when she noticed what he was doing. "You can't do that!"

Peyton quickly stepped back, eyes wide. He opened their connection, the familiar warmth radiating from Alice's chest. She felt it then, the wild magic that emitted from the fabric. It was Fae origin.

Kyra wiped at her cheeks once more, her skin taking on an ashen shade. "This fabric, they're made of..."

"Our victim," Dr Anderson finished for her. "We're not sure how yet, but the DNA matched perfectly."

"I've never... I don't know..." Kyra said, voice hoarse. "Skin is used regularly in black magic, but nothing like this."

"You think you'll be able to recognise the magic residue from a second body?" Peyton asked, his hand in his pocket.

Kyra shrugged, just a delicate shift of her shoulders. "It's possible. If I get to the body early enough I may be able to tell you more."

Alice checked her phone when it beeped a voicemail. "If there's already a second body, we're running out of time before there's a third."

Kyra looked up, features tight. "Then let's go."

(CHAPTER BREAK)

THE SMELL HIT Alice before she even exited the car, the wind carrying the scent of blood and death. The sun was hot

above, the rays blinding as spectators watched from the steps of Britain's oldest library.

"Well, this is public," Peyton murmured as they approached.

A white tent that had been erected, hiding the scene inside the large children's park on the centre green. On the same square there were two museums, three famous restaurants and a theatre which made it heavy with tourism footfall.

"Detective Peyton, Agent Skye," a uniformed officer nodded in greeting. "They're just through here." He pulled up the police tape, allowing them to walk beneath.

"She's with us," Alice said before he could stop Kyra.

Cameras flashed, the crowd shouting excitedly in the distance at the drama.

Kyra hesitated. "I'll stay back a moment," she said in a whisper. "I need to feel the area."

"Okay, join us when you're ready."

A dark hand passed through the tent, Brady's large body following quickly after. "Nice for you two to join us," he grunted, eyes flicking to Kyra. "That the black witch?"

"She's getting a feel for the area," Peyton repeated as he passed into the tent, Alice quickly behind.

The smell was stronger inside, as if it were concentrated in the tight space. Lights had been set up, facing the large climbing frame with attached yellow tube slide.

"I would like you to meet Jane Doe." Brady looked down at his notepad. "A child found her just over an hour ago."

"A child?" Peyton growled.

"Yes. She got caught on the body on the way down the slide. At the end he pulled at a loose thread around the nose thinking it was a giant toy. It was his mother who realised and reported."

"How did the killer manage to plant this body with no one noticing?" Alice muttered, kneeling to take a better look into the dark slide. "There must be CCTV facing this direction?"

"We're working on it." Brady crossed his arms. "How did the meeting with the pathologist go? Anything that can help with here?"

"It was interesting," Alice replied, staring at the bound legs that draped over the edge. The female body was covered in the same fabric as the last victim and even with the forensic lights trained inside, Alice could barely make out the shape. "Where's Jones?"

"Here!" Jones said with a cheery grin, his goggles placed on his head but the dark red marks remained around his eyes. "You miss me?"

"Do you think we could remove the top half of the slide?" Alice stepped back.

Jones nodded his head, smile growing. "As in cut it off? You think you can do it without disturbing the scene beneath?" At Alice's nod Jones shot out of the tent, returning seconds later holding a protective sheet. "Peyton, stand here." After Peyton put on gloves he made him hold one side of the sheet before he moved to the top of the slide, balancing at the entrance to grab the other half. Once they held the sheet taut he gave Alice the go ahead.

"Acri ignisiam." Alice hovered her fingertip on the yellow plastic, carefully concentrating her power to a small point. The first side took a few minutes, the second was almost off before the slide creaked. Brady grabbed the top as it began to slip towards Peyton, lifting it off as if it weighed nothing and settling it to the side.

"Nobody touch her," Jones snapped. "I need to process

everything before the coroner arrives." He ran out excitedly to grab his gear.

"She's not as malformed as the last," Peyton said as he knelt beside Alice.

The woman was placed on her back, knees bent to the side and her hands clasped together, as if she were praying. Her nose was only slightly elongated, the tip sharp enough it pierced through a gap in the weave. She was small, barely five-foot.

"Anybody else think she's posed?"

"John Doe was also posed," Brady said as he stood. "It was reported he was sat at a table with a china tea cup."

Alice looked at Brady with a frown. "A tea cup?"

"Hmmm, the gentleman that found him noticed a table with a china cup set in the alley. He knocked the table over in panic when he realised he was dead."

"But why a slide? It hides her."

"Yes, but you could say John Doe was also hidden considering he was in a dark alley behind a busy concert," Peyton added.

Brady shook his head. "Do we know what animal the last victim was?"

"No, and we may never know." Alice had seen enough. She stepped away, wanting to put space between herself and the body. "Once they're dead we can't force them to complete their shift."

"What about bloodwork?"

"Shifters, witches and druids can't be identified through DNA. They all come back as human, or even animal for shifters if they're transformed." It was how they remained undetected before the war.

"We're relying on his dentistry records," Peyton added.

Brady contemplated that for a moment. "What about when they're stuck mid-shift?"

"His bloods came back human, which was why valerian root was flagged."

"Hmmmm." Brady turned as the tent opened, and Kyra stood there with a tear stained, but determined face.

"Hello," she said, cautiously stepping inside.

"Detective Brady, this is Kyra Farzan, independent necromancer," Alice introduced them. "Detective Peyton you already know, and the crazy man outside dressed in all white is Jones, the Forensic Scene of Crime Officer."

"That's... different," Kyra said when she noticed the woman wrapped in a peachy fabric.

"Did you find anything?" Alice urged her.

A shallow nod. "A dark residue is present, the same as the last."

"How can you tell?" Peyton asked in his usual callous tone. It came across as rude, unless you knew him.

Kyra's head snapped to him, eyes narrowed. "I just can." She tugged on her braid. "If you would excuse me," she glared at Peyton. "I need to step closer to the..."

Brady and Alice stood to the side while Peyton clenched his jaw.

Her examination was thorough, her attention on the inside of the slide silent as she once again pushed her aura from her body.

"Strange," she said quietly a few minutes later, almost to herself.

"How so?" Brady asked.

When Kyra looked up, a delicate pink hue flushed her brown cheeks. "Nothing, it's silly."

"Nothing is silly," Alice said flicking her eyes to Peyton

who still trained his attention on the dark witch. "We need any leads we can find."

"Well, the way she's been posed... it's familiar."

"Familiar how?"

"Have any of you ever read anything from..." she paused. "Where was the other body found?" she asked, dark eyes brightening.

It was Peyton who answered. "He was having a tea party."

"Were his hands rested on his knees, palms up?"

Brady narrowed his eyes. "Actually he was, how did you know?'

Kyra bit her lip. "You need to look at Freya Wilson, she's a thriller author. Her latest novel depicts these exact deaths, down to the skinning." She flicked her gaze to the slide then back again. "Naked, skinned, wrapped like a mummy and then posed."

"Interesting," Brady growled, tapping his pen down in his little black book. "What was the name of that author again?"

"Freya Wilson." Kyra shook herself, the colour draining from her face. "Excuse me." She swept past the tent flap and back outside.

Alice found her by the police tape, the spectators moved on. "Hey, are you okay?"

"I'm sorry," she said on an exhale. "That was unprofessional." Kyra raised her face to the sun, closing her eyes. "It's harder when it's fresh, but I can confirm it's the same magical signature as the last."

"It's not unprofessional, I'm pretty sure I puked on my first case. They all laughed at me for weeks."

Kyra's mouth twitched. "That Detective Peyton may be able to tell you more, he may feel human but I would put

money on the fact that he's not. He has also stolen some of the fabric from John Doe."

Alice raised her eyebrow, about to respond when a flash of white hair caught her eye.

Xander stood off to the side, arms crossed as he watched her through wrap-around sunglasses. He wore a suit, the fabric black in stark contrast to his pale hair. She raised her arm and he moved forward, ignoring the uniformed officers who asked him to stop.

"It's okay," she said when an officer placed his hand on Xander's shoulder, his other reaching for his belt at Xander's growl. "What are you doing here?" she asked.

Xander remained silent, his attention on Kyra who continued absorbing the sun's rays. He frowned, tilting his head.

"Xander?"

Kyra blinked, flinching when she noticed Xander staring. Face flushed she stumbled back, and then stared in return.

"Kyra?"

Kyra blinked. "Erm, I'll go see if anybody needs my assistance." She looked towards the floor, cheeks burning as she moved back into the tent.

"Who's that?" Xander asked, his eyes tracking her until she was out of sight.

"That's Kyra... she's working with us on this case."

"She a dark witch?" he asked, even though it sounded a statement.

"Xander, what are you doing here?" she asked once again.

He shook his head, eyebrows pinched. "I was passing through the library and heard the commotion." He

shrugged, but his attention kept moving back towards the white tent. "What happened?"

"I can't say."

She expected Xander to complain, but instead he just nodded. "Understood."

"Alice?" Peyton called.

Alice moved her head to respond, and Xander was gone when she looked back.

"You going to tell me about the fabric?" Alice asked Peyton when he moved closer. "Like the sample in your pocket?"

Peyton smiled, just a small arch of his upper lip. "No, not yet. Who was that? I've seen him around that boyfriend of yours."

Alice smiled back. "You got the address for that author?"

CHAPTER
ELEVEN

Peyton pulled up outside the large house, the tall brick walls that surrounded the property keeping away prying eyes. The metal gates were open when they arrived, but as they followed the gentle bend of the drive the road disappeared from view.

"They've been following since we left the city," Peyton murmured, bending the mirror to try and get a better look, but couldn't.

Alice knew, she had noticed the black car carelessly following them for miles. They had made it obvious, close enough to tailgate when they were on the motorway. "They haven't followed us on to the property."

Shit. Shit. Shit.

"Is there something you should be telling me?" Peyton asked as they both exited the car, his pale eyes staring at her from across the roof. "Why would they be following us?"

"Just so you know, the universe doesn't revolve around me."

"Alice, we're connected. I felt your anxiety thirty

minutes ago." He opened their connection, the warmth soaking over her for a few seconds before he locked it back tight. It was long enough, the link calming her nerves.

She knew who it was, had seen them in the mirror.

"It's just some guy who I had a disagreement with." Which was the truth considering she punched Chester's balls into his throat. But it wasn't him she was worried about, even though she knew how powerful he was with or without a wand. No, it was the woman in the passenger seat who was his keeper.

She hadn't seen them in months, which meant something had changed.

Shit.

Peyton narrowed his eyes before he moved to the open gate. "They're still here."

"And they will be our problem when we leave," Alice said, turning towards the house just as the front door swung open.

"Hello?" a woman cautiously greeted from the threshold. "Can I help you?" She wore a silk dressing gown, her pale, almost white grey hair pinned up elegantly.

"Afternoon, I'm Agent Skye and this is Detective Peyton. We're here to see Freya Wilson."

The woman blinked, almost startled. "I am she, how can I help you?"

Alice knew Freya was supposed to be in her late seventies, but the woman before her looked barely fifty. Both her throat and fingers were bare of any jewellery, as were her ears. Unless she wore magic infused jewellery in her hair, the woman looked two decades younger. Surgery was good, but not that good.

Peyton seemed to think the same as he pulled out the book in question, bought from the closest bookstore.

Flicking to the back he glanced at the photograph. "Mrs Wilson," he said with a smile, "we have some questions regarding your latest book."

Freya broke into a grin, stepping out onto the porch while closing the front door behind her. "While I appreciate you're fans, I don't allow people into my home so could you please..."

"I'm sorry, I think you misunderstood." Peyton showed his badge, lifting it to the light. "We need to talk to you regarding..." He looked back at the book. "Blood of the Moon."

Freya tucked the silk around her, eyes flicking between them. Her chi stretched, brushing across Alice and Peyton in what she disguised as a greeting amongst magic bearers, but Alice knew it was a strength test and had already concealed her own. Freya's frown deepened, eyebrows pressed together as she tried to figure out what Breed they were.

"Of course, if you would like to join me." Freya held the door open, clicking it closed behind them as soon as they entered. "Would you like a drink? Tea? Coffee? Gin?" she chuckled.

"No, thank you," Alice and Peyton said in unison.

Inside the house was dark, the thick curtains drawn across all the windows. Lavender and dust tickled her nose, more so when they sat down on an old fabric Chesterfield. A desk sat towards the back, a typewriter in the centre with a pile of paper beside it.

"I must apologise about the curtains, I suffer from debilitating migraines and the darkness helps."

Freya clicked a button and the fireplace crackled into life.

"Now," she said as she sat in the armchair opposite.

"How can I help you?"

"Do you read the news?"

"The news?" she frowned. "What's this about?" She looked between Alice and Peyton.

Peyton smiled gently, easing her nerves. "We were wondering if you've received anything interesting in the last few weeks? Fan mail? Gifts? Etcetera? Anything out of the ordinary."

"Did my agent call you?" Freya looked away, hands shaking. "I asked her to keep it a secret."

"Keep what a secret?" Alice asked. When Freya remained silent she leaned forward. "Mrs Wilson..."

"It's Ms. I've been Ms since my husband passed." Freya played with the hem of her dressing gown.

Peyton and Alice exchanged a look.

"I'm sorry to hear about your husband," Alice said carefully.

"You shouldn't be," Freya smiled, "he lived a happy life." A single tear glittered down her cheek. "My apologies, I get carried away sometimes." She wiped it away with her sleeve. "To answer your question I've been receiving threats, more so of late."

"Threats?" Peyton urged. "What kind of threats?"

"Oh, you know, the usual." She gently clasped her hands together, the nails long and painted black. "Recently the letters have become rather dark, quoting my own words back at me. I write criminal thrillers, which involves me describing crime scenes in graphic detail. I didn't expect the threats to repeat that."

"In what way?"

"It would have been best if I could show you, but I've burned them all as soon as I received them. They would start with stating they were my biggest fan, and

wanted to honour my work by murdering me in the same way."

"I'm sorry, have you been receiving these threats for long?"

Freya laughed, the sound short and hollow. "Over the years I have received similar letters, harmless mostly. Blood of the Moon was my latest novel, have you read it?" When neither Alice nor Peyton answered she continued. "It's about a collection of shifter murders across New York and the trial of the one sentenced. He's a man who was brought up by his uncle, a hunter. He learned to skin as a child and became fascinated with shifters. He grew up to be a famous trophy collector."

"So he hunted and skinned shifters?" Alice asked.

"I never said that," Freya smiled, "but that's the thriller part. The killer is never who you expect it to be."

"So the killer would skin them as they would an animal for a trophy and what... wrap them up and pose them for the police to find?"

"Ah, so you have read my novel," Freya smiled. "Yes, they were posed as an added insult to the investigators. To mock them."

"What about the fabric?"

Freya's smile tightened. "Creative inspiration."

"To confirm, you haven't kept any of the letters?" Peyton asked.

"No, I couldn't bear it."

"Why haven't you called the police?"

"Because it had all been a bit harmless."

"I'll organise witness protection, if your fans are going to this extent..."

"NO!" she interrupted Peyton. "No, thank you. I don't want or need police assistance. I'll make a state-

ment but I have no interest in witness protection at this time."

"Ms Wilson..." Alice began.

"No."

It didn't take long for Peyton to write down her statement, reassuring her he would pass on the details to the station. It wasn't until they were back outside, Freya safe behind her front door before Alice spoke.

"You heading straight back to Scotland Yard?"

"Hmmm." Peyton stepped toward the open gate, checking the road before returning to his car. From his expression she knew the Knights had left. "What do you think of Ms Wilson?"

Alice didn't hesitate. "Her hands were young."

"Excuse me?" Peyton frowned.

"She's in her seventies, yet her hands look as young as mine." Alice stared at her own, the nails short, and bitten to the quick. Ms Wilsons, on the other hand, were well looked after, manicured.

"I don't understand."

"Hands are the hardest to make look young, along with the neck. So how did she do it?"

"Good genes?"

Must be amazing genes, Alice thought, looking back at her own hands. *Fucking amazing genes.*

Alice pulled off her jacket, her phone falling from her pocket and into the wet mud. "Oh, bloody hell." The mobile flashed when she touched it, showing several missed messages and texts. She always had it on silent, not wanting to risk any noise when she was either on a contract, or on an investigation.

"You okay?" Peyton asked as he opened the car.

"Ye...ah," she said with an obvious hesitation.

Peyton paused, his hand in his pocket. "The fabric feels like Fae."

Alice looked up, her phone clasped in her hand. "You thinking an Object of Power?"

"I'm not sure," he grunted. "That witch didn't really help."

"Maybe, maybe not."

Her phone flashed once again in her hand, a message from Mac.

'Come pick him up. Now!'

"Shit!" She sent a quick reply, asking him for details. She saw him start to reply, but then nothing.

"Sam?" Peyton asked, lifting an eyebrow at her nod. "Elduin says your roommate is like the wind. Strong, fast, and unable to be caught."

"Very poetic," she muttered. "We need to sort out how this fabric..."

"And discuss the doorway you witnessed before, but I also understand loyalty. We have no active leads right now and I'll try and figure out the weave."

"Okay." She tied her jacket around her waist. "You able to drop me off at Club X?"

CHAPTER TWELVE

Alice had always thought it was strange how busy Club X was in the daytime. Not as busy as the night, the darkness bringing in all kinds of clientele. However, the daytime was busy nonetheless considering they specialised in erotic dancers.

So when Alice arrived and the club was closed, she panicked.

"Hello?" She banged at the locked door, fist on metal hard enough to hurt. The entrance faced a large square, with busy restaurants and shops. She was bringing attention to herself, the loud and consistent banging echoing across the pavement. "Hello?"

A small buzz, followed by a growl.

"Alice, it's open."

A click, the door opening with a slight push. Raucous shouts filled the entrance, louder when she entered into the main room. Tables had been pushed to the edges with no care, leaving dents and scratches in the expensive wooden floor. At least two chairs were smashed, splinters showered over the blood smears and splatters. A wolf lay uncon-

scious, but from the steady rise and fall of his chest Alice knew he would be fine.

"What's going on here?" she shouted, calling her magic to her palms when an aggressive looking wolf snarled in her direction. She immediately looked him in the eye, maintaining eye contact until he dropped to his stomach, head bent to expose his throat. The show of submission made her stomach twist, but in that moment she was grateful.

"YOU!" A woman with pale blonde hair snarled, nails elongating into claws as she stomped ungraciously across the floor. Her boots crunched the broken chairs, scratching the wood further. "THIS IS ALL YOUR FAULT!" She lifted a full-shifted claw, swiping at Alice in a whip of speed.

Alice stepped back, a claw a whisper from her nose as a leopard tore through the room and tackled the woman to the ground.

"RANGER!" Mac snarled, running after the leopard who turned round with a mouth full of sharp teeth.

"What the fuck is happening?!" She hesitantly approached Sam, making sure his leopard caught her scent before she grabbed his scruff and pulled him away from the woman who lay beneath him on the floor. Her mouth stretched, fangs elongated as she fought her anger to shift. "Mac?"

"I don't know!" He turned his attention to the woman, crouching until he was closer to her face. "Olivia," he snapped. "Do. Not. Shift."

Alice felt the power from his voice drift over her, like a heavy water current. It wasn't as harsh or sharp as an Alpha, but he was still a strong dominant.

The woman ignored him, her nose becoming a snout, drool dripping between her pointy teeth. It meant she was a dominant too, maybe even stronger than Mac.

"ENOUGH!" Alice shouted, making every wolf flinch, including Mac. Olivia whined in the back of her throat, turning her face towards the tables.

Mac shot Alice a warning glance, his eyes reflecting back his own wolf.

Great, she thought. *I seem to have pissed everyone off.*

"Sam?" She tugged on the leopard. "What's happened?"

A ripple appeared over his fur, obscuring the beautiful rosettes. Lifting her hand she stepped away, allowing him the space to shift back. Over the few minutes other staff members entered the room, hovering around the edges. Two she knew were new, vampires from what she guessed from their dark eyes. Another dancer was a predatory cat, and another a falcon who watched the event unfolding with only a little interest. All the waitstaff were wolves, and their hostile gaze was aimed at her alone. They prickled against her skin, but she refused to acknowledge them.

"Alice," Roman said from the back. "You okay?" He pushed through the crowd, much to the grumbles of the others and crushed her in a hug. He had grown even bigger in the weeks she hadn't seen him, his frame filling out until he was almost the size of his brothers.

"Roman," Mac said, his voice vibrating with a barely controlled rage. "Can you enlighten me with what the fuck happened?" He swept his gaze across the room, mouth tightening at the broken furniture.

"Erm," he mumbled, shuffling from one foot to the other as he stared at Mac's throat. "I think you should let Ranger explain."

Alice paused, wondering who the bloody hell Ranger was until she remembered it was Sam's stage name.

Sam groaned, climbing to his feet. A cut slit his top lip and a bruise darkened the golden skin across his left pec.

But they were already healing, the majority clotted and sealed from his first shift.

"Why did you call her?" he said with uncharacteristic venom. "What a fucking joke."

"That's it," someone called from across the room. "His pretty little whore witch is here to save the day!"

"HENRY!" Mac snapped, turning the full extent of his rage to the man. "GET ON THE FUCKING GROUND." The man dropped immediately to his stomach.

It looked strange on a full grown adult.

Mac returned his attention to Sam, ignoring Olivia as she climbed to her feet, her face and hands completely human. "I called her because if I didn't you wouldn't have stopped until Paul was dead."

The wolf Alice noticed when she first entered groaned. Paul, she assumed.

"You weren't listening, and we both know your animal doesn't listen to my dominance," Mac continued.

Sam shook out his hair, the long blonde strands tangled. Olivia smirked, tilting her head as she turned to Alice, but she didn't look her in the eye, keeping them lowered. She was beautiful, taller than Alice by a good several inches with a bust and butt to be envious of. Her blonde hair was pale, as pale as Sam's which went well with the dark blue of her eyes.

"You shouldn't have called her," Sam said, his voice softening as he moved to stand behind Alice, his chin resting on her hair. She immediately began to stroke down the arm he circled around her stomach, calming him, calming his leopard. "That wasn't fair."

"What happened?" Mac asked again.

Sam remained silent, as did everyone else.

"No one? Really?" he snarled. "So you think it's appro-

priate to trash my business? In front of customers? HUMAN CUSTOMERS!" He raised his voice, his wolf taking the lead. "NEVER MIND THE COST IT IS TO REPLACE EVERYTHING, THE AMOUNT OF MONEY WE'VE LOST BY JUST CLOSING FOR THE EVENING!" He began to pace, face flushed. "Everybody get to work on repairing the floor. Every single bottle smashed, chair broken and walls dented will be replaced or repaired, and it's coming from all of your wages."

A chorus of cries, complaining that it was unreasonable.

"ENOUGH!" Mac growled. "This was everyone's fault. No one stopped Paul and Ranger from fighting, and I know many of you would have spurred them on." He carefully caught everyone's eyes, waiting until they dropped their stare. "We do not discuss pack business here, that is one of the rules."

Mumbles, but the majority of the staff began to tidy up.

"You," Mac snapped at Sam, finger pointed. "Follow me into my office now. Paul will follow when he's able to walk again."

Sam's arm tightened, but he released her. "I'm not leaving Alice here."

"I'll stay with her," Roman said, raising his chin. "She will be fine."

Sam stared, the amber of his irises glowing until he nodded. "Baby girl, I'll be right back."

She watched him go, confused with everything. What had happened for Sam to react so violently? He wasn't a fighter, not really. Punching out leery men who wouldn't leave her alone when they were younger didn't count. He preferred to use his words, yet Paul remained dazed on the floor, the wolf shaking his head with a cry.

"Stupid bitch," Olivia said with a flick of her hair. "Doesn't even realise this was all about her."

"That's enough," Roman sighed, pinching the bridge of his nose.

"What?" she whined, hands on her shapely hips. "It's because of her the pack is broken. She needs to take responsibility and fix it!"

"What are you talking about?" Alice asked.

Olivia tilted her head, lip lifting in a snarl. In a burst of speed she howled, launching herself forward. Alice barely had time to brace before Roman jumped in front, flooring Olivia with little effort. He panted, skin undulating as he fought for his own control. He whispered something to her, too quiet for Alice to hear.

Alice grabbed his shoulder, using touch to centre him. He relaxed, but not before she noticed that red tinge in his eyes, and his voice was deep and smoky when he finally spoke.

"Sorry," he mumbled.

Veins appeared beneath his skin, black and pulsating.

A memory flashed, of a great Daemon with wings of darkness, clear enough Alice dropped her hand.

Lesser. She remembered Lucy calling those that were forced to transcend that were not druids. *Creatures who have Daemon tendencies.*

Was that what Roman was? A Lesser? Was he more effected than they all originally thought? She really hoped not.

"What happened here?" she asked him when he calmed himself down, his features back to normal.

Roman took his time to respond, jaw clenched. "Olivia, go help clean."

Olivia growled, but she climbed to her feet and walked off.

"Roman?"

"Look, I can't speak here and Sam will be back in a minute. Come to the Compound tomorrow, I'll explain everything."

Alice hesitated. She hated that place. "Roman, I..."

"Please?" he begged. "I promise I will explain everything, it will help."

Alice noticed Sam skulk in, making a bee-line towards her with a face of thunder.

"Okay, I'll come tomorrow."

Alice wasn't sure what to make of the flash of relief across his face.

CHAPTER
THIRTEEN

Alice hummed, window open and hair whipping in the wind as she followed along, not so well, to the pop song that played on the radio. A radio that barely functioned until Sythe had worked his magic. She would have to thank him.

At least something was going her way. With all the crap she had to deal with, she would take her beloved car actually working as a win. Especially as Sam had been suspended with no pay, which meant her wage would have to pay for all the bills. Sam would never put himself in a position without money, not when he had experienced homelessness. But that didn't mean he could survive on savings.

She had no idea when he would return to work, of even if he could return after the damage he did. He still hadn't told her exactly what had made him react in a violent way, and that's what worried her. They told each other everything.

They had argued over it, one of the worst fights they

had ever had. Just before he stormed away she promised she wouldn't bring it up again, but she never said she wouldn't interrogate the wolves from White Dawn. Something had upset him, and she was going to find out what. He acted like her protector, not understanding she would do anything for him. He was her best friend, her brother. But he was also someone who self-destructed when left alone with his own mind.

"What the fuck..." Alice slowed her car until it stopped, unable to tear her eyes away from the two men who walked naked into the surrounding trees of The Compound. The drive in front of the house was packed with more cars than the space could hold. Many had resorted to parking on the grass, their tyres ripping the wet green from its roots.

"Alice!" Roman ran over, opening her car door and tugging her arm before she could protest. "You made it!"

"I said I would." She noticed a woman in the distance, also naked as she ran across the clearing, breasts distractingly bouncing free. "Is the whole pack here?" she said before adding, "and why are they naked?"

"I think so," Roman mumbled, looking away.

"No, wait." She pulled out of his grip. "You said you would explain to me what happened last night, you didn't say it would be in front of the whole pack!" She didn't actually know it was the whole pack, but there were a lot of cars.

"Look, It was just some stupid fight. Paul called you some horrible names and Sam reacted badly. But I know who can fix it."

She didn't care Paul was calling her names, she was well aware the pack blamed her for their Alpha's punishment, and she was too tired with their shit to fight it. She

had forgiven Rex for his role in the situation, and Roman was largely a reason for that. But her patience wasn't infinite. If they were starting to go for Sam she needed to put an end to it.

His statement registered. "Wait..." Eyes narrowed, she faced him. "What do you mean, 'fix it?'"

Roman lifted his head, tilting his ear to the air as if he heard something she couldn't. "Come on, you're going to miss it." He ran towards the woods, the same direction as the others. He stopped at the first tree, looking back to see if she was following.

"Fuck sake." Alice debated her choices. She did not want to be anywhere near the pack, but Roman had said he could fix it. "Shit. Shit. Shit."

"Come on!" he called with a grin, a gust of wind catching his hair to give him a boyish charm.

"Ugh, fine!" she shouted back. "But I'm not getting naked!" Shifters thought nothing of baring their flesh to the world, it was the norm since they were naked when they transitioned from one shape to another. But sometimes, packs or groups of shifters forget everyone else was very much a prude.

She was more comfortable than most, but that came with living with a leopard who thought he was god's gift to men, women and anything else he set his eye on. That didn't mean she was comfortable amongst a group of strangers who thought it was appropriate to talk about the weather with their dicks on full display.

"Roman, what is this?" she asked as he walked her towards the sound of music and laughter. The trees weren't thick, the path clear but that didn't stop the spike of anxiety that twisted her stomach.

She had run through the same woods, had fallen.

That was in the past, Rex forgiven. Yet, why did she feel she was being hunted again?

The forest wasn't large, only a small strip that separated The Compound's two large fields. One was the white zone, as Roman explained beside her, a field for children and vulnerable wolves. The one they were headed to was classed as the red zone, as it was the furthest from the safety of the house. Their land connected to other shifter packs, but even with Xavier culling those believed to have been involved with The Master's cult, White Dawn was still the largest.

Alice paused at the edge of the trees, not sure what to make of the festivities that presented her on the larger field. Fifty or so wolves, not all naked some even in wolf form. They all sat or stood in a large circle, the centre stripped down to bare earth, surrounded in crudely created wooden posts. Flowers decorated the edges, some even placed delicately in the women's hair and around their throats in a chain. Spikes cut into the ground, flames dancing as the clouds threatened to darken the early afternoon sky.

She took her time, sweeping her gaze across everyone who turned to stare at her on the edge, Roman howling in greeting beside her. His eyes were alight when he turned, his startling irises a circle of red much like when Kyle lost control.

"You ready?" he asked, holding her hand in an iron grip. She would have thought he held her for comfort, but from the tightening of his fist she thought it was to stop her from running. What the fuck was he afraid of? She couldn't outrun a wolf, never mind the fifty that watched her with both hostile and curious eyes.

Ready for what? she thought, but her voice didn't respond as her attention settled on the twin Alphas that stood to the side, watching her with different expressions. Theo, the scar that split his face red against his pale flesh watched her with horror, while Rex gave his usual poker face.

She approached, her boots crunching the grass and twigs as the twin Alphas stood up in greeting. Mac caught her attention from the left, his head shaking carefully from one side to the other as Theo stood forward.

Mac didn't want her to do something? Do what?

"What is this?" Theo asked with a tight smile.

You tell me? she thought, but instead she remained silent before her mouth got her into trouble.

Maybe that was what Mac was warning her about?

"She came because I asked," Rex growled in a voice that caused the hair at the back of her neck to stand on edge. He angled his head, nose scrunched as he scented her from across the dirt circle.

Her eyes settled on Roman beside her, who shrugged with a frown.

An old woman tugged at Alice, handing her a rope made of fresh flowers. "Usually you would be bathed beneath the moon, and covered in flowers picked by our female elders," she explained. "But we assumed you wouldn't be traditional."

Alice couldn't remain silent anymore, panic starting to flare at the overwhelming attention. "Traditional what?"

Rex nodded, his long hair sweeping forward in a half bow. "Our mating ceremony."

"Did you just say 'mating ceremony?'" Alice choked. "You have got to be fucking kidding me?"

"What?" Roman scowled, tightening his hand in hers.

"Rex, you never said anything about a mating ceremony? You said you could help her if she came?"

"A witch can never be an Alpha's mate," someone hissed.

"I will never see her as Beta!" another added.

"This is bullshit!"

Howls and shouts erupted around her, but Alice cut them all off with one sharp glare that ended with Rex. "I will *not* mate you."

"She doesn't know?" Theo asked his twin, nostrils flaring before he returned his attention to Alice. "Rex started the bonding process, and while the mating connection takes time to be accepted it leaves the remaining pack vulnerable. It was why we've been having a few problems with neighbouring packs trying to take over territory."

"How did he start the bonding process?" Alice felt like she was on Mars. "What the fuck is going on? Why are shifters so draconic?"

"You gave me permission," Rex growled, deepening his voice as his eyes glittered in memory.

A flush burned across her body. She had given him consent for sex, and by goddess she wished it hadn't have happened, but for mating? Hell no. "Are you telling me that the thirty seconds we spent together was enough for you to assume I agreed to mate you?"

A few chuckles that immediately stopped at Rex's snarl.

Alice shifted the hair off her shoulder, keeping her head high even as her heart raced. She knew it was a low blow, but she wasn't feeling pretty friendly in the situation.

"Do I not get a choice?" She desperately looked between the brothers, but neither Roman or Theo would look at her. "You're Alpha Theo, not..."

"I'm still Alpha," Rex interrupted. "My twin can't take the role unless he defeats me in battle."

"Where's Xavier? He would never accept a witch as an Alpha's mate." Alice carefully took a step back, but some of the wolves had moved behind her. Not threatening, but there all the same. "I'm sorry, I don't want to be your mate." She raised her voice, so every wolf could hear. "I'm not your Alpha."

"We know that," a woman purred to the side. She stood up, naked but for the flowers in her long, pale blonde hair. "Which is why I challenge you for the right to mate with the Alpha."

"Oh, Olivia," Alice muttered, her attention naturally dropping to the large, dark nipples of the women she met only the night before. "Fan-fucking-tastic."

"Me too!" Another woman climbed to her feet, her modesty covered in a sunflower patterned dress. She was younger, barely out of her teens. Another followed quickly, taking the women up to three.

"Alice, may we speak in private?" Rex asked, hair covering his expression. "Please," he added quietly.

He went to take her hand, which she immediately snapped away, crossing her arms.

"Follow me." With hard eyes he moved towards the privacy of the tree line.

"I don't want this," she said as soon as he nodded that they were out of ear shot. "What the fuck were you thinking?"

"We both know I wasn't thinking," he snapped, the first sign of real anger she had seen in... forever. "I hoped it would have helped, our mating would create a strong pack. Right now the pack magic is damaged because we haven't finished the ritual, as Alpha I need to repair it."

"Then turn it off!" Not that she had any idea what she was asking to be turned off, she knew nothing of pack magic.

"It can't be turned off," he said, insulted.

"Rex, this has nothing to do with me," Alice said, desperately sweeping her gaze across the waiting pack.

What the fuck had she gotten herself into?

"Doesn't it?" he growled, taking an aggressive step forward. "This is *your* fault."

"What?!" Alice felt like he slapped her. "How can It be my fault?"

"Because of you I've lost everything, my brothers trust, my pack, even my fucking dominance. If it hadn't been for you, it wouldn't have been ruined."

Heat at her fingertips. An overwhelming power threatening to break free. "You did all those things to yourself, Rex," she said, her voice darker, smoky. "You made the deal with The Master, not me."

"No..."

"You endangered your own pack."

"NO!" he roared.

"You almost killed me because of your problems." She swallowed back the power, her chi pulsating along with her heartbeat, ready. "Your problems, Rex. Not mine, and definitely not your younger brother's who went through hell because of your choices."

"YOU OWE ME!" Rex snapped. "TOGETHER WE COULD HAVE DESTROYED HIM, YET YOU DID NOTHING!"

She punched him, hard enough he staggered back with a red welt across his jaw. Her hand screamed in pain, the angle wrong and her thumb possibly bruised, but she didn't care.

"How dare you," she whispered, barely controlled rage

making her voice warble. "There is no one to blame but yourself."

Rex cooled his features, betraying nothing. "You can't just walk away. The pack bleeds as it waits for the connection to be completed. The only way that it can be repaired is if I take a mate, or my declared mate dies."

"Then take a mate, just not me."

Rex growled. "You might think us beneath you because we can't do magic in your sense, but pack magic is natural. An Alpha's job is to control the strength and flow of the pack magic, helping packmates control over their animal. It stops them being overwhelmed with instincts. It's why you'll very rarely find low dominance shifters outside a group or pack, or you'll see the packs of weak Alphas destroyed from the inside. The pack magic calls to you as I chose you beneath the light of the new moon. You have to answer otherwise you will jeopardise the dominant flow of my pack, and I will not let that happen." He bent, making them almost nose to nose. "And you know the lengths I would go to for my pack."

Alice straightened her spine. "Is that a threat?"

"You need to show them you have the strength to lead them by my side. If you wish to mate me, you need to win."

"So I have to lose?" Alice looked back towards the women, three strong shifters who were both stronger and faster. "Witches don't mate."

"Packs aren't just shifters. Humans, witches and even some Fae have mated in."

"I don't love you," her voice cracked. Actually, right then she hated him.

Rex's features tightened, but he still betrayed no emotion. "Not all mates choose love, some mate for convenience."

"Convenience?" Alice laughed, the noise on the edge of hysteria. "It's always nice to be just a convenience, I guess."

A pulse beat against the skin on his cheek. "I'm sorry, if there was another way..." He allowed silence to finish his sentence.

Alice looked away, her chi vibrating as she fought the anger that threatened to spill. "You're not sorry."

CHAPTER FOURTEEN

Theo had taken a seat on a newly placed bench, Roman quietly talking beside him. Leaving Alice to stand alone Rex took his place beside his brothers, the women hissing beneath their breath. Theo noticed the welt on his twin's jaw, the mark almost healed.

A man stood forward amongst the crowd, his dark skin covered only in a pair of blue denim jeans. Black hair covered his chest, thick and coarse.

"Sire," he said with his eyes trained forward. "I wish to leave White Dawn." Murmurs behind him, the wolves looking to one another before Theo stepped forward, placing a heavy hand on the man's shoulder.

Claws pierced through Rex's fingertips, but his voice remained calm. "Trey, this can be discussed after..."

"No," Trey interrupted, dropping his chin at Rex's growl. "I will not be a part of this, and for that I state my official resignation."

"And where will you go? Strays are not welcome here."

Trey began to speak, but immediately snapped his mouth shut.

"He will go with me," Theo said, features settling into a resolute expression. Squaring his shoulders he stepped in front. "I will no longer stand and watch as you destroy White Dawn's honour."

"Theo?" Roman began quietly, looking between them both from his seat on the earth. "What are you doing?" Rex interrupted.

"You destroyed us this past year," Theo continued with a renewed strength. "Possibly even before then. White Dawn was once the strongest, most powerful predatory pack, and now look at us." Theo pulled an aura, his dominance leaking across the pack until they all, one by one fell to their knees or lower. "It's because of you your own brother was taken as leverage and packmates were murdered."

Rex gritted his teeth as he felt the influence, their dominance equal. "I did what I had to do, for our survival..."

"Is that what you tell yourself?" Theo snapped. "For their survival? Or yours?"

"And what exactly would you have done?" Rex aggressively stepped forward, his intention clear as he stuck a finger out. "We will never know because you ran away."

Alice lowered herself to her knees, wanting to be below the eyeline of the two feuding Alphas. She had never seen a dominance fight, but it looked like that was about to change.

"Ran away? I left because you know what would have happened if I had stayed. I chose to leave so we didn't have to fight. I chose you over my pack. But that's not going to happen again. I forgave you for your reckless decision before, listened to your excuses with rose-tinted glasses. But I will not stand around as you show an outsider that

we're no better than senseless animals. You cannot force a mating."

"We both know mates don't always agree at the beginning, which is what the mating dance is for." Rex turned towards the pack, making sure he had their attention. "I chose us an Alpha female, one powerful enough to protect us."

"Oh, you mean by kidnapping me and gifting me to a cult to sacrifice?" Alice mumbled beneath her breath. "Real fucking romantic."

"Alice?" Theo asked, the power in his voice giving her pause. "Do you wish to continue with the mating dance?"

All eyes fell on her.

She carefully shook her head from side to side. She had no interest in being anyone's mate, especially Rex's.

"Then before the pack, I, Theodore Wild officially challenge Rexley Wild for the position of Alpha of White Dawn."

"Theo..."

"I will not be part of this, Rex." Theo raised his voice. "Your corruption has grown within the pack, weakening us until we were seen as prey to the other packs. Fight me, and we shall allow nature to decide what's best."

"Please don't do this."

Theo closed his eyes, cheekbones sharp. "You've given me no choice." A series of cracks as he shifted into a large brown wolf, the end of his tail black, as if it were dipped in ink. It was the fastest shift she had ever seen, the whole transformation taking thirty seconds or so. Theo snarled, ears pinned to his head as he bent into a crouch.

"So be it." Rex jumped, shifting mid-air to hit his twin, his shift taking slightly longer as an identical wolf emerged in the blur of teeth and claws. Blood sprayed the crowd, one

that watched with their full attention as the Alphas went for the throats.

Alphas were born, not made. They were naturally stronger, faster. Rex and Theo both equal.

Roman crawled towards her, eyes bright with red tinged tears.

"We need to go," he whispered. "I'm sorry, I didn't know," his voice broke. "This isn't safe."

"What's happening?" Her eyes couldn't track the wolves, their movements a brown smudge with flashes of white and red. It wasn't like the documentaries, where they paused to circle each other and snarl, it was a full on brawl. Blood had wet the earth, an alarming amount that didn't seem to effect either's ferocity at which they attacked.

"This is all my fault..." Roman's eyes flicked behind her, widening to saucers.

Alice turned just as the air shifted, enough that the teeth struck her left shoulder and not her throat. Biting back a scream she flung her arm out, fire pulsating at her fingertips.

"VENTILABIS!" The teeth ripped out of her shoulder, the pain piercing as Alice let out a small cry. Left arm weakened she tightened it to her body, pulse strong as she felt an overwhelming warmth soak into her shirt. With her right arm she reached back, pulling her sword from the hidden sheath against her spine.

The wolf that had attacked her was small and white blonde, its face scorched until blackened skin had appeared beneath the fur.

"Olivia's within her right to fight you for right as Alpha female," one of the pack members said with a shrug. "It's our way."

"It's not our way to attack someone like that," another answered.

"I don't want to be Alpha female." Alice gritted her teeth. "I'm not a shifter."

Olivia's wolf howled, shoulders hunched as she prepared to attack again, her teeth stained red. The pack stepped back, opening up the circle until they surrounded them, as well as Rex and Theo.

Great, Alice thought. *This was exactly how I felt I should spend my Saturday.*

A dark wolf appeared beside her, his coat as dark as night with arctic eyes circled with red.

"Roman?"

He glanced up, his wolf recognising her with a familiar bark. He was larger than she remembered, almost twice the size. Before he could have been just a domesticated dog, and a small one at that. But with his head hitting her at her hips, he was almost the size of his brothers.

Roman let out a howl, what looked like smoke puffing out from between his sharp teeth. Olivia howled in return, her attention on Alice as she dug her claws in the earth, launching herself once again. Roman's tail knocked Alice to her knees, quick enough that Olivia's snapping jaws missed as Roman sliced down her flank, deep enough she collapsed. "ROMAN!" Alice tried to pull him back, but he had already bitten down on Olivia's stomach, ripping her to shreds. When her hand brushed against his scruff he turned and barked at her, his eyes closer to red than blue as he turned back to his feast.

"The fight's almost over." A man stepped in between them, dark arms raised in submission as Alice held her blade in front.

Alice kept him in her sight, turning her head slightly so she could watch the Alphas. One of the wolves had pinned the second with his mouth around the other's throat. But even as the bottom wolf struggled, teeth didn't pierce flesh.

"Come on, come on, submit," the man whispered, ignoring her sword.

She pulled away, noticing it was Tyler, Rex's second. Trey stood closely beside him, their features similar enough that they could be family.

"What's happening?" She couldn't tell the two identical wolves apart.

It was Trey who answered. "Theo would never hurt his twin, but Rex needs to submit for it to be over. If he doesn't..." he let the end of the sentence drift off.

Theo bit down harder, closing off Rex's airflow.

After several minutes, everyone, both those in wolf form and human howled as Rex finally collapsed beneath the jaws of Theo.

Theo dropped his twin, leaving him breathing heavily in the dirt and blood as he turned towards the pack, his howl louder than all the others combined. He started to shift back, the transition taking painfully longer as Alice watched pale flesh rip through fur. Theo stood naked, skin covered in sweat. The wounds he received in the fight were a bright pink, partially healed. His scar, that Alice though was just on his face, travelled down his torso and criss-crossed his left thigh.

Bending over to Rex he whispered something, the wolf moaning low in his throat before he began to shift back too.

The crowd was silent, the only sounds from the wind against the leaves and the wet sloppy snarls as Roman devoured his meat. Theo settled his attention on his

youngest brother, pulling him back by the scruff as pack mates silently cried at what remained of Olivia.

"What happened here?" Theo asked, his wolf vibrant.

A finger pointed. "It was the witch, it was her fault!"

Fifty sets of predatory eyes turned to Alice.

Oh fuck!

CHAPTER
FIFTEEN

"Alpha!" A man puffed, holding a naked woman against his chest. "I found her in the forest."

The woman coughed up blood, her hands squeezed around a knife that protruded out of her stomach. "Olivia," she choked. "She killed... Briana's dead."

Roman whined in Theo's clutches, snapping at anyone who got near.

"DOWN!" Theo barked, forcing Roman onto his back, stomach exposed.

"Olivia attacked the witch," another packmate nodded in Alice's direction. "She attacked from behind and Roman defended her."

"Hmm," Theo bowed his head, eyebrows drawn together as he sighed. He took the woman from his packmate's arms and gently laid her on the floor. In one clean movement he pulled the knife from her stomach, then forced her to shift to heal the majority of the damage. When the newly shifted wolf climbed shakily to her feet he faced the remainder of his pack, shoulders back, chin lifted as he

swept his gaze across the crowd. “White Dawn, I am Alpha, and my word is law.”

A chorus of howls in agreement.

“Rexley Wild is to be exiled from our lands, and White Dawn will start fresh. Our reputation was tainted, but we’re going to claw it back. We were once the largest, and strongest pack in Europe, but those leeches that corrupted our pack are gone. We will be the strongest once more.”

Roman rolled onto his stomach, head settled on his front paws. His eyes were crazed, jaws snapping at anyone who moved too close.

“Sire, what about Olivia? Roman...” someone asked.

“Olivia murdered her competition in the middle of an Alpha battle.” Theo made sure his voice carried across the field. “She also embarrassed our hospitality to an outsider who doesn’t know, or understand our customs. I asked Roman to protect her, and he did as his Alpha asked. Her family may bury her body, but it will not be on White Dawn land. Are there any of you that oppose this?”

The wolves murmured between themselves before eight or so stepped forward.

Theo, with eyes of ice growled. “Then you can leave, you’ll have an hour to get off our land until you’re hunted down for trespassing.”

(CHAPTER BREAK)

THE WIND WAS BITTER, her body tense as she waited for Riley to pick her up. She had wanted to get out of there as quickly

as possible, so when she discovered someone had clawed her tyres she thought she might explode.

Tears burned her eyes as she tried to control the shivers that wracked her body, shooting pains across her shoulder. She was tired, but at least she was no longer bleeding. Being close to a pack of angry wolves while wounded wasn't the best idea, even though it was their fault.

Roman prowled in the trees behind her, every now and then coming over to bump his nose in her hand before running back. The rest of the pack stayed away, shooting her curious glances when they left for their own homes. Which was good, because she was no longer friendly.

Alice perked up when she heard a car, but immediately cursed when she noticed who was in it. Xavier parked beside her beat up Volkswagen, his car flashy and expensive. It was something she wouldn't have expected from a man like him, one so raw and primal.

"Just the witch I need to speak to," he said, orange eyes bright. "How interesting that you're here." His eyes narrowing onto her shoulder. "With bite marks too."

"Yes, how interesting," she mumbled, hand itching to palm her sword that was tucked neatly back in her sheath.

"What happened?" he demanded.

She wasn't fond of his tone, but answered anyway. "Talk to your pet."

"Also the reason why I'm here, it seems I've been giving him too long a leash." He paused, watching the wolves scramble away in their cars with a slow growing grin. He was their judge, jury and executioner after all. "You owe me a favour," he said once they were alone once more.

Wild magic sparkled inside her chi.

Bom. Bom. Bom. Bom.

Alice shrugged it off.

"Regret's a powerful thing." It was getting to the point she should have kept her mouth shut and allowed Xavier to execute Rex. It would have made her life easier.

"Shifters have been disappearing over the last few years, which isn't unusual amongst nomads. But recently it has come to my attention those shifters had turned up dead, murdered."

"Murdered?"

Xavier thrust a newspaper at her, the front page crumpled.

'The Shifter Slayer has struck again!' it read in large black typography.

"This needs to stop," he growled, stripes appearing across his skin before disappearing.

Bom. Bom. Bom. Bom.

Alice turned, the urge to run towards something overwhelming as wild magic teased her fingertips.

What the fuck?

A snarl, Xavier appearing in her eyeline. "Pay attention," he clicked. "You owe me a debt."

Alice blinked, shaking her head. "Sorry." She was already on the job, but if she didn't admit that to Xavier it would get rid of her debt to him. Two birds, one stone. "You said years? How many exactly?"

"Eighteen in the last two years or so, all skinned and wrapped."

"Eighteen? Fuck." That meant the 'Shifter Slayer' had been working for longer than they initially thought. "Why are you only now reporting this?"

Xavier's nostrils flared, jaw clenched. "It took me some time to come to this information. I know you've been hired

as a Breed Consultant for Spook Squad, or whatever stupid fucking name they're called."

Shit. "What exactly do you want with your favour?"

"As soon as you've hunted down who's doing this, you call me," he growled. "I get to take them out."

Bom. Bom. Bom. Bom.

"I'll see what I can do."

Bom. Bom. Bom. Bom.

"Do you hear that?" she whispered as her head turned back towards the clearing. She saw the car pull up beside her in her peripheral, but all she wanted to do was move forward.

"Alice?" Riley touched her shoulder before she hissed out in pain. "What happened?"

Claws pierced through Xavier's fingertips, but he remained silent, his orange eyes watching Riley with caution.

"It's... beating," Alice murmured. "Can you hear the beating?"

Bom. Bom. Bom. Bom.

"I..." Riley's eyes turned liquid silver, mouth curved into a snarl. "There's Shadow-Veyn in the area." He shot off in the direction of the red zone, Alice tearing after him without a second thought. They cleared the trees quickly, finding themselves in the clearing within a matter of seconds.

The beating intensified, originating from the iridescent oval that floated a foot from the centre. It shimmered, symbols flashing in a circle below it, scorching their patterns into the earth before changing to another.

"Is that?" she began as her wild magic sung along with the hum.

"An active portal," Riley finished for her. "Yes, and that's a hellhound, classification D."

The beast snarled, circled by several wolves. The wolves snapped aggressively, but didn't approach. The Hellhound was twice their size, possibly bigger than the last one she encountered. Its head was void of fur, skull a pale grey colour etched with marks and lines around the hole where its nose was supposed to be. Red eyes sank into hollow sockets while smoke floated between exposed ribs. Spikes poked out of its back, the sharp bones an extension of its spine.

"D?" Alice shouted. "What the fuck is a classification D?"

What happened to A though C?

The hound snarled, showing off three sets of razor sharp teeth.

Alice palmed her blade. "Riley, here!" She handed him her sword, the glowing runes along the steel pausing as it switched hands before renewing their glow in a slightly different shade. She wasn't stupid, she knew Riley was trained in dealing with Shadow-Veyn, unlike her who still wore the scars from last time.

Riley's tattoos blazed down his arms and across his throat, the marks echoing along her sword as the usual runes morphed into druid glyphs. It was curious, but she didn't have time to think about it while the hellhound howled an ear-splitting cry.

"Don't let it escape," Riley said just as he jumped forward, knocking the wolves away before they could suffer a fatal bite. Her sword pointed tightly in his larger grip.

Alice shouted at any wolf that got too near. "Stay back!"

The hound howled once more, but this time something

responded, and it wasn't the wolves. A dark blur jumped through the portal, smaller than the first but just as horrifying. It's red eyes settled on the closest wolf, lips peeled to reveal black gums and sharp teeth.

'Listen out for the hounds.'

Was Lucy trying to warn her?

She lifted her hand, her palm already engulfed in flames that sparkled with wild magic. A wolf reared back, inches from the hounds poisonous teeth.

Alice thrust her hand to the left. *"VENTILABIS!"*

The wave of scorching heat pushed the beast back, enough for Alice to tackle the wolf out of the way of large snapping jaws. With a grunt she rolled, taking the hit in her already painful shoulder.

"ADOLEBITQUE!"

The chi shot from her fingertips, concentrated into a line that she forced to circle the hound. Wolves barked at the flames as they crackled and danced in the wind, trying to bite their way through until wild magic snapped them away.

"You okay?" Theo appeared in her eyeline, a hand held out to help. She accepted it, allowing him to pull her back up to her feet.

"One bite will kill you," she hissed out a breath, wondering how much the shifted wolves could understand. The fact they continued to try and fight her fire she guessed they understood very little. "Pull your wolves back."

Theo narrowed his eyes, jaw set. "That thing is on my land. It's attacking..."

"Their bite is poisonous. If you don't believe me, ask Rex and Xavier." They had witnessed it before.

Both the men she named stood to the side, arms folded

as they watched the action. When neither protested her statement Theo howled, calling back his wolves just as Riley thrust her sword through the larger hounds throat. As soon as its head separated, the body began to dissipate back into the earth.

Fire was a roar in her ears as it started to spread, eating up the grass and branches within reach. “Shit!” She called the magic, teasing it back into line before the smaller hound leaped over the flames, taking down a wolf. “SHIT!”

Alice ran over, waving her arms. “Oi, ugly!” The hound turned its head, the wolf struggling below it. “That’s right, over here big boy.”

She had no idea if it was a boy or not, she had no interest in fact checking. The hound stepped back, watching her with tiny eyes in large, dark sockets. Smoke drifted through the gaps in its sharp teeth.

“What are you? Classification A? B? Don’t tell me you’re a C? Those guys are the worst!” She slowly backed away from the pack, its gaze following her every move. “Come on.” She was prepared when it tensed its back legs, allowing herself to be knocked down into the earth.

Fire pulsed around her, but it wasn’t enough as she felt drool burn like acid across her skin, foul breath choking. She thrust her hands up, her palms going straight though the gaps in its ribs and into his chest cavity.

The hound snarled down at her, its fangs too close for comfort.

“VENTILABIS!”

Her wrist caught on a bone as the hound was launched into the air, bony tail alight. A glint of silver, Riley appearing beside it. With one swing the hound was cut in half, each side falling apart to reveal its blackened organs inside. Her fire continued to burn, creeping towards the

body before the hound dissipated into the earth, just like the other.

Alice recalled her magic, the mud beneath her feet burnt and crunching when she climbed to her feet. The iridescent oval pulsated, the symbols beneath a scorched mess as they overlapped one another.

How do I turn it off? she thought. It was literally a floating cloud with no definitive structure. *What the...* Alice blinked, the dark figure inside the oval large, with pointy horns and batlike wings arched above broad shoulders.

Bom. Bom. Bom. Bom.

"Alice? Are you okay?"

With a loud pop the portal collapsed, the cloud turning almost liquid before disappearing altogether.

"Alice?" Riley rushed to her arm, checking where the poisonous spittle had landed. He covered it with his palm, the light burning just as hot as he murmured something under his breath. He twisted her wrist, checking her single tattoo. "Looks like you have the right ink."

He handed back her sword, his tight t-shirt ripped to pieces as well as the flesh beneath. His own tattoos glowed, concentrating closer to the wounds as a sickly green goo was expelled. It hissed at it hit the ground.

"How come mine didn't do that?" she asked, looking at her arm.

"Because you weren't scratched or bitten." He lifted a finger, brushing it along her bottom lip.

"Where have the beasts gone?" Xavier asked with a rumble. "The last one disappeared before too."

Riley didn't turn, his eyes mirrored as his own beast fought for control. He didn't like to see her hurt. Breathing heavily he said, "It's not supposed to be Earth Side, so it's returned to the Nether." He turned his head slightly,

lashes low. "Convenient considering the increased sightings."

Xavier tilted his head, orange eyes flashing. "Noted." He turned his attention to the twins. "Congratulations to the new Alpha. I'm sure the correct paperwork will be organised and an appropriate hierarchy will be assigned."

"It will," Theo replied, looking between them. "I assume there will be no problems?"

"I'm sure if there are, I'll be available to fix it." He stretched his bare feet, his shoes lost somewhere as he crushed the mud beneath his toes. His eyes met Alice. When he just stared she nodded, acknowledging their earlier conversation. "It's interesting that you didn't die, especially since I last saw you beneath a lightning storm riddled with poison."

Alice sat straighter, but didn't comment.

An open mouth chuckle, his teeth sharp as stripes flared across tanned flesh. "Rex?"

"Yes," Rex nodded, the wolf strong in the colour of his irises. "Until we meet again."

"No," Alice began as he turned to follow Xavier. "Rex, whatever you believe is between us is over. I had forgiven you for what you did before, but this?" She shook her head, emotions running high. "No, this is different. You mean nothing to me."

Rex flicked his eyes to hers, a snarl lifting his lip. "You fucking bitc..."

Before Rex finished his sentence Riley lifted a heavy fist, and connected it to Rex's nose. Blood gushed, but Rex straightened, not stopping the flow as he tried, and failed to meet Riley's eyes. Riley may not be a shifter, but his beast was enough to win in dominance. Which was interesting.

"Now that punch wasn't for Alice, because she can take

care of herself as she's one deadly fucking female," Riley said with a controlled anger. "In a fight, my money would be on her every single time."

Blood soaked down the front of Rex's bare chest, nose slightly crooked.

"No, I punched you because you're an arsehole, and if you ever hurt her again, you'll be a dead one."

* * *

She let out a frustrated breath, irritation causing phantom pains across her chi. Her host was long gone, replaced with the emptiness she had felt for... for as long as she could remember.

"More questions?" she muttered, stroking down Vlad's naked chest hard enough to leave marks.

He let out a hiss, but didn't move.

"Tell me, why now?" Vlad asked, jaw clenched. "Why here?" He gestured to the rolling hills in the north of England.

She leaned forward, her lips close enough she could feel his velvet touch. Touch was something she had missed. Intimacy in one's flesh.

"Do you crave your destiny?" She licked at his lips, but still, he didn't move.

"Yes," he growled. "I have dreamt of it."

"You were born for this, gifted it. And there are those that wish to take it away."

"I will crush them."

"Your true self needs to be released. You were not meant for such a mundane life."

Vlad sucked in a breath, pupils dilated as her nails dug in, drawing blood.

And still, he did not move.

"A life where you have nothing, mean nothing." She lifted a bloody finger to her lips, painting them in red. "I can give you what you want." She kissed him, pushing his own blood onto his tongue. "Power."

"Answer my questions, Pandora," he snarled, his hand reaching up to curl around her throat.

She laughed, even as he tightened his fist. It mattered not, she could easily find another host. But she liked the red-head, even if her features were slowly changing. Her nose was becoming more narrow, and her ears were taking on a slight point. Was her original image coming through? She didn't know what she used to look like. She didn't remember.

"Why now, you ask?" She pulled out his grasp, knowing she could only do so because he allowed her. Or that's what she would allow him to believe. "Because you needed someone to unlock your power."

"And that would be you?"

She reached for his pendant, the coin, the seal. The power welcomed her touch, savouring as it tasted her magic. It knew what she could do.

Her memories were broken, taken from her long ago. The magic that created the seals called to her, as if familiar. She suspected the same magic was what took away her memory, and breaking the seals would release those memories. She would know for sure why she was locked away, and who she truly was.

"How do you know this if you don't remember?"

"I said I have no memory of my life before. But every Fae can feel where the wild magic leaks the strongest, and I have spoken with many those of mine blood."

"Why do you want to do this?"

"Because..." Another crack as she increased the pressure. "I want my memories, and helping you will release them."

"So you gain from my ascension," he sniggered. "Which means you need me."

She tightened her smile.

Patience, she told herself. She needed her memories, and only then could she become whole again.

So for now, she did indeed need him.

"Do it. I'm ready." Sweat dripped down his face as she pressed one more time, pushing her limited power into the cracks.

A flash of light, the seal separating in two.

Vlad screamed, crashing to his knees just as memories long lost swirled around her mind. They rushed through her, flashing across her vision until tears blurred. She remembered him. Her love. She also remembered where he had gone, imprisoned just as she was.

The emptiness inside her ached, hard enough her hand touched her breast as if she could comfort the pain.

Her memories were still broken, missing. She needed the rest.

Fists pounded into the dirt as sweat drenched across Vlad's whole body.

When he looked up, he smirked. "The power, it speaks to me." His voice was deeper, harsher as he climbed to his feet. He looked at his arms, the sweat floating off his skin. With a click of his fingers it shot like bullets in all directions, missing Pandora by a bare millimetre.

She ignored the strands of her hair that fell to the earth.

"Pestilence," she whispered his new name. His destiny. "The power, what is it saying?"

He caught her eye, his irises shattered. "It says we need to find the others."

CHAPTER
SIXTEEN

The car was warm and comforting when Riley pulled up in front of his place, but her stomach rumbled at the promise of greasy food.

She should have gone home. Yet there she was, following Riley through the front door and towards the large kitchen at the back without a word of protest. She didn't want to go home because she was embarrassed, knowing Sam would blame himself for what had happened.

Dark woods, pale walls and green plants greeted her as she passed through, her hands hooked on her arms as she looked down at the mud caked on her skin.

Riley pulled out a stool from the centre island, nodding for her to sit down as he started to unpack the food from the paper bag.

"I'll make a mess," she said quietly.

Riley chuckled, bending over to grab something from a lower drawer. "I've had to clean up worse than mud in here." He reappeared with a candle just as Alice took her seat. It was a thick pillar candle, an off yellow that had been

used numerous times before. He stuck it in the centre before he sat down opposite, unwrapping his oversized burger.

Alice couldn't help her smirk. "How romantic," she said with a chuckle. With a flick of her wrist she lit the wick. *"Lumenium."*

"Fast food by candlelight," Riley said with a wink. "You can't say I don't treat you, sweetheart."

Alice laughed, the sensation growing from her stomach before warmth spread across her body. Riley watched her with humorous eyes, narrowing when she stole a few salty chips and shoved them ungraciously into her mouth.

"Do you know," she said once she had swallowed. "That no one has ever treated me to a candlelit dinner."

Riley lifted a single eyebrow. "We had candles at the restaurant the other night."

Alice sucked on the paper straw, enjoying the little bubbles pop across her tongue. "That's not the same."

"No? How so?"

Alice opened her mouth to speak, but then couldn't answer. Shaking her head she went back to eating her own burger and chips, enjoying the comfortable silence. It wasn't until she had finished hers, and Riley his second, that she wanted to explain.

"Riley..." she began.

"You don't need to justify anything to me," he interrupted. "I know you would have had a reason to go. Although, next time I hope you warn me if you're getting mated. I would have brought a gift or something." Riley laughed as Alice bundled up a tissue napkin and threw it at him.

"Shit!" she hissed out in pain, her shoulder protesting at the movement. Riley jumped up from his chair, cleaning

his hands with the napkin before coming over. He gently moved her hair, checking the bite marks that throbbed.

"Hmmm, I didn't know you were into biting."

Alice's pulse spiked, but not from pain as his warm breath settled across her skin. "Ha fucking ha."

Riley double checked her arm, the small burn seemingly fine before he stepped back, cleaning up what remained of their meal and gestured for her to follow him up the stairs.

"I'll be able to get a better look under the bathroom lights," Riley said as Alice sat on the edge of the bath just off from his bedroom.

A blush prickled her cheeks as he checked her shoulder once again. "You won't need stitches," he murmured quietly. "Maymal left some ointment here somewhere, that will help it all heal faster."

Alice smiled at the mention of the older woman who doted on Riley like he was her own. "The lavender smelling stuff? Is she around?"

Instead of answering Riley carefully removed her ruined t-shirt. "You'll need to wash off before I can apply it." He gently removed her jeans, the fabric caked in a thick layer of grime. They slipped off her legs with ease, as did her socks as she left her dirty boots by the front door. His hands stroked up her legs as he stood, so soft yet she felt it everywhere. Pulse still raised she sucked in a breath when he bent his body over hers, his lips close.

His chi brushed purposely across hers, the sensation causing shivers down her spine.

With a reluctant groan he uncurled to his full height, his own jeans tight across his groin as he turned on the large shower that stood in the corner.

Alice reached for the hem of his own shirt and tugged it up above his head. As soon as his chest appeared she spread

her palms across it, fingertips tracing the tattoos that flashed beneath her palms. When she looked back up, his eyes were liquid silver.

"Alice," he warned, voice deliciously deeper.

She quietened him with a kiss to the centre of his chest, just to the left above his heart.

Riley gently tangled his hand in her hair, tipping her head so he could easily claim her lips. The kiss was slow, powerful. As soon as he stopped she moaned, trying to pull him back as he chuckled. He quickly stripped out of his jeans, as she did the rest of her underwear before he stepped into the shower, using his back to protect her from the spray.

The second kiss was hotter, their tongues dancing before he turned his attention to her neck, nibbling the skin between his teeth. Bones melted she allowed him as much access as he wanted, the shower the perfect temperature as he made his way down. Tapping on her right foot he brought it up, placing it on his shoulder while he knelt on the tile. Grabbing the soap he lathered up his hands, starting with her calf and massaging his way upwards.

Alice grabbed at the bar on the wall, her breathing laboured as he swapped to her other leg, repeating the painfully slow, yet luscious journey up her left calf.

"Riley," she moaned as his circular movement brushed onto her inner thighs. She had never been so aroused, his fingers teasing the one place she wanted him to be. Stubble scraping across her belly, he slowly moved up her body, washing as he went.

"Clean your shoulder."

She didn't have to be asked twice. Moving beneath the shower completely she allowed the warm water to sweep the dirt from the bite mark, the skin surrounding it red, but

no longer as sore. Hair wet she grabbed the shampoo, quickly washing it through and throwing her head back to rinse it out. Arms lifted it pushed her chest out, which Riley took advantage of as she felt his lips suck around her nipple.

"RILEY!" she squealed, pushing him back with a laugh. She grabbed the soap, starting across his broad chest.

Let's see if he likes it, she mischievously thought.

She dropped to her knees.

Riley tensed, hands moving to grip the bar along the side with white strained knuckles.

She washed up his legs, ignoring the groan from the metal as he tightened his fists. The bar continued to strain, tiles cracking as she washed precariously close to his hard length. Her tongue snaked out, sliding along his shaft just as the bar pulled free from the wall with a crunch. Next thing she knew he had lifted her up, back against the cold tile and entered her in one thrust. She was so ready for it, her tissues swollen and aching.

"You..." He thrust again, Alice tightening her legs around his hips. "Make..." He pulled out, teasing her as she moaned low in her throat. "Me..." He slid back in, but oh so slowly. "Fucking..." Alice shuffled, trying to make him move faster. "Crazy." His lips touched hers as she held on, her orgasm hitting her with surprise as she clenched firmly around him.

The shower shut off, the air cool as he dropped her onto wobbly legs. Silently he wrapped a fluffy towel around her, drying her quickly before he picked her back up, carrying her to the bed and dropping her in the centre. She pulled him down, shoulder forgotten as his warmth engulfed her. Their chi's blended as one, pushing her into another orgasm as she felt his fingers searching below.

"Riley!" she cried, wanting more. Needing more.

Without argument he slid back in, and she had never felt so complete in her life.

~

ALICE LOOKED OVER HER SHOULDER, the bite mark covered in a lavender smelling ointment that felt warm against her skin.

With a rip she pulled at her t-shirt's neckline, separating the shoulder seam with little effort. Tugging it over her head she carefully arranged the extra fabric, tucking it in so it created a weird stylised asymmetric design that left her shoulder open. It wasn't bad, and her wound had space to breathe. Her jacket would cover the rest when needed.

"Shit," she muttered to the mirror. Her jacket was in her car. "Bloody hell."

Her jeans were still damp after being cleaned in the sink, but not uncomfortably so thanks to the radiator. With her sword strapped over her t-shirt she was set, sort of anyway.

The climb down the stairs was quiet, as was the hallway and kitchen. Stomach rumbling at the sight of a chocolate muffin on the kitchen counter top Alice walked into the adjoining dining room, following the sound of voices.

"Coffee?" Riley appeared in the doorway, cup held in his hand.

Alice made an animalistic sound, stealing the coffee and bringing it to her lips with a moan.

"Well, good morning, sweetheart," he said with a deep rumble, a feather light kiss placed on her neck.

A warmth grew from her gut, and she wasn't sure whether it was the coffee or not. She had woken up

wrapped around Riley like ivy, half draped across his chest with his thigh pushed between her legs. He had stroked down her back, slowly at first before it developed into more. The sex was lazy and slow, the kind where she felt he had given her a full body kiss.

Someone cleared their throat, loud enough she realised they weren't alone. Blush burning across her cheekbones she bit her lip, tugging strands of hair behind her head as she observed the room. It was a large study, and every Guardian was present except Jax. Axel and Kace stood in front of six screens and the biggest computer Alice had ever seen at the back. The screens took up the whole back wall while Sythe and Titus placed red pins onto a world map just to the left, concentrating around Russia. Xander stood at the centre table, paperwork and notes piled in front of him. The right was covered in weapons as well as a thick metal door.

"Morning," she said, her voice surprisingly strong. "I have to get to work, but I may need a ride."

"Sythe recovered your car, he's made it safe to drive for now," Riley said as Sythe lifted his head in a nod before returning to the map.

That fixed her lack of jacket problem.

"What is this room?"

"Central control, it's where we plan everything."

"Alice," Xander greeted as he stepped forward, pale eyes trained on her. "Jax has translated the paperwork." His gaze moved away, eyebrows pinched before he quickly returned his attention to Alice with a frown.

"So he figured out what language it was?" Alice asked as Xander handed her the original notes and letters. "Where is Jax?"

Xander's eyes flicked to behind her shoulder, the crease deepening between his brows.

"Xander?" she asked as she checked behind her, but saw nothing but air.

"Jax has many talents," Riley answered instead. "One is translation. All the papers depicted different variants of the apocalypse from different eras and languages."

"Yes,' Xander said, shaking his head. "And every story centres around this." He pushed at the papers until the drawing of a coin appeared, the centre cut out in a diamond. "It's called a seal."

Stomach twisted Alice concentrated on the image, a sweat breaking out across her skin.

"This seal is what connects you to War, once broken it will ignite an unknown power that has the possibility to tear down the veil between realms."

"Because that's what The Dragon needs, more power," one of the other guardians muttered, but Alice wasn't sure which one.

"From what we've studied," Xander continued, "was that it doesn't necessarily mean the end of the world, but to renew it."

"Renew?"

"The original Elementals were cursed because they were never supposed to have magic. Not like native magic that originates from here such as druids and shifters. The curse was for the Elementals to wipe the slate clean, to remove the magic that was originally gifted to the chosen humans. But now there are numerous realms, with a veil between them all keeping the balance to help compensate. If the veil fell..."

"It could destabilise everything," Riley said.

Alice crossed her arms. "And what does that mean?"

Riley and Xander exchanged a look. "We're not sure."

"I wasn't born just to destroy everything."

"You actually were, at least, your family was." Xander pushed the drawing closer. "Everyone from your bloodline had the same ability and potential."

Alice stared at the seal, nausea and discomfort assaulting her stomach. "This seal, what is it?"

Where was it?

Riley touched her arm, her hands soft. "We don't know."

"But," Xander sighed. "It's what Dread was searching for, and in the end it was one of the reasons he was executed."

CHAPTER
SEVENTEEN

"You're late," Brady growled when she finally made it through the barriers. It was rush hour at Kings Cross, the large train station heaving with thousands of tourists and commuters. "The Vic's been rushed to hospital."

"What do you mean the Vic's been rushed to hospital?" Alice bent beneath the yellow tape, the voices loud and echoing across the station. "I was called because there was a third body."

The police had closed off two platforms, both trains stuck on the tracks until they had processed the scene. Cancellations flashed up across the departures display board, creating havoc amongst those waiting.

"We were called for a body, but first responders found a pulse before we got here." His eyes dropped to the bite mark, the cream leaving her skin slightly shiny. His attention then dropped to her crudely created top. "So... date with Riley go well last night?" he said with a slightly inquisitive tone.

He was asking whether she was wearing the same clothes as the night before. She was, but that wasn't the

point. At over six foot four and built like a wrestler Brady looked anything but a gossip. However, Alice knew his wife Michelle was, and she was at home with the new baby.

"Did you really want me to go home and change?" she said, trying to hide her smirk, but also confirming his suspicion. She wouldn't really tell him what happened, but she knew it would make his wife happy. Michelle was an amusing character that Alice would call a friend, and if the gossip made her send Alice more baby pictures in exchange for details, then it was worth it.

Brady grunted. "No, you're already late. Let's get back to work."

The train on the left had its doors wide open, Jones carefully dusting the buttons on the outside for prints.

"Our Vic was found around six this morning by a..." Brady flipped through his notepad. "A Miss Cookie Pie, AKA, Beatrice Everette."

Alice smiled at the name, not having to ask what Miss Pie's or even Miss Everette's occupation was considering King's Cross, and the connecting station St Pancras was famous for the sheer amount of sex workers.

"Your black witch is around somewhere, she said something about needing quiet." Brady looked back towards the crowd. "Not like she's going to get anywhere quiet here."

"It made sense to call her." Alice had called Kyra as soon as she knew herself, knowing she could be an asset in such a strange case.

"No, it was the right call," he nodded. "The Vic had the same M.O. as the previous two. Miss Everette found him sitting in a two seater with a table. The train wasn't due to leave until seven, and had been there since five forty-five where a total of eighteen passengers passed through the

barriers. We're trying to see if they used their own credit cards or those anonymous train cards."

"Partially shifted and wrapped in a woven fabric?"

"Yes. Miss Everette thought it was an unaccompanied bag and was about to go call for assistance when she noticed the shape." He flipped the page. "His arms were resting on a laptop on the table, beside a hot coffee."

"Because that's not weird." Alice frowned. "Aren't the trains checked?"

"Usually, yes. An Inspector is supposed to walk the train to make sure no one is left behind."

"Usually? So no one did it today? How interesting."

"Quite. CCTV is being arranged, but it takes time."

Jones shuffled back, his white overalls squeaking. "Train CCTV is atrocious, we'll be lucky if we can get anything from it." He carefully placed his equipment into a clear plastic bag and handed it to one of his team members with an uncharacteristic sigh. "Don't expect much from the scene either, it's a high footfall area which can mess with the evidence." His eyes dropped to her top, a smile teasing his lips. "Good thing O'Neil isn't here, he would be pissed."

"Her clothes don't affect her ability, and at least it's not the same shirt as the other time." Brady grunted.

Jones pulled down his hood and goggles. "You talking about the bees?" he chuckled.

Alice crossed her arms. "Shut up, we went bowling!"

O'Neil thought it was a great idea for the team to regularly meet up to 'bond.' The last time they went bowling and she wore one of her favourite tops. It had two bees on the front with their faces covered in honey like a sheet. Beneath was the lettering 'BOO BEES.'

"Where's Peyton?" As soon as she mentioned his name a warmth grew from her chest. He had opened their

connection. She immediately found him towards the centre hub, his notepad out as he tried to talk to a few witnesses. His frustration spread through her, tingling the wild magic within.

The city was one of the most multi-cultural places in the world, and both stations connected London to other parts of the country, as well as France, Brussels and The Netherlands. It made the area full of tourists, which meant many language barriers.

"If you would excuse me." Jones waved as he approached Peyton and the older Chinese couple, speaking quietly. After a few minutes the couple sat back down, calmer.

Jones shrugged when he moved back towards the train, mumbling something about his grandmother as he continued to process the scene.

"Alice," Peyton frowned as he joined them. "You read the news this morning?"

"No, I've barely had time to brush my teeth." Her phone went off at six-thirty, but she had been too busy to hear it.

He unfolded a page, ripped from the morning's newspaper. "Take a look."

AUTHOR FREYA WILSON reclaims her title as bestseller after a decade of flops. Blood of the Moon is setting records across the globe gaining accolades everywhere from the United Kingdom, United States to Australia six months after its initial release. Must be a shock to Hellfire Publishing House who had only recently terminated her contract.

. . .

THE ARTICLE READ beside a picture of Freya herself grinning outside her house, book clutched to her chest.

"Wait, she was dropped from her publisher? I wonder why she never mentioned that?" Alice handed back the paper. "Guess the copycat is boosting her sales."

Peyton hadn't closed their connection, the warmth familiar yet strange at the same time. She felt him in her very essence, which meant he probably felt her too. It's what she assumed being soul-bound with someone would be like, except their connection wasn't out of love.

"What you thinking?" Peyton moved closer, her wild magic electric as it recognised him. He still had the fabric in his pocket, Alice could sense it.

"I'm thinking she knows more than she's letting on." As did Peyton.

Brady clicked his neck, facing them with a frown. "There is no connection between the homicides and Freya Wilson."

"Doesn't mean she doesn't know more," Alice shrugged.

"You're right, and if we go by the book this is only the third victim of eight."

"Eight?" Peyton frowned. "Why eight?"

Brady shrugged. "It's not explained why, but the eight are over the space of one month."

"Shit," Alice muttered. That was a lot of homicides.

A soft voice came out of the train, talking to Jones. Kyra stepped down, her dark hair tightly braided, brown skin ashen.

"The spell doesn't originate from witches," she said with confidence, chin tipped up as she spoke to Brady. "I believe the process is Fae in origin, and then been adapted by a black witch."

Alice looked towards Peyton, who hesitated before

confirming. "She's right. It's definitely Fae, but as of yet I'm not sure what."

Brady seemed surprised at his verification. "Anything else?"

Peyton cut off their connection, her heart immediately aching at the loss.

She shot him a warning look.

"Whoever is doing this is forcing them to shift," Kyra continued, voice soft considering her words. "Then skinning them in their half-form. It took me some time but I remembered years ago I researched the process. It's one of the old ways that's been banned, even amongst approved dark witches."

"Why would they want to do that?" Peyton asked. "Skin them in half-form?"

"The old ways would use the skin in many incantations and potions. There was also some skin-walkers who could shapeshift when they wore the skins. But skin-walkers are all but forgotten this side of the world."

"The skins aren't worn, they're used to create the fabric they're wrapped in."

Brady adjusted his blazer. "Then why..."

"Shifters have an amazing ability to heal and pause aging," Alice interrupted, remember the wolves only the day before.

Kyra frowned. "Pause ageing?"

"Shifters age slowly," Alice answered. "It's like they stop ageing at thirty." They didn't actually stop aging, but it was hard to tell their true age until they were in their last section of life which was around two-hundred. Poor fertility was relatively common amongst Breed, especially compared to humans who in return had a shorter lifespan.

Even witches, who were the closest in DNA lived to on average one-hundred and fifty.

"Pauses ageing?" Peyton parroted, head shifted off to the side. "It pauses ageing."

"Peyton, what do you..." the words died in her mouth.

"Hey, you okay?" Kyra nudged her bare arm, her hands ice cold.

Alice shook her off. "Erm..."

Chester stood amongst a few people curiously glancing over the police tape, his red hair blazing beneath the LEDs. He faced her, lip tipped in a smirk.

"If you would excuse me, I'll be right back." Alice moved automatically towards him, her gaze quickly taking towards the surrounding crowd. Chester's handler wasn't there. "Fuck!" She bent beneath the tape, pushing past the crowd into the very busy central hub. "Fuck. Fuck. Fuck."

It took her a few seconds to find him once again, the fine hairs on the back of her neck standing on edge at the smile that arched his lips, the emotion fake and not reaching his eyes. As soon as he caught her attention he moved, walking down a tunnel full of children on a school trip.

"Hello again," he nodded his head in greeting, green eyes bright. "I don't have long."

"Chester," Alice croaked, sweat dripping down her neck. "What are you doing here?"

The children chattered amongst themselves, lined up against the station tiles as the teacher studied the train map.

His eyes widened as his smile stretched his cheeks. It made her think of a doll. A lifeless doll. "You remembered my name," he said with an uncomfortable innocence that

resembled the children around them. "Do you want to play?"

"How's your balls?" She remembered well how she used his own anatomy against him.

His face hardened, jaw clenched. "You broke my nose last time." His hand went into his long trench coat.

Shit.

The children shuffled around, impatient.

She needed Chester to remain calm, especially as he was so unpredictable.

"Are you alone?" she asked, trying to get him to move. Her own hand itched to go for her blade which was strapped to her back, partially hidden beneath her hair. The black straps were tied around one shoulder and her waist, the damaged shoulder bare.

"Oh my, is that a sword?" One of the school children pointed. "Can I touch it?"

"Wow!"

"Can I have a go?"

"Are you a police man?"

"No idiot, she's a police *woman*!" The children chattered.

A teacher shooshed them, moving them along when she noticed Alice and Chester's stand-off.

Alice could hear a train coming, which meant the tunnel wouldn't be quiet for long as she already noticed a rush of people approaching.

"What are you doing here, Chester?" she repeated. "Has something changed?"

"I said I wanted to play." He pouted. "But I can't play, can I? But I've been told soon." He brought out a knife, the end sharp. He kept it close to his hip, beneath the eyeline of the passing commuters. "You need to find it first."

"Find what?" Alice asked as she stepped back, hoping he would follow. He was unpredictable, and with easy reach of a lot of innocents.

Confusion creased his brow. As soon as there was a clearing he jumped, the knife flashing as he rushed forward. Alice let him come close, her arm coming up to knock his hand as it slashed against her chest.

"I can't wait to cut your pretty little face up," he whispered, his arm pinned before he pulled free.

Alice hit out, slamming him against the white tiles as she tried to disarm the knife. People bumped into them, making it harder to hold as they scrambled for control. She was nudged, pushed just as Chester thrust the knife once again.

"Fuck!" She dodged, barely. The knife scraped down a tile, cracking it.

"This is fun." With a heavy boot he kicked, his foot connecting to her stomach with enough momentum she slid across the floor. People jumped out of the way, swearing and muttering at the inconvenience.

Peyton appeared in a burst of light. "Alice, what?" He recognised Chester, his hands glowing as he helped her to her feet.

Chester stepped back, teeth bared. He spun on his heel, running further down the tunnel towards the waiting train.

Both Alice and Peyton ran after him, but from the rush of wind she knew it was too late. They skidded to a stop just as the train disappeared into the black hole, leaving the platform empty.

"Shit, I need to call the next station!" Peyton looked around.

"There's no point, he's long gone." Alice paced, realising he had cut her across her arm. A thin slice, barely a graze.

She wiped at the blood, the wound already clotting. "Fuck! Fuck! Fuck!"

"Alice, who was that?" Peyton asked, anger hardening his gaze. "And don't tell me he's nothing. We're connected, remember!" He thrust their connection open, his power causing her to stagger.

Alice grit her teeth, stepping closer to the wall to allow the new crowd to wait patiently for the coming train. "He's a Knight," she said, keeping her voice low.

"A what?"

"They're called The Knights," she said slightly louder, the platform becoming busier once again.

"And you've kept this from me?" He thrust a hand in his hair, tugging at the strands until his ears appeared. The pointy tips red.

"It doesn't affect my job, and we have other important things to deal with."

His eyes narrowed, tone hardening. "You think I care just because of Spook Squad? You insult me." His voice seemed to growl, his faint accent thickening. "Alice, who are they? What do they want?"

Another train arrived along with a gust of air. She waited until it had left, and the crowd had dispersed enough they had a gap until she spoke again.

"They're assassins dating back to King Arthur..." the rest of the words caught on her tongue. They were still in a busy train station with hundreds of people flowing around them. "Look, this isn't the time or place to discuss this."

"Hey," he growled, "we're connected. If there's something you need to tell me..."

Alice clenched her jaw. "Another time, Peyton."

He caught her arm in an iron grip when she turned

away. "No, if this is important to your safety you need to tell me."

"Why? This is my problem to deal with."

He strengthened their connection, reminding her about the vulnerability between them. A vulnerability that she had created by accident.

"Shut it off," she said, facing away. "I said, shut it off!" She closed her eyes when he strangled the link, her chest aching at the sudden loss.

"Your problems are my problems."

Alice clenched her jaw. "I'm sorry." He was her familiar whether either of them wanted it or not. "They're after me because I'm an Elemental."

Peyton frowned, shoulders tight. "An Elemental?"

She bit her bottom lip. "I'm a true descendant of one of the original witch families. Draco."

Peyton paused, his blue eyes meeting hers. The intensity of his gaze was hard to decipher. "Fuck!" he finally said when the silence stretched. "You're destined to become War."

He pushed her gently back, her spine curving along the wall and out of the way of the commuters walking. An old lady sat alone on a bench beside them, her attention snapping up from her knitting. She glowered at them until Alice smiled and waved.

"There are things you keep a secret," Peyton whispered against her ear. "And admitting you're an Elemental is one of them."

Alice shoved him back. "Don't you dare talk to me about secrets."

Peyton laughed.

"Hey, there you are!" Brady shouted, appearing beside

them. "What are you doing?" He looked between them with a scowl. "Is there something going on between you two?"

Peyton shook his head. "No, sir. We chased someone suspicious, but unfortunately they lost us on a train."

"Alice?" Brady asked, brows crossed. "Do you have a description?"

"No, sir, they were too fast."

Brady growled. "Then stop train watching and get back to work."

CHAPTER EIGHTEEN

Alice could hear the shouting from the drive, her car barely parked before their voices carried through the house.

"Why are we even having this conversation?" Sam screamed from the kitchen when Alice pushed open the front door.

"Because we need to talk about us!" Ash cried back. "I told you I can't do this anymore." Something slammed on the counter. "I don't want to share you!"

"Let me repeat myself then, I don't want to be exclusive!"

A loud bang, crash as something else clattered to the floor.

"Now look what you've done!" Sam shouted once more. "Stop trying to change me, Ash. I am who I am. I'm not a one person man..."

Alice pulled the front door closed again, leaning her forehead against the cold wood.

She was tired.

Her shoulder ached.

Her chi pulsated. Underused, or overused, she wasn't

sure. But she hadn't felt the need to recharge in months. Knees weak she slowly slid onto the floor, sitting on the step. Exhaustion was a vacuum, both physically and mentally.

There was no break, no holiday or pause. Everything just kept coming. It was if the universe hated her, or, at the very least disliked.

Chester was a warning she couldn't ignore. If he had hurt someone it would have been her fault.

The Knights were waiting for her to find something, but find what?

"You giving up already?" A masculine voice asked. "Pathetic."

Alice snapped her head to the side. She hadn't heard him walk up, but Jax stood to the side of her car, arms folded across a barely covered chest.

Alice stuck up her middle finger. "Fuck you."

What's with these men? she thought as she glared. *Have they ever heard of modesty?*

"What an original come back," he sniggered. "A car has been watching this house for the last few hours, and you're sitting out here with a 'kill me now!' sign flashing above your glowing blonde head."

"Do you know what Jax?" she said as she stood. "For a man of few words, you sure have a lot to say."

Jax was one of the Guardians she didn't trust, not that she trusted many of them. He was always quiet, a constant controlled anger that seemed to hate the world.

He jumped over the bonnet of her car in a burst of speed, eyes turning liquid silver in his anger. On Riley it made her excited, on him it made her nervous.

"Does Riley know you're here?" she asked, stepping

away from the door. She didn't want to be cornered... just in case.

Jax's eyes narrowed at her movement, the colour returning to normal. "You're going to destroy everything." He pulled something out of a bag, throwing it at her.

The box hit her chest, her arms scrambling to catch it. In her hands was the box found at the bottom of Dread's things. It felt... heavier than she remembered.

"It took me some time to unlock it, the language," he hesitated. "It's difficult, as were the documents I had to translate. I warn you it may not be what you expect."

Alice sighed, hugging the box to her chest. Pressing her ear to the door she heard silence, not the screaming match only minutes before.

"Do you want to come inside?" She had questions, ones she didn't want to ask out in the open.

Jax nodded his head, his beautiful honey brown hair covering the single scar that split his face.

The kitchen was empty, the floorboards upstairs squeaking as Alice collected the plates and cutlery from the table and stacked them on the counter. Dinner had been abandoned, the hob still boiling the water until she turned down the dial.

Jax quietly sat down, his hands carefully placed palm down on top of the kitchen table. So she was able to see them? She wasn't sure. Once Alice had sat opposite, the box placed between them did he start.

"Before I open it, I need to explain the story behind it."

Alice licked her dry lips, remaining silent. Nerves fluttered in her stomach, and for why she didn't know. It was just a box, what could be in it that made a Guardian of the Order look so uncomfortable?

"The reason you couldn't read the letters was because it

was written in Celestrian."

"Celestrian?"

Jax nodded. "The humans also have another name for them, angels."

Alice dropped her eyes to the box before returning them to Jax.

"Celestrials are from Aetherna, the fourth realm."

"Wait, there's a fourth realm?"

Jax sat back, the chair squeaking beneath his weight. "Aetherna is the true realm, the one that created Earth Side. At least, according to the celestrials, the pretentious bastards. Celestrian isn't a language you can learn, only be born with."

Which meant Jax had been born of a celestrial.

"Wait, then how did Dread..."

Jax pulled out a single feather, the colour a soft dove grey. "I believe he was a fallen celestrial, also called a fallen angel. Those cast out of Aetherna to live amongst the humans as one of them. The Fallen retain some of their power, but their genetics are almost identical to that of a human..."

"And therefore can be turned into a vampire," Alice finished for him.

"Exactly," he agreed. "Celestrials are watchers, the keepers of history. They believe they were the first true consciousness, even before the Fae."

Alice thought back to the poem. "'The watchers," she quoted, "'the winged gods observed from a height...'"

"Winged gods? Maybe once they believed themselves to be gods, but that's long been forgotten," he sniggered. "The prophecy was written as a warning, one that was ignored."

"What started it? The Gemini twins..."

"The Gemini twins tore a hole in the veil between Earth

Side and Far Side. It allowed wild magic to leak into this world, but also allowed the first twin, Lorelei to gift humans the power of the elements. Aerwyna, the second twin then gifted the same humans the power to amplify their new magic through blood and death. In doing so it unbalanced everything."

"That's right, the twins were punished by The Creator, as were the humans with ..."

"The Creator never punished the humans," Jax interrupted. "In creating the original hole it disturbed the whole fabrication of the veil which separated, at the time, the three realms. The effect was cataclysmic to the natural flow of magic, and threatened to devastate everything. It was The Creator who was the watcher of the veil, and so he needed to restore balance. He had no choice but to allow the humans of Earth Side to retain magic that was not meant for them."

"The Creator was a celestial?" Alice asked, leaning forward.

Jax ignored the question.

"Aerwyna in a fit of rage constructed weapons for the Elementals, and encouraged them to follow the path of destruction. She would whisper and urge, but again, this was against the balance of everything. So another celestial, another watcher was sent to stop her permanently."

Her blade burned against her back, as if it knew it was being spoken about. "Jax, how do you know all this?"

He ignored her once more.

"Hadriel, instead of destroying her, became her lover. Together they stole beasts from Far Side and corrupted them, twisting their image into something from night-

mares. They created their own creatures who could drift through the veil with ease, wreaking havoc amongst the people and absorbing souls. Aerwyna and her lover wanted to rule, not just Earth Side, but all three realms. She was powerful, a dark princess, sorceress and along with his celestrial magic they almost did."

"Except she was banished back to Far Side by her sister."

"Right again. Lorelei, the light princess in atonement for her sisters deeds used the last of her remaining power to create one more realm, The Nether. She would imprison everything her sister and her lover created, forcing them to live in darkness. But to do so she needed something powerful at its core, and the celestrials were all too happy to give over their traitor. They threw Hadriel down into the darkness, his own power trapping him inside it forever."

"I don't know why, but this story seems familiar to me." Alice touched the box, the wood hot beneath her fingertips.

"Like I said, the prophecy is a warning that can be interpreted many ways. But in the end it depicts the fall of the veil. Seals were crafted by The Creator, designed to mute the Elementals magic to the point they were not at risk and therefore restoring balance once again. It would be up to the individuals to decide whether they accepted it or not. However, Aerwyna's influence was still there, and the seals would eventually corrode or break. It all pointed to the inevitable, so throughout time it would be reset."

"Reset? How can they be..."

At Jax's expression she understood what he meant by 'reset.' She knew Elementals were descendants of the original witch families, and only one from each would inherit the curse. When one died the magic would be passed to another descendent.

But who said she had to embrace the power of War?

"Your seal was what Dread was searching for, it's what all his research was about. If someone were to break it by mistake it would unlock your full power, and then you could potentially destroy everyone."

Alice sat quietly for a moment.

"How do I stop my seal from breaking?"

Where the fuck was her seal?

"According to the scribes, You don't. It will always break unless reset."

"I don't believe in fate."

"Then you better figure it out, because we won't let the prophecy happen."

Jax stood, the chair scraping against the floor. He leant across to the box, surrounding it with his palms. A glow appeared beneath his skin, so bright Alice squinted.

"This is a memory box, and Dread made it for you." Emotion in Jax's voice, intense and rich and something she could not quite put her finger on. "Celestrials have the ability to remove or copy memories, and so Dread left you this. To unlock it you just..." His fingers pressed into two spots on each side. The box clicked open, and Alice lost her sight.

He calmly barked out orders into the handset, fist clenched as the lights flashed past the tinted window as his driver expertly manoeuvred the tight suburban streets.

He was going to be too late.

He knew it.

Knew it the second he received the voicemail in the middle of the night. He had warned his friend about the consequences of dark magic, had experienced it himself in his other life. Had

lived with his mistake for close to a millennia. Yet, his friend ignored his warning, and now he was racing across the city hoping he was wrong. That his friend hadn't done something he would regret.

"Faster," he growled to the driver, knowing the car was going as fast as the machine possibly could. His back twitched, long unused muscles forgotten as instincts called for him to call his wings, to fly faster. But they had been stripped long ago, and because of it he knew he was going to be too slow, too late.

His frustration turned to worry, then vaulted into anger. Closing his eyes he concentrated on the subtle rumbles of the car against the road, on each tyre screech as they turned towards the nicer neighbourhood in the human district. Preparing himself.

The night was silent when they pulled up outside the house. No alarm, no movement or even a breath other than from his own team. Men, hired specifically for their loyalty to him. He knew they would do as they were told and ask no questions. It was a favour they owed him, and he always collected.

It was the Breed way, and he had been Breed for more lifetimes than he could truly remember.

The subtle scent of mugwort brought his attention towards the front bedroom, the window wide open, but no-one was inside. His chest ached, strong enough he would have thought it was a heart attack if he wasn't already dead.

"Caution, red," he warned his men as they all slowly approached, muscles tensed as he fought the urge to run through the house. The front door was smashed, his eyes able to pick up the glass shards across the floor with precise detail, even in pitch-black. He smelt the blood before he turned his head, his throat burning at the proximity of the life source. It was a reaction he hated, but he couldn't control the carnal urge as his fangs

punched out from the top of his gums, growing until he struggled to close his lips.

His eyes tracked the droplets, leading into what he knew was their kitchen, and with a shallow nod he allowed one of his men to push at the door, his gun drawn as light flickered beneath the frame.

"Clear."

He walked into the kitchen, taking in the broken cupboard under the sink, the door hanging off its hinges while bleach bottles decorated the floor. A pool of red was to his right, the moonlight through the window causing it to glow.

He heard a heartbeat.

"Stay back," he growled to his men, holding his fist in the air as he carefully made his way into the garden. The backlight brightened at his movement, settling on Lily who was hunched forward, her once white nightdress tinged with pink. Beside her was the heartbeat, little Alice who sat on her heels, eyes wet, but vacant.

"Alice?" he said, softening his voice as he slowly approached, not wanting to spook her. He knew Lily was already dead, but gave her a cautionary glance anyway. "Alice? It's me, it's uncle Dread."

She didn't look up, just continued to stare at her mother. The wind whipped at their hair, tangling the pale blonde strands together. At her feet was a teddy bear, the fur ruined.

"Sir, the house is clear," Nix, one of his men said.

He nodded in acknowledgment, knowing the answer before he even asked the question. "Jackson and the boy?"

"Not inside."

Zeph clutched a sword in a tight fist. "Is the child okay?"

Alice looked up at the mention of her father and brother, her bottom lip trembling. As he had done hundreds of times before, he reached down and picked her up, her skinny arms wrapping

around his neck instantly. He settled her head in his neck, her breath cold against his throat.

She didn't cry, or moan. Nothing. There was no reaction, and that worried him.

"Sulphur," Raphael hissed, his burnt amber wings rustling behind him. "The place stinks of it."

"There's no summoning earth," Zeph muttered, gaze sweeping the garden with militant precision. "They might have been sent from elsewhere."

With Alice wrapped around him like a weightless vine he re-entered the house, keeping her faced away from the blood and gore. It didn't take long to climb the stairs, the master bedroom just down the hall. Quickly and efficiently he sat Alice on her parents bed, her eyes partially closed. She shivered, her teeth chattering before he covered her in the duvet.

Once she was settled he carefully opened the hidden cupboard, searching inside for Lily's sword. Grimoires and books were also stacked at the back, but he left them, knowing he would take care of the house until Alice came of age. She could do with it what she wished, but until then it would stay there, unoccupied, waiting.

Alice was asleep when he picked her back up, changing the duvet to an easier to carry blanket. Wrapped up he lifted her in his arms, sword carefully pointed away.

"What are your orders, Nahaliel?" Nix appeared in the doorway, eyebrows pinched. His voice was deep, and woven with such loyalty it couldn't be bought. His wings were as black as the night, almost hidden in the darkness.

"You know I no longer go by that name," Dread snarled, but at Alice's flinch he calmed his voice. "There are no more orders, we were too late."

Swallowing hard he cradled Alice closer. He had been friends with her father since he was a man barely grown. He had been

with him through everything, from meeting the love of his life Lily, to the birth of their first son Kyle, and then the birth of Alice.

He didn't know what Jackson had done to result in this, but he hoped he could find peace in knowing Alice would be taken care of. He couldn't have children, and had never wanted the responsibility. But looking down at the sleeping child he knew he would give his life for her without a second thought.

With a heavy heart he looked towards his men, their wings poised and weapons ready. It was the first time he didn't feel envy, feel the emptiness at his back from the loss of his wings. Because if he hadn't fallen, he would never had met Jackson, and therefore never had saved his little girl.

"There is nothing more to be done."

A CRY ESCAPED Alice's throat, her eyes blinking away the memory that wasn't hers. Hands hot she dropped the box onto the table, the top snapping open. She was alone, Jax gone as she brushed the wet tears from her face. Inside was a key.

Hand shaking Alice picked up the thin, golden key, recognising the design immediately. It was just as thin as the other one, with the lines curved like an eye, what would be the pupil cut out and replaced with blue glass instead of red. Leaning over she pulled open the kitchen drawer, finding the other key and placing them both on the table. They were both too thin for a normal lock, but together...

Alice placed the blue key on top of the red, pressing down until they slot into each other perfectly. The pupils lined up, the glass turning from blue and red to purple.

Dread had given her a key. Now all she needed was the lock.

CHAPTER NINETEEN

Alice stirred her coffee, the spoon turning in a clockwise motion. Freya Wilson sat across the table, hands clasped and resting on the table, fingernails painted black. She sat eerily still, staring at both her and Peyton without even a cursory glance to the two-way mirror to her right. Brady sat behind the glass, watching.

The interview was taking place at Scotland Yard, the room soundproof but equipped with the latest microphone and camera equipment. Everything was recorded, every twitch of the muscles, bite of the lip or stutter.

"You sure you don't want one?" Alice asked Freya, gesturing to the mug.

"No, thank you," she said, smiling. "Will this take long?"

"Not too long," Peyton said, sipping his own coffee. "Remember, you're not under any kind of caution." They had no evidence Freya was involved, so she agreed to the interview voluntarily after a little pushing on Peyton's part. Alice wasn't sure why Brady had decided to sit out, allowing her to take part instead. She had no training in

interrogations, so she decided to sit back and keep her chi stretched, reading Freya through her third eye.

Peyton clicked a button on the desk.

"Okay," he began, looking at his watch. "Time is 15:21, Monday tenth of June. Present in the room is Detective Constable Raeran Peyton, Independent Breed Consultant Agent Alice Skye and..."

Freya moved forward, bending towards the microphone that stuck out from the desk. "Ms Freya Wilson."

"Could you please give your date of birth."

"Erm," she coughed, clearing her throat. "Twenty-sixth of February, nineteen-forty-nine."

Peyton smiled. "Thank you. Now, the reason we have invited you here is to clear up some information you told us from our last visit. Do you remember when that was?"

Freya looked between them. "Yes, last week you came over to my house to ask me about my latest book."

"Exactly," Peyton continued. "We were coming to ask you about the murders within your book that were being replicated in the real world. Strange, isn't it?"

"I guess so..."

"So strange that the sales of your book Blood of the Moon have skyrocketed and outsold the majority of the rest of your work combined."

"How convenient," Alice added. "Especially considering your contract with your publisher had been terminated only three months after its release." Alice pushed out her aura, feeling Freya's flinch at the connection.

"Those sales were earned," Freya said, tone deepening as she flicked her eyes to Alice then back. "That book was a masterpiece of literature."

"Freya, can I call you Freya?" Peyton continued without waiting for her to confirm. "Is there a reason you failed to

mention that your publisher dropped you after fifteen years?"

"I didn't think it was relevant. They're still obliged to pay me for the books they've released on my behalf until they return my rights."

"Why did they drop you? In fact, don't answer that, I have the answer right here." Peyton opened the thick folder Alice knew to be full of meaningless paperwork. It was meant to look full, when in reality it was empty of information bar a couple sheets. "We contacted Hellfire Publishing House for a statement regarding the reason you were dropped, and they were all too happy to oblige to separate themselves from these murders. It says here that they decided to let you go after the release of Blood of the Moon due to continuous creative differences. Quite nicely put considering."

"Professional," Alice agreed.

"They also go on to state the increasing aggression towards their staff from you, Freya." He looked up from his notes. "Which was also what your agent said." He slipped over a statement. "The same agent who has gone on record stating they had never seen or even heard from you regarding any threatening letters."

"That's a lie!"

"So which is It Freya? Is your agent lying or are you? Where are these letters?"

"I've told you!" she shouted, tears glistening her eyes. "I burned them."

Peyton snapped the folder shut with an audible slap. "So where did you first hear of the Loom of Life?"

Freya's eyes widened, smile tightening. As quickly as they came, the tears disappeared and her chi flared. Alice caught it, the energy push weak, almost as weak as a mage.

As if she knew Freya concealed her chi, tightening so Alice could no longer feel it.

Her carefully composed face dropped, but only for a second. "Loom?"

"From your book?" Peyton pulled out Blood of the Moon. "I actually enjoyed it, so thank you."

"Oh, that," she chuckled, looking away. "I read it somewhere." Her fingers clenched, remaining on the table.

Peyton shook his head. "Where?"

Freya hesitated. "I can't remember. Are we almost done here? I have a book signing to get to."

"I find it interesting how you go into great detail of the loom, accurate detail too. The Loom of Life is actually a Fae artefact long forgotten. Did you know that?"

"No," she muttered. "I didn't." Freya went to stand when Peyton held out his hand. "I think I'm done..."

"Now," Peyton continued. "Wrapping the deceased in fabric made from their own flesh is dramatic, and unnecessary. I'm sure this book you used for research, being so accurate would have stated that once the fabric is woven, the weaver already benefits from the sacrifice's life force."

"This interview is over," Freya snapped. "If you wish to continue I would like a solicitor."

"You're not under caution," Peyton reminded her, looking at his watch. "Interview suspended at 15:59." He clicked the button on the desk. "You're free to go Ms Wilson, good luck with your book signing."

~

"YOU HAD way too much fun doing that," Alice said as she pushed open the door into the fresh air.

"A little," Peyton said, following her behind as he loos-

ened his tie. "I was pushing her harder because we just got news the third Vic hasn't woken up and they don't think he will. Apparently the leader of the shifters is there trying to help."

Xavier was there? Alice thought to herself. *How did he find out?*

"She knows something," Peyton continued. "We just need to get her with some physical evidence."

Alice had agreed, explaining to Brady that she was too weak in power to achieve the spell alone. Which meant they were looking for at least one other person. "Let us hope Jones finds something." They just needed a fingerprint or hair, anything substantial that put Freya at the scene, otherwise they couldn't get a warrant to search her premises. "Brady seemed happy with the progress."

"That's because there's two bodies, a third if our Vic dies, and only days away from another. Oh, and we have no active leads."

"How many are we expecting?" Alice hadn't had a chance to read the Blood of the Moon, and Brady was working on bullet points for the team.

"Eight in total if we go by the book, one for each moon phase."

"And does that match what you know of the loom?"

Peyton grunted. "I'm still working on it."

"That..." Alice paused, noticing Freya waiting on the street for a black cab.

"Hey baby girl!" Sam waved at her from across the street.

"Sam!" Alice welcomed his hug, wrapping her arms around his shoulders as he lifted her in the air and swung her around. "You ready?"

"Of course! It was my idea to treat my favourite girl to a

hot drink," he smiled, wiggling his eyebrows at Peyton. "You can buy your own coffee, pretty boy."

Peyton grunted, his attention on Freya who had finally hailed a cab. She shot them a scathing look, pulling away into the busy city traffic.

"Rain check? I'm meeting Elduin."

Sam placed his arm around Peyton, who quickly shrugged it off. "You sure you don't want to join us? Of course Elduin's welcome too."

Peyton shook his head. "Busy."

Alice grabbed Sam's hand, pulling him away. "Come on!"

Only a short walk away and Alice grabbed a seat by the window while Sam went to the counter, ordering their drinks. When he placed a hot chocolate in front of her she sighed, curling her cold hands around the warm mug.

"You look cute," she said when he had taken his own seat opposite. His hair was a shiny straight curtain draped over his shoulder. Black circled his eyes, drawing everyone's attention to their beautiful, unusual colour.

Sam looked down at his own hot chocolate. "Look, Alice..."

"Don't," she warned, knowing what was next. "I don't need an apology, it's not your fault."

When he looked up, his amber eyes were hard, angry. "It's because of me you went to The Compound. He tried to force a mating, Alice. What sort of arsehole..."

"He didn't try and force anything," she stopped him. "Because I wouldn't let him." She reached over to his hand, him flinching at the contact before he crushed her palm with his, his leopard prowling behind his irises.

I hate those fucking wolves, he said without words. *They've brought us nothing but shit.*

Alice decided he needed to hear it out loud. “It’s over,” she squeezed his hand. “I have forgiven Rex for everything else, but this... no.”

“Roman called...”

“And he had nothing to do with it.” Alice released his hand, using a small spoon to eat the cream on her hot chocolate. “Besides, we have another issue to deal with.”

Sam dramatically groaned. “What’s happened now?”

“We’re being evicted.”

Sam stared, his lip twitching before a laugh escaped. “I didn’t even know we could! Isn’t there laws against that sort of thing?”

Alice sucked on her spoon. “No idea.”

Sam sighed. “We have some sort of luck, baby girl.”

“Hmmm.” Alice sipped the chocolate, savouring the sweet flavour. “Why don’t you talk to me about Ash? I heard you guys arguing last night.”

Sam wiggled his eyebrows. “We weren’t arguing for long.”

Alice laughed. “Oh yeah, going by the squeaking from your bedroom until the early hours of the morning, you were *real* busy.”

With a chuckle Sam tried his drink. “With Ash it’s... complicated. He wants me all to himself, but he doesn’t understand that I’m not just gay. I’m... I don’t even know, I’m still exploring that myself. I don’t even think I want to be in just one relationship, or any romantic relationship at all.”

“I know you don’t want a full on relationship, but maybe you should let him ... oh, I don’t know... love you?”

“Hmmm, funny.”

“No, seriously.” Alice sipped at her hot chocolate, savouring the rich flavour. “You’re worth loving Sam.”

Sam paused, thinking her statement through. "You're my favourite, baby girl. You know that?"

Sam's phone vibrated, Ash's name flashing up.

"You going to answer?" Alice nudged it towards him. "I heard he was a stallion."

He smiled. "I'll be home later, I want to talk about that box you left on the kitchen side." Sam kissed Alice on the cheek, clutching the phone to his chest. "I love you, and I really think you should take your own advice."

Alice blew him a kiss goodbye. "Maybe I will."

CHAPTER TWENTY

Alice entered the lift, the warm paper bag of noodles and chicken wrapped in her arms. It felt right to call Riley, to meet him at work with dinner. Not that the cheap takeaway could really be called dinner. But it was also an excuse to see him. She was... strangely excited. She wanted to tell him about her day, about her suspicions and know his thoughts. He mattered, unlike any other man had in that way.

Alice looked up at the reflection of herself on the metal lift doors. Her makeup was hours old, the eyeliner slightly smudged and her hair looked barely brushed. Her clothes were decent at least, professional, with a black trousers and jacket that made her white cotton t-shirt acceptable. She had strapped a knife to the outside of her thigh while her sword lay flush to her back, hidden.

Riley was continuing to split his attention between The Spike and Blood Bar, with the latter being run by a manager until he could be back fulltime. The building was tall, made from glass and steel that looked as sharp as the businesses that rented the eighty-or-so floors. Financiers, solicitors and bankers flashed across the

digital screen as she went up and up, until she hit the top floor.

The door slid open, Alice stepping out as Kace appeared from behind one of the glass partitions on the left. His eyes flashed when they met, nostrils flaring.

"You need to stop this," he snarled, tugging at his dark red hair. "Do you not know what you're doing?"

Alice paused. "Excuse me? I'm just bringing dinner..."

"You're killing him." He moved closer, towering over her with his height.

But she wasn't as easily intimidated. "Back off," she snapped. "What's this about?"

"You need to fuck off," he said with a smoky growl. "His beast is more volatile since you turned up, and considering he usually has complete control that's saying something. You don't get it, but each time we turn there's a chance we won't come back. It's why there's a rule that we can't have relationships."

Alice paused. "What?"

Kace continued, snarling down at her. "The rules are there to keep us strong, and Riley is sacrificing himself, as well as us to be with you." He shifted his head, eyes swirling silver. "And guess who has to put him down when he can't turn back? Us."

"Stop it!"

"Guess you really are War," he rumbled, walking away.

Alice stood, chest tight as tears burned her eyes. Her legs moved forward, but she felt hollow as she placed the takeaway bag onto the receptionist desk. "Erm, can you give this to Mr Storm, please."

The receptionist smiled, taking the Chinese. "Are you not...?"

Alice turned away, almost running to call the lift that

was luckily still on the top floor. Inside was empty, the steel box feeling confined as the metal doors slid closed.

"Alice?"

She heard his voice, but the lift had already begun to descend.

Moving to the back, she wrapped her arms around herself as if she were to break. People filtered in as they went down, until it was almost full when they hit the ground floor.

Riley was waiting, almost panting with eyes completely liquid silver. People quickly moved around him, his attention on her as she fought the tears that threatened to spill. When it was just them he stepped inside, waiting until the door closed before hitting the emergency lock button.

"We need to talk about this," he said with a deep growl.

"Your silence on the subject is enough, it seems." She tried to unlock the door, but he stood in the way. She let out her own frustrated growl. "Then talk. Tell me how I'm irritating your beast! Or how every time you transform you're closer to never coming back. Tell me..."

"Who said you irritate my beast?" He dropped his head, teeth bared as he planted each palm on the mirrored metal behind her.

Alice clenched her fists. She wanted to hit out, her anger and pain manifesting as she struggled with the information. "Tell me I'm wrong, tell me that being with me doesn't make you change more," she said with an acerbic edge. "TELL ME!"

The tears burned when they released, making her angrier that the situation had brought her to tears in the first place. If being with him was making his beast react, then them being together was also slowly destroying him. The thought made her sick.

"Please, Riley," she said, voice breaking. "You're making me the monster I'm trying so hard not to be."

"You, the monster?" he laughed, the sound hollow, emotionless. "My beast doesn't become irritated around you, sweetheart." His voice deepened, the tattoos that peeked beneath his dark tailored suit glowing as power vibrated around her. "My beast is enamoured by you."

"Please," she whispered, voice wet.

Her tears were salty when his lips met hers, his tongue pushing through as he pushed all his emotions into the kiss. She opened for him, putting everything she had in it as her heart ached deep within her chest. Her chi was on fire, seeking his until his merged in an overwhelming sensation that caressed across every part of her skin. Her hands somehow found their way around his neck, tangling in his hair as his hands clamped down on her hips. She kissed him as if he were the only man left on earth. And then she stepped back, breaking their connection and reaching around to unlock the lift doors.

Riley was silent, watching her in the reflection as she stepped out and walked away without looking back. She was trying everything not to be War. She could not be the reason for his destruction.

~

THE SKY HAD DARKENED and the street lights were on by the time Alice made it home. She was numb, the tears dry and her face was swollen and red.

"Sam?" she called into the house, needing her best friend. The kitchen light was on, but he wasn't there when she checked. "Sam! You home!?" she shouted louder, looking at Dread's paperwork that he had organised on the

table. The key rested on top, with a sticky note attached to the stem.

THEY EYE IS *the logo for a specialised bank!* It read in Sam's scruffy scrawl, followed by an address in the financial district. *This is some super suspicious shit, baby girl!*

"GOOD WORK, SAM," she muttered, placing the key back down. The house was empty, meaning she was alone with her thoughts all night. With a heavy sigh Alice reached for her phone, deciding to be productive rather than sullen and research the bank when a voicemail popped up.

HEAVY BREATHING GREETED HER.

'Shit!' Sam's voice whispered quietly, followed by a pained sound. His breathing crackled, sounding wet as if he fought for every breath.

'Where are you?' Another voice echoed, feminine, female. *'Come out, or your friend dies.'*

Alice controlled her own breathing, the pulse in her throat beating violently as she strained to listen.

A loud screech, so loud she almost dropped the phone, followed with a crash.

'This will teach that little witch a lesson,' the feminine voice laughed, louder than before but slightly muffled. Footsteps, heels clicking on the hard ground, possibly concrete.

Ice cold, Alice stiffened her weak knees, listening as she heard something being dragged across the floor, disap-

pearing into the distance. She knew what that something was, but didn't want to articulate the thought.

She listened to the voicemail through twice more, anger breaking through her numbness in a violent wave.

'This will teach that little witch a lesson.'

She knew that voice.

CHAPTER TWENTY-ONE

Magic vibrated her fingertips, so strong it was a sharp pain that forced her to clench her fists.

"Steady it down," Peyton said, placing a heavy hand on his shoulder. "You're like a fucking beacon." His touch weirdly calmed her, his own magic mingling with hers. Alice sucked in a breath, holding it until her pulse settled into a more regular pace. She had no intention of inviting Peyton, but he had known something was wrong and literally appeared in front of her with an audible pop. Their familiar connection was a problem, but right then she was grateful.

His commander Elduin quickly followed, lip lifted in a snarl to reveal his sharp, but short canines. They were both wearing what they explained was armour, but unlike any armour Alice had ever seen.

The silver plates covered them from neck to toe, with small spikes down the arms and claws at the edge of their fingers.

"If you can't handle this, then leave," she said, her voice steady and calm. "I'm not here as part of Spook Squad."

Peyton angled his head, and what looked like barbed wire wrapped around his throat, moving up until it formed a crudely spiked crown with a ruby resting against his forehead. With his pale eyes and silver hair, he looked terrifying.

Elduin's headpiece was similar, but less ornate.

"I've listened to the voicemail, I'm more than aware of your intentions," he said quietly. "But you must be prepared for what we may find."

Alice shifted her shoulder, dislodging his hand. She knew what he was saying, and refused to acknowledge it.

The gate to Freya Wilson's house was locked, the metal thick and heavy. The walls were tall, almost twice the height of Alice yet Elduin scaled them with little effort. With a raised eyebrow he leant down an arm, allowing Alice to pull herself up and over the brick.

"Why didn't you just poof?" she asked.

"*Drifting* takes a lot of energy. Energy we can't waste," was Elduin's reply, his voice thick in accent.

Peyton landed quietly beside her, eyes scanning the grounds as well as the dark house. It was late, the streetlights barely reaching the front door as they approached.

Elduin mumbled something beneath his breath, the words alien and musical. A ball of light appeared in his hand, floating until it passed through the lock. With a click, the door swung open, the scent of dust, books and lavender wafting immediately out.

"Neat trick," Alice whispered, the ball of light floating just above their eyeline. The same as their visit before, the curtains were pulled and the rooms were covered in darkness. The little light illuminated the books that were piled high in every corner, covering the armchairs, the fireplace and the desk at the back.

"They're all of her own book," Peyton mumbled, flicking open one.

Elduin growled low in his throat as he dropped to his knees, ear to the floor. "Can you hear that?"

Alice watched, his arse in the air as he swayed, face crushed to the carpet. "No..."

Peyton opened their connection, and beneath the white noise that pulsed through her head she heard it, the drums. Faint, but there.

"The drums?"

"Older Wild magic pulsates when concentrated," Peyton explained. "It can sound like a drum beat to those trained in noticing such things."

The words registered in Alice's head, her stomach clenching. The only wild magic they knew was the loom, and if the drums were beating, they were being used.

Tinkerbell reacted to her panic, bursting into life in a blast of sparks. The blue ball danced around her head, giving off some extra light.

"It's below us," Elduin said.

It didn't take them long to find the stairs leading down to the cellar. They had been left wedged open, wards marked with blood written across the wooden door. Many were damaged or faded. Alice took a second to examine each one, knowing they were dark magic. She recognised the curves and lines, having memorised them from her mother's grimoire. They weren't just dark magic, they were death magic.

One symbol glowed, igniting.

"Shit, she already knows we're here." She pushed out her hand. *"ADOLEBITQUE."* The door slammed back into a kitchen cabinet, collapsing beneath the heat of her flames.

It would take her time to remove the deadly wards, time they didn't have.

"Well, there goes our silent approach," Peyton grumbled.

At the bottom there was light, a bone chandelier high on the ceiling highlighting the wooden-panelled walls in the large, perfectly square room. The air was stale, but covered with the overwhelming scent of flowers that came from the fifty or so vases of lavender that decorated the protruding shelf in the centre of every wall corner to corner.

A large pentagram was engrained into the concrete floor, fresh blood covering the elemental points as well as more wards and symbols.

"Careful where you step..."

Elduin shot over to the other side, water splashing only seconds later. The wooden panelling created an illusion against the wall, hiding the deep bath in plain sight. Dark, congealed water sloshed over the side, covering the concrete and thickening on impact, turning into sludge. Elduin emptied more of the water, pulling at something deep inside.

"I don't think he's breathing." Elduin pulled once more, Ash appearing from beneath the dark depths. The water continued to thicken, sticking to his skin as Elduin carefully placed him on the floor.

"Is he okay?" Alice asked, the sludge moving across the concrete towards them from the bath.

Peyton said something Alice couldn't understand and Elduin quickly lifted Ash onto his shoulder, running back up the stairs.

"The walls are an illusion," he said to her in English. "There must be a hidden door."

The sludge began to sizzle, burning as it approached.

Alice frantically ran her hands across the shelves, knocking off the vases as Peyton checked the opposite wall. The flowers fell into the sludge, immediately wilting before turning black.

"It's over here!" Peyton called, pulling at the inbuilt shelf. Alice jumped, landing beside Peyton with her palms slapping the panels. One of them shifted, and voices floated out.

"What do you want me to do?" Freya cried.

"What's wrong with you?" Another voice joined in. "Were you trying to get caught?"

"Have you felt her power, Sister?" Freya wailed. "She was feeling for my chi! She knew I had something to do with it."

"So you took someone she *knew*?"

"She's here! The wards won't keep her out for long!"

"You've already put us to shame with writing your little book. How long really did you think this would last?"

Alice gestured for Peyton to stand back, the sludge kissing at their heels. *"VENTILABIS!"* The panels crumpled at the push, forcing open a doorway.

Freya sat on her knees in the centre of another pentagram, her white gown drenched in blood. A large screen was before her, the woman on it surprised before it flashed black.

Freya climbed to her feet with a shriek, a ball of green arcane coating her hands. She thew it towards the ceiling, the arcane bursting into fragments. Alice hurled herself to the right, covering Sam who was tied to a table.

"ARMA!" Her shield popped into existence around them, protecting from the green arcane that weakly rained down.

Freya snapped the cord at her neck, the pendant glow-

ing. She had hidden her chi within a crystal, hiding her true power.

"PEYTON?" she shouted.

A sword appeared in Peyton's hand, the blade curved. He launched himself towards Freya, the pentagram at her feet flashing as he stepped over. He was thrown, crashing into the corner and knocking over a candelabra, the candles falling.

Another shot of arcane hit Alice's shield, stronger than before, followed by a feminine chuckle.

"Fuck, fuck, fuck," Alice chanted, carefully checking over Sam who remained unconscious.

Bile irritated the back of her throat. The muscles were exposed on his legs, the skin cut from high on both thighs. His knees and elbows were broken at an impossible angle, but she wasn't sure if that was on purpose, or the fact he was stuck in mid-shift. His ears had elongated, pushing through his blonde strands that had been clumsily cut to just below his jaw.

"Okay, okay..." Using the knife on her thigh she cut the bonds, but she was unsure how to safely remove him.

Smoke tickled her nose.

Peyton circled Freya, struggling with the pentagram that forced him back each time. Fire crackled in the corner, the candles catching on the woven fabric that draped off a large wooden structure.

The loom.

It was pure white, the threads a metallic gold that reflected the image of the flames that began to eat at its frame.

Peyton appeared beside her, armour blackened as dark magic began to corrode at the metal. "The protection spell..."

Alice dropped her shield, the chi rebounding back with a snap. "Protect Sam." Peyton looked between her and the flames, bowing his head. A familiar warmth grew from her chest, wild magic magnifying as she pulled from their familiar connection.

The loom creaked, the golden threads breaking one by one.

Alice turned, trusting him to get them out of there. "It's over Freya." Alice stepped her toe towards the edge of the circle, preparing herself as the spell flung her back. She twisted as she fell, rolling back onto her feet, her blade in hand. The runes down the steel flashed, shifting shape as she lifted it up.

Freya watched, eyes round in panic as she tried and failed to control the flames from within her pentagram. They moved past the protection lines, threatening her feet as she staggered back.

The spell would only protect her from those who wished her harm. The fire, however was a natural element unmanipulated and without intention.

Alice would only have to wait her out.

Lightning sparked at her fingertips, somehow attracting the fire that covered the whole left side of the room.

"Please," Freya cried, hugging her arms to her chest. She looked frail, her age showing as she heaved in large sobs. "I was only doing what I was told!"

Alice felt the intense heat begin to curl up her leg, reaching her outstretched palms. The real fire mingled with her own, the blue flames absorbing the red.

"How? How?" Freya stuttered. "What are you?" She dropped to her knees, the bones in her shoulders visible through her thin skin. "Let me serve you!" Her skin began

to peel, melting from the intense heat as it circled around her.

Alice would have felt sorry for her, but then she remembered the victims partially drowned and stripped of their skin. She remembered Ash lost beneath the water, and then she remembered Sam.

"ALICE!"

The fire roared in her ears, stirring her rage and compelling her to finish it just as wild magic pulsated through her blood stream. They amplified each other, witch and Fae. She could taste it, the magic, the limitless power.

Freya fell beneath the heat.

Kill her.

A voice, a whisper.

"ALICE!" Peyton appeared beside her, teeth bared and skin pinkening. "LEVEL IT DOWN!"

He shouted in her face, yet his voice was distant, distorted.

Make him kill her.

He cut their connection, the warmth gone but the wild magic was already hers.

Kill them both.

"ALICE!"

Peyton collapsed to his knees.

Alice blinked, the flames dying instantly. The surrounding concrete creaked from the loss of the heat, cracking and threatening to collapse around them.

The roar was gone, but Peyton wheezed, weakened at her feet. She reached for him, his face red, blistered. "Are you okay?" He pulsed beneath her fingertips.

"Fuck this familiar shit," he managed to croak, eyes hard when he looked up.

Alice laughed, because if she didn't she would cry.

Freya moaned, passed out and flesh burned, but alive.

She wanted to be angry at Peyton for stopping her, but she wasn't. Freya had broken one of the rules, rules created by The Magicka for the protection of their own Breed. It didn't matter that Freya didn't die at Alice's hand, because there was only one punishment for practicing black magic.

Death.

Alice just hoped they skinned her alive first.

CHAPTER TWENTY-TWO

Peyton crossed his arms, the armour long gone and replaced with his usual work attire of a shirt, slacks and a long black coat. The skin on his face had been cleaned, and a non-stick plaster had been applied. The female nurses had gasped when he had walked in, fawning over the wound as if he had been sliced in half instead of a small burn. Alice wouldn't have been surprised if they had kissed it better.

With a sigh she rested her head against the wall. They were outside Freya's private hospital room, handing her over to the covering officer while she received treatment. Apparently she had second degree burns across sixty per cent of her skin, but Alice didn't care, all she wanted to do was find Sam.

"They won't let you in yet," Peyton murmured beside her. "They need to fix him up."

"What, so you can hear my thoughts now?"

Peyton chuckled, "no, but it's where I would be if I were you."

Alice grunted, the scent of soot and burned flesh

mingling with the metallic tang of bleached stainless steel that was the hospital. “She never said why.”

Peyton turned to face her.

“Freya,” Alice said. “She never said why she did what she did.”

“You mean why she wrote a book about her own crimes?”

“Yeah, I mean was it for the youth? The publicity?”

“Sometimes there doesn’t need to be a reason,” Peyton said after a pause. “Sometimes people are just evil.”

“Maybe.”

It took an hour for them to report and hand over, the paperwork side being dealt with at another time. Mouth dry she made it to intensive care, finding Sam’s room with little effort.

“Can someone call security please!” A doctor shouted to a panicked nurse, the phone receiver already at her ear.

The anti-violence enchantment that adorned the walls glowed red, blurring as it activated. Xavier stood over Sam, mouth open and sharp teeth barred. He snarled, and Sam began to convulse.

“SECURITY!”

Alice held out her hand. “Wait, he’s trying to help.”

Sam suddenly shifted into his leopard, his animal pissed off and angry as he staggered to his feet, confused.

“AGAIN!” Xavier roared, claws piercing the mattress as he gripped the edge of the hospital bed. “SHIFT AGAIN!”

The enchantments on the walls began to throb, confusing Xavier’s Alpha effect with violence. He was pulling an aura, forcing Sam to shift between one shape and the next to jump start his healing. The shift back to human was slow, slower than usual as each bone broke and reformed in to the correct shape. Skin appeared to grow

from nowhere, starting at the balls of his feet and working its way up his legs. Alice looked away, hating the part in the middle where there was neither fur or flesh to cover the exposed bone and muscle.

Security appeared, nudging Alice out of the way before she caught them at the door.

"WAIT!" she shouted, blocking them with her arm. She called her magic and the anti-violence enchantment shot like a bullet through her skull. Alice clenched her jaw through the pain. "Stop it!" she cried with a defiant sort of despair. "He's helping."

She rounded on the two guards, her hand ablaze in warning. It was dangerous to interfere with a shifter mid-shift, especially as it was Xavier who was controlling the shift as Sam had thankfully passed out.

The security guards stepped back, wary. Xavier prowled into the hall, eyes that of his tiger as he bared his sharp teeth in warning.

"Sir, you're going to have to leave," the one on the right said, hand close to the taser on his hip. "And you too, ma'am."

"I will leave," Xavier said after a pregnant pause, his tone gravel-rough. "But she stays with my leopard." He pointed to Alice.

The guards shared a flicker of uncertainty. The left guard dropped his gaze to the floor, a shifter.

"I think that's quite enough," a nurse said, moving the guards away once the situation had settled. The enchantments stabilised into their patterns now there was no longer a threat of violence.

"You," Xavier snapped at Alice for her attention. "Is the one who did this dead?"

Alice lifted her chin, the pain in her head gone but the

metallic taste at the back of her tongue still prominent. "No. She's been arrested and will likely be executed by The Magicka."

Xavier's warning smile turned into a snarl. "That wasn't what we agreed. She's mine to kill. Flesh for flesh." Stripes appeared across his tanned skin.

"There was another, a black witch involved." It was only a second, but Alice knew who it was.

"Tell me." A demand from the Alpha amongst Alpha's.

"She's called Christine Shade, and she's one of Frederick's."

Xavier's smile stretched, making her blood run cold. It was hard to believe he was both man and animal, because all Alice ever saw was the brute tiger.

Without a word he stalked out.

She knew her debt had been paid for saving Rex. It was the Breed way, to offer a favour as payment. It showed integrity and was the preferred way amongst the older Breed.

"You can go in now," a nurse quietly said as Alice found herself staring into the window. "He's stable."

"Thank you," she replied automatically. "Oh, his friend, the other man..."

The nurse tightened her smile. "I'll find out for you."

Sam lay on his back, his now shorter blonde strands a halo against the stark whiteness of the pillow. While she had been distracted with the guards someone had dressed him in a hospital gown, his legs bare, the newly formed skin a bright pink. His shift back and forward had helped him recover, and as long as they kept him clean he wouldn't even scar. Wires attached to his chest, beneath the gown that connected to a machine. From the beeping she guessed it measured his heartrate.

He groaned in his sleep, his hand twitching as if reaching out. Alice carefully curled herself onto the bed beside him, resting her head on the corner of the pillow. She stretched her legs, arms wrapped around herself as tears burned her eyes. She listened to his steady breathing, thankful that he had survived.

She wouldn't know what to do if she had lost him. It was Sam who had brought her back from the safe space in her mind, the place she created to protect herself as a child. And in return she had taught him to love himself, to see himself as someone of worth and not what his father taught him to be. He was her sunlight in a world of darkness, her partner in crime.

She closed her eyes, arms tightening around herself as if she could hold herself together, conscious not to touch him.

She must have fallen asleep, because the next thing she knew fingers brushed though her hair.

"Hey, baby girl," Sam quietly whispered, his face red and puffy from crying.

"Sunshine," she whispered back, telling him how much he meant to her, and that she had almost lost him.

Sam smiled, but it was edged with sorrow. "As you are my starlight." He rested his forehead against hers. "Ash never woke up, and they don't think he ever will."

Alice caught the sob in her throat. "I'm sorry."

Sam nodded, his skin stretched across his cheekbones as tears came hot and fast. "The doctor said I'll be fine, I had shifted in time before there was any lasting damage." Sam swallowed hard, eyes darting around the room. She could feel his panic building.

"Hey, hey, look at me." She tangled her fingers in his shorter hair, keeping his attention. "I'm here, you're okay."

Sam didn't deal well with hospitals, not since spending

so much time in one as a child. She watched the abuse he suffered at the hand of his father flash across his eyes, the cuts, bruises and broken bones. Shifters didn't scar, yet Sam was covered in faint silver lines. It was a punishment, that if he cried his father would put salt into the wounds, sealing them into his flesh forever. He had embraced his past as much as he could, used it to build himself into a strong, independent man who made Alice proud.

"Look at me," she kept saying even as his pulse raced, visible against his throat. "I was thinking we should run away."

Sam blinked, a small smile tilting his upper lip at her attempt of a distraction. "Run-away where?"

Alice shrugged, as much as she could from her position on her side. "I don't know, somewhere hot where no one knows us. We won't have a house for much longer, so the timing is perfect."

"You moan every year that your skin burns, and you get freckles across your nose." He bopped her nose in emphasis. "And there is someone here you wouldn't want to leave. Someone who may even let you move in with him."

Alice settled herself back down onto the pillow. "You're all I need."

Sam chuckled, but his breathing became laboured, eyes rounder. "You don't run away, baby girl. You meet destiny head on, it's what makes you better than everyone else."

Alice subtly clicked the nurse call button. "Maybe destiny can go fuck themselves."

"That I agree with." The heartrate machine beeped loudly.

A nurse came in, silencing one of the machines. "Mr Murphy, are you okay?"

Panic overwhelmed at the sight of the nurse, Sam pulling at the wires attached to his chest.

"Sam, look at me again." Alice forced his attention once more. "It's just you and me."

Sam breathed in, then out. "I'm okay." He closed his eyes. "I'm okay." He began to shake.

"I'll go get a doctor," the nurse said, running out of the room.

"I hate hospitals," he murmured after a few minutes.

"They hate you back."

Sam snorted.

The nurse reappeared, followed by a doctor. "Mr Murphy, we're going to give you something to help you sleep."

Sam didn't acknowledge the doctor, keeping his eyes closed until they had left, the medicine injected into his drip.

"I'm okay," he repeated. "I'm okay."

Alice stroked through his hair, watching his eyelids twitch until she thought he was asleep.

"Guess it was my time to be broken," he mumbled with a deep sigh.

Alice wanted to smile, but she couldn't seem to do it. "I'm sure it won't be long before it's my turn again."

CHAPTER
TWENTY-THREE

Alice double checked the address on the sticky note, then looked down at the pavement at her feet. Lines had been raised to look like an eye, the same artistic design as her key.

With a frown she checked the two buildings beside it, both tall glass and steel towers with a steady flow of people. The oversized door she stood at, on the other hand, appeared to have no one enter or exit for the last thirty minutes. It looked out of place with its Victorian style and colourful stained-glass features, and when she approached, the sign simply read *'I.'*

Alice reached for the long brass handle, the door swinging open as a man stood in the doorway. He slowly stepped aside, holding the door as Alice entered, closing it immediately behind and resuming his position in the corner, hands clasped in front of him. His suit was black, tailored and expensive.

"Welcome to *I*," the woman behind the only desk greeted. "Please could you sign in." She produced a book, heavy enough it made a thwack noise when she

placed it on the wood. The pages were old, worn and blank.

"What is this place?" Alice asked, looking around.

The room itself was thin and long with black and white chequered tiles. They climbed half way up the walls before changing to just white. Other than the desk, there was nothing else, the room completely bare. There wasn't even a computer or phone, just the single book.

"Sign in, please." The receptionist placed a quill down, the tip a shiny black.

Alice carefully picked up the quill, the feather long, white and surprisingly heavy. With the tip she signed her name, date and then hesitated. "I'm sorry, I don't know the time." There wasn't a clock.

The ink immediately disappeared, leaving the page blank once more.

The receptionist stared, her perfectly painted lips a bright red. "Purple or green?"

"Excuse me?"

"Purple or green?" the receptionist repeated, turning her head slightly to the left, to indicate the purple door that Alice hadn't noticed, then slightly to the right, to indicate the green door.

"Huh? Oh!" Alice rummaged in her bag, finding the key. It had separated, so she clicked the two pieces back together. "Purple." She held it up so the light from the fixture high on the ceiling shone through.

A click, the green door changing back to chequered tiles.

"Your number is three-hundred and sixty-two. If you would follow me."

The purple door opened into a perfectly circular room, including a round table in the middle. The walls were cut into various sized numbered squares, the number three-

hundred and sixty-two already sticking out. Right in the centre of the square, below the number was a keyhole.

"Let me know if I can be of any assistance." The receptionist made no noise as she left, the purple door sealing behind her.

Alice stood, her stomach recoiling, clenching as she touched the outside of the box. It was shiny, metal but textured like a soft suede. She carefully lifted it from its section, placing it on the table in the centre. The key slid in without any resistance, the box hot to touch as she turned it with a click. The lid popped, opening.

Hand shaking, she lifted the lid, vomit fragrant on her tongue as her stomach continued to twist. She could hear whispers, voices too quiet to distinguish as she lifted the first piece of paper.

She studied the photograph of Dread and her parents.

Her mum stood in the middle, smiling to the camera with both her arms wrapped around her husband, Alice's father and Dread. Her stomach was swollen, heavy and her feet bare as she dug her toes into the thick grass.

Dread grinned from ear to ear, fangs showing as he held a 'It's a boy!' balloon in a tight fist. Beneath were more images of her family, of Kyle as a child, and then Alice a few images after. Dread appeared in some, looking younger even though she knew that was impossible because vampires didn't age.

End them.

Alice jumped back, frantically looking around the sealed room. She was alone, yet she could still hear the voices, the whispers.

End them all.

Was she losing her mind?

With a deep breath she closed her eyes. The voices faded, but her stomach ache remained.

The door hissed open.

Alice turned, frozen as the receptionist walked in with a large glass of water. She carefully placed it on the table without looking down, head straight. She left without a word.

Alice groaned, pinching the bridge of her nose.

What was wrong with her?

She pushed the glass away, instead reaching inside for the next set of photographs. More of her father, some alone, working at a desk while others were with a group of men she didn't recognise.

"Is that..."

Alice frowned at one photograph in particular. "Ugh." She crumpled it up, not wanting to see the relationship between Mason and her father.

The last thing in the box was an A4 brown envelope, a small bulge at the bottom. She tipped the envelope upside down, hand stretched out as something hit her palm.

FIND THE OTHERS.

Alice collapsed to her knees, throat constricting as she heaved.

FIND THE OTHERS.

FIND THE OTHERS.

FIND THE OTHERS.

FIND THE OTHERS.

FIND THE OTHERS.

Heat burned her palm, her chi igniting with an overwhelming strength that rattled the surrounding boxes. The photographs flew from the table, all floating to the floor.

She immediately dropped the coin, it rolling until it landed against the wall with a thud.

It was her seal.

"What the fuck!"

Alice crawled on her knees, scooping it up with the envelope, careful not to touch it with her bare skin. Slapping the envelope onto the table she guzzled the water, drinking every last drop.

"Shit."

Bending down she picked up every photo, noticing a piece of paper with bold, black writing.

Marc Jacobson
Jamison Smith
Daly Judd
Glenn Herbert

36 Matlier Road, Berkshire
89 Priv Avenue, York Dire
49 Whitby Road, Little Birmingham
Unit 102-106 Guild Street, London

Alice frowned, flipping the piece of paper over. It was another photograph, a grainy image of a man huddled in a large coat. It had rained, the camera picking up the blur of the water droplets as the man had lifted his collar up as protection against the cold. He had turned towards the camera, his eyes looking into the distance as a cigarette glowed orange in his mouth, highlighting his pink tipped nose.

Alice stared, examining every line on the man's face with great detail.

Dread had kept a big secret.

Because if she believed the photograph, then her father was alive, and according to the time stamp at the bottom the image was taken only a week before her trials, a week before Dread had been executed.

ALICE RAN out into the open air, her chest constricted as she struggled for breath. She leant forward, resting her hands on her knees with her head hung low. The envelope was tucked into her bag, the voices quiet as she clutched the photograph of her father.

A microphone was thrust in her face.

"What can you tell me about Mr Storm?"

Click. Click. Click of a camera.

Alice snapped to attention, walking away as the man followed.

"Please answer some questions!" he shouted, drawing attention.

Click. Click. Click.

"Where's Mr Storm? You guys have an argument? Is that why he isn't with you? Where did you first meet?"

"No comment." Alice turned a corner, carefully manoeuvring the busy streets full of well-dressed workers.

"How long have you been dating Mr Storm? Are you serious?" He hounded her with questions. "Look, bitch. If you don't answer, I'll just make some shit up and then... AHHH"

His camera burst into flames.

"WHAT THE FUCK!"

Everyone turned to see the commotion.

Alice ran, no longer caring if she hit someone or if she

tripped. She just needed to be in a place without so many eyes. Her legs began to burn before she stopped, the crowds dispersed as clouds covered the sun, taking with it the warmth. She was numb as she climbed into a black cab, her chest tight and stomach twisted around a block of ice. She felt the seal through her bag, an unknown, yet familiar presence that begged for her touch.

Phone in hand she scrolled, clicking Riley's name.

"Alice?" he answered immediately. *"Where are you? You've not been answering my messages and then the thing with Sam..."*

"Shit, I shouldn't have called you."

"What's wrong?"

She had wanted to hear his voice, for him to tell her it was all okay. Alice stared at the back of the drivers chair, voice devoid of emotion. "I'm sorry, I shouldn't have called you." *"Alice, wait..."*

She hung up, quickly finding her brother's number. The call wouldn't connect, which meant he was in The Nether.

"Here you go, Ma'am," the driver said as he pulled up in front of her house. "That will be..."

Alice thrust a twenty pound note in his face, mumbling for him to keep the change.

It took her seconds to climb the stairs, even less to run into the bathroom and to sweep everything off the sink with one swing of her arm. She carefully placed her fingertips onto the mirror, her reflection pale. She didn't know Kyle's summoning name, and never wished to know. Their names bound them, and she would never want Kyle to experience being a slave ever again, to be forced into doing someone's bidding.

"Xahenort, I call you through the reflection." The glass

pulsated beneath her fingertips, her third eye picking up a swirl of colour as it concentrated in the centre.

"Xahenort, I call you."

She waited.

"XAHENORT!"

"Bloody hell woman," Lucy snarled as his image appeared on the glass. "So impatient."

Alice stepped back, anxiety twisting her chest. "I need to speak to Kyle."

"Why can't you speak to me?" His nostrils flared, a frown creasing his brow. "I wanted to discuss our next night out."

"Please," Alice begged.

Lucy leant forward, his image distorting. "What happened?"

"Alice?" Kyle appeared, pushing Lucy out the way. "What happened... your eyes?"

Alice immediately touched her face, hand shaking. What was wrong with her eyes?

The scry ended, her reflection returning. With a gasp she looked at her irises, the emerald green glowing.

A pop of pressure, Kyle appearing beside her.

"Tell me what happened." He went to touch her, his hand hesitating before it brushed her shoulder.

Alice thrust the photograph at him.

Kyle stared at it, silent. His own eyes teasing red, jaw clenched as he studied every detail. When he turned it over he roared, a thunder that rattled the bathroom. His hand grabbed onto her arm, and with a static pop they both drifted.

* * *

The portal pulsated, black swirls forming along the silver arch.

"Why can't you feel them?" Pestilence growled. "The others?"

She ignored his question, concentrating on the portal as she locked it into place. She was yet to remember how to make them permanent, but the temporary doorways she had opened would be enough. Without more Horsemen they didn't have the power to break down the veil, but she could send power down to the Nether Underworld, allowing some of the smaller creatures to leak through. She wanted them to wreak havoc, to distract as Pestilence grew in strength.

"Pandora?" A hot breath against her neck. "Answer me."

Smile tight she turned, gently cupping his lightly stubbled cheek with longer, slimmer fingers than before. His eyes, ones that looked broken, stared at her with a controlled anger. He wanted more power, his impatience frustrating. She needed him, needed Pestilence to bring down the veil between the worlds so she could find her love. She didn't remember his name, just like she didn't remember her own. But the ache in her chest grew

when she thought of Him, and she knew he was imprisoned in the Nether somewhere. Her memories gave her that, at least.

Which meant the veil needed to fall, and she would make sure of it.

"You were already connected to your seal." She watched his lip lift into a silent snarl, hands clawed. "You have been influenced by it since a child, you understood what it meant when those around you became sick and fevered. When your anger could create boils and cysts. You have always known what your destiny was, even if you didn't know how."

"Nothing influences me," he growled.

She ignored him. "The others are yet to embrace or even encounter theirs, and when they do, I will know, as will you."

His fractured gaze flickered to the doorway. "Why the portals?"

"There are many Breed imprisoned beneath our feet, and they would serve you well if you released them. The portals are signs that the rift is coming, a sign for them to prepare for what is to come."

"I don't trust you."

Pandora laughed, the sound like bells. "What makes you say that, my darling?" He shouldn't trust her, because as soon as she got what was hers, she would destroy him. "I want the veil to come down just as much as you."

He tilted his head, his eyes on the edge of sanity. Power flowed through him, whispering to him. She could feel it.

"You don't care about the veil falling," he said, matter of factly.

"I need the veil to fall." She allowed the truth in her words to echo. She needed the veil to fall, because there was no other way to release the imprisoned. To release her love.

"You're up to something." His eyebrows grew heavy. "I know it."

Pandora flicked at her hair, attempting to move away before his hand snaked out, holding her wrist in an impenetrable vice. Water moved down his arm, over his hand and onto hers. She knew if she moved, it would freeze.

"Pestilence, my darling," she soothed, trying to calm his rage. "We are in this together, all the way."

Jaw clenched he leant forward in a kiss, his lips hard against her own. She allowed it, knowing it was a sacrifice she was willing to make.

A gasp of air, her chest tightening with warmth.

Pestilence hissed, jumping back.

Another horseman had just connected with their seal.

CHAPTER TWENTY-FOUR

Alice crashed to the cold concrete floor, her head dazed as she tried to understand her surroundings. Kyle panted, fists clenched as he pushed at the metal fencing that enclosed the large dark warehouse.

"I saw him Alice, lying there, covered in blood." He began to pace, his bare feet catching every loose stone. "If he was alive, why didn't he help you?"

Alice climbed to her feet, her bag slung loosely on her shoulder. She hated drifting, the recovery taking its toll as she waited for the dizziness to fade.

"If he were alive," he continued. "Why didn't he help me?" Kyle pushed at the fence, the metal bending from impact.

He stepped over it, shoulders taut beneath a tight black t-shirt. His arms were bare, the tattoos that helped control his Daemon side on full show around his wrists. Alice looked down at her own hand, the tattooed glyphs similar. While Kyle's were bands, Alice's was vertical, the pattern starting from her wrist and ending just shy of her elbow.

"Where are we?" she asked, following him across the forecourt.

"This is Unit 102-106 on Guild Street. According to your information this was the last address connected to dad."

The warehouse had no name or indication of what could be inside. There were no other outbuildings or trucks, nothing but the singular large building. A single light glowed from one of the top windows, the rest dark.

The door took little effort to unlock, the inside just as sparse as the outside. It was open plan, one floor with metal stairs climbing up to an overlooking glass office. They were silent as they climbed up, the door at the top already open to create a halo of light.

Alice cautiously stepped inside, Kyle a dense energy at her back.

The air to her left shifted, a knife flashing before she caught the wrist. Using the attackers own momentum she kicked out, sending them staggering towards the glass. Unfortunately the man recovered quicker than she anticipated, charging again with the knife pointed straight. Kyle growled, moving past her to catch her attacker halfway, pinning him to the wall with a heavy arm.

"Son?" The man dropped the knife when Kyle slammed his wrist. "Son, is that you?"

Kyle stepped back, emerald eyes surrounded in red. "Dad." The single acknowledgment held so much anger, so much rage that it darkened his tone.

"What happened to you?" their father asked, reaching out to touch his son's face until

Kyle snarled a warning. He moved behind Alice, creating a violent shadow. He touched his wrists, jaw clenched as he fought the anger that continued to bleed into his eyes.

Jackson looked between them, his eyes hovering over Kyle's tattoos that disguised the worse scars, the scars that hid where he was chained. He was older, his dark hair peppered with grey. "So," he began, his own tone clipped. "You found me." His attention settled on Alice. "You look like your mother."

From the curl of his lip Alice knew it wasn't a compliment.

"I suppose you should come inside." He moved back, gesturing for them to close the door behind them. The office was all one room except the bathroom, which was a single toilet and sink just off to the right. The carpet was threadbare, marks where there once was a desk had worn to concrete. Light sockets hung loosely from the ceiling, the wires open. Chairs stacked in the corner, a camping bed beneath with a miniature fridge and large duffel bag.

Jackson pulled one of the chairs from the stack, sitting on it as he faced his children. "I've seen you in the papers," he sneered at Alice. "When did you start using the family name again?"

Alice swallowed, her throat tight. "Eighteen."

"You should have kept the name Dread gave you."

Alice had been happy with the name given to her by Dread, but at eighteen she was an adult, and wanted to feel connected to her lost family.

Jackson crossed his legs, resting his hands on his knee. "You shouldn't have come, I don't want you here." His foot tapped, the shoes surprisingly new.

Alice absorbed the rage that threatened to spill. How could he be so hostile?

End him, the voices whispered. *Find the others.*

Alice clutched at her bag, trying to silence her seal.

Jackson noticed the motion. "From the state of your

eyes I guess you found it," his tone hardened. "It's in the bag isn't it? It's influencing you already because you're weak, you always were."

"Dad..." her voice cracked.

"No!" he snapped, pointing his finger. "You don't get to call me that. I hope you know this was all your fault. If you hadn't been born your mother would still be here."

"Enough," Kyle whispered, voice hoarse.

Jackson ignored him, sitting forward to clasp his hands. "Your power scared us, scared your mother enough that she studied dark magic to learn how to suppress yours, but nothing seemed to work."

"Enough," Kyle repeated.

Alice remained silent, her chest aching, breaking.

"You were three when we were told you inherited more than just the Draco genes. It was then we were given your seal by a celestrial, he explained who you were destined to become." Jackson began to chuckle darkly. "It explained so much."

"You left us," Kyle snapped. "You left us to die!"

"NO!" Jackson burst from his chair, hard enough it toppled over. "No, that's not what happened. They were only supposed to take Alice, that was the deal!"

"Deal?" Alice choked. "You made a deal?" She felt numb.

"Your mother wasn't seeing sense, she was obsessed with protecting you." His words came thick and fast. "You were influencing us to argue, to start a fight. It was always about you. The seal was supposed to suppress your power, to help us control you but it never worked, you were too strong. So in the end I sought help, and was advised that to stop it, you needed to die."

Alice hugged her arms around herself, as if it would

stop her heart from hurting. "That's how Mason found out, you told him."

He turned his head, looking away. "I did what I had to."

"Stop blaming a child for your failings as a father," Kyle snarled, his t-shirt tearing. "You were supposed to protect us, and instead you sold us to the highest bidder who had no intention of allowing the magic of an Elemental to go to waste." Wings erupted from his back, the feathers sharp as blades. "It was because of *you* mum was murdered, and it was because of *you* I am what I am."

Jackson stepped back. "You're a Daemon!" he said in disgust.

"ENOUGH!" Kyle thrust forward, his wings angled for balance as he lifted Jackson by the throat. "You are a pathetic excuse for a father. You tried to sacrifice your own daughter because you weren't strong enough."

"Kyle." Alice placed her hand on his shoulder, careful of the spikes on the arches of his wings. "He's not worth it."

Jackson scratched at Kyle's hands, his feet dangling from the floor. He was dropped, knees cracking against the floor as Kyle stood back, shaking.

"You're right," Jackson wheezed. "I wasn't strong enough. I wasn't strong enough to kill her when we first found out, and because of that I've lost the only women I have ever loved, and my only son has become everything I'm trained in destroying."

Kyle shifted to the window, staring down into the darkness. "We're not alone."

Jackson laughed, climbing to his feet, deep mahogany eyes trained on Alice. "You were supposed to be taken. Just you. If you died, the prophecy would have been paused, and your mother wouldn't have had this guilt."

The window cracked, a dart sticking out from Kyle's

arm. He reached over and pulled it out, dropping it to the floor.

"Kyle?" Alice ran over, stemming the blood that flowed from the small hole. Black lines appeared beneath his skin, slowly creeping down his arm. She turned to her father. "What have you done?"

"I've done what I should have all those years ago," Jackson replied.

Kyle frowned, his hands grabbing Alice's hands as a look of concentration flashed across his face. He collapsed to his knees, Alice falling with him.

"Ventilabis!" She pushed her hand out towards their father, pushing him back with a burst of flames as he went for his knife. He smashed into the stacked chairs, collapsing into a pile. *"ARMA!"* Her shield popped around them, breaking instantly at the lack of connection to the earth. "SHIT!"

The stairs creaked, the door smashing open. Chester grinned, a sniper slung over his shoulder.

"Why, hello there," he grinned, his eyes alight. "Guess what time it is?"

Two others flanked him, one male and one female. They held their guns out, trigger finger ready.

"Time I beat the shit out of you again?" Alice warned. She flicked her eyes to Jackson, who groaned from the corner just as Kyle began to convulse, eyes rolling back into his head.

The man she didn't recognise chuckled, lifting his gun up.

Chester pulled out a small vial, holding it to the light. "Tick tock." He threw it to the woman, who caught it between two fingers.

"Is this it?" the man laughed. "This is what everyone

was talking about?" He adjusted the thick strap across his chest. He held a pistol, but a large blade sat comfortably on his hip.

The woman placed the vial in a pocket. "Come with us, or your brother dies."

Alice slowly stood, hands raised in submission. Her chi pulsated, but she kept it concealed. "What did you shoot him with?"

Chester moved forward with a pair of handcuffs, the metal oxidised, giving off a dark blue hue. He reached over, grabbing a wrist. She immediately pulled her other arm up, slamming the heel of her palm into his nose with a crack.

The man lifted his gun, and then another dart stuck out of Kyle. "Looks like time's almost up."

"STOP!"

Chester pulled her wrist harder, his grip so tight she was surprised it didn't break. Ignoring his nose which gushed blood he snapped the handcuffs onto her wrist, the specialised metal immediately muting her magic. As soon as the second cuff clicked into place he pulled her against him, mouth to her ear in an intimate whisper.

"I'm going to have so much fun playing with you." He punched her in the kidney, the pain dropping her to the floor.

CHAPTER TWENTY-FIVE

The ceiling glowed, runes constantly activating every time she made any movement. They washed over her stone cell in red, followed by blue, then green, yellow and finally purple.

Alice rattled the chain that connected to the furthest wall from the wrought iron door. Thick manacles wrapped around her wrists, the blue-black metal warm against her broken skin. Her chi coiled inside, dormant as the metal retrained her in more than just movement.

The sound of whipping bounced off the stone walls, echoing down the corridor. Her own back winced, the memory of her own torture only hours old. She had screamed, the pain unbearable yet she heard no screams just then, no cries of pain or any acknowledgment at all.

Easing back she settled against the cold stone, her shirt ripped to shreds to reveal her raw skin beneath. The runes on that wall ignited, giving off the red hue first before the others quickly followed. Blue, green, yellow and purple.

Alice had laughed when she had first realised that the three walls, the ceiling and the floor were warded in

different colours. She had no idea if it was intentionally or not, her knowledge on the specific symbols lacking. But it was something she used to highly amuse herself when she was last strapped to the wooden table in the centre, the floor giving her a yellow halo as she received thirteen strikes of the whip. Red, blue, green, yellow and purple. Always in that order.

Her cell was a fucking rainbow.

Alice pulled at the chain, hissing out a breath as the manacles bit into her skin sharp enough to draw blood. The room glowed, the runes activating once again.

"Oh, bloody hell," she moaned as the colours flared. It wasn't like she had any idea on how to escape and the wards didn't seem to do anything but blind her.

Alice pulled at the manacles some more, coating her blood around her wrist so it would slip out.

"That won't work, you know," a voice mused from the cell opposite. "Not while you're attached to the wall."

Alice ignored her, instead pulling as hard as she could.

The left manacle tightened.

"Fuck. Fuck. Fuck." Alice tried to pull harder, but her hand started to become numb, her bone creaking.

"Told you," came the snarky chuckle. "If you relax it will go back."

Alice stared at her hand, watching it swell. After a few minutes the manacle released the pressure and pins and needles assaulted her fingertips. If it had tightened even further she was sure it would have broken her wrist.

"Hey," the voice whispered after a few minutes. "You there?"

Alice remained silent, the distant whipping continuing its rhythmic thwack, thwack, thwack. The wards turned off, coating her cell in complete darkness.

"Hey," the voice said slightly louder. "Over here." Something scraped across the floor, hitting her cell door. "Are you the one that broke Chester's nose?"

Alice shuffled along the floor, the chain scraping so she could see more clearly out the gaps in the door. The wards flared back to life as she sat cross legged, facing the woman opposite who seemed to lounge in her own cell, no binds. The woman had thrown a plate.

"Fucking hate that guy," the woman continued, tugging at her pixie cut hair, white Alice guessed from the reflection of the colours from the wards. "He's not playing with a full deck, complete psychopath." She paused, looking at her well-manicured nails. "He isn't safe, and should never have been approved as a Knight."

"You think he shouldn't be approved as a hitman?" Alice couldn't help her laugh, but stopped when her ribs began to ache. He had hit her there a few times too.

"We're assassins, not hitmen. We only take on contracts that agree with the moral code."

"Hired killers have a moral code? Now that's amusing."

"It wasn't always like this, you know," the woman said, sliding closer to her cell door. "We are... were protectors of the people. Have been for centuries. We have three tenets, protect the innocent; slay the corrupt; defend the realm."

"Defending the realm by murdering people?"

"You have no idea what we do," she snapped, leaning forward to grip the wrought iron. "Shit!" She let out a little yelp, snapping her hands back as steam rose from her palms.

Fae, but Alice couldn't tell what type.

Darkness covered them once more until Alice waved her arm. Red, blue, green, yellow and purple.

"We're not just assassins, and we're very careful with the contracts. This isn't about money..."

"But you do get paid?"

"You think food is free?" she laughed, carefully checking her palms. "We're not interested in cheating husbands, stock brokers or bankers. We care about justice. Abusers, rapists and murderers. We take out evil that would otherwise fester and grow."

Alice remained silent.

"We fight for what is right, we don't torture." She looked around her surroundings, upper lip lifted in disgust.

"If you're a Knight, why are you down here too?"

"I refused to take on a job." The woman flicked her purple eyes to Alice, head slanted. She lifted her shirt, showing a mark directly over her heart like a stylised sun. The skin looked red raw, painful. "We're bound to the guild for a service of time. We're connected to each other through the leader using a specialised orb that dates back to a very different time in magic."

"Why would you choose to bind yourself to something like that?"

"Because it was a honour to be welcomed within The Knights. It gave many of us reasons to continue in our existence, to pay penance for past deeds. Now, however they seem to welcome any meat head with a hard-on for weapons and death."

"Corruption can do that," Alice muttered, testing her manacles once again.

They plunged into silence, the whipping no longer echoing. The second time the manacles tightened they took longer to release. Alice couldn't help the cry that escaped, the bruises and cuts protesting at the force.

"Why do you keep trying?" The woman asked when Alice finally dropped her head.

Alice remained silent, studying the bindings at her wrist. She didn't understand how they worked, the metal solid, shiny the whole way round with no markings or engravings. There wasn't even a clasp.

"You're War? Aren't you?"

Alice jerked her head up.

"Did you know The Knights were originally created by King Arthur back in the early sixth century? Their sole purpose was to hunt down people like you. He killed innocents because he was scared of what *may* happen." She moved her back towards the wall, turning her face side on. "The Elementals all went into hiding, and The Knights adapted over the centuries into defending the realm in other ways. But then Ciara was born..."

"Ciara?" An artificial light flared.

Heavy boots hit the stone floor. "MIVIANA!"

The woman hissed, jumping to her feet as a man approached, a torch wrapped around his head. "Brett you bastard, let me out."

"You know I'm not allowed," the man called Brett growled, folding his arms over his chest. "You should do what you're told then this shit wouldn't have happened."

Miviana pouted, her face flushing as she looked him up and down. "Brett baby, you know this isn't right," she purred, eyes teasing. "Let me out and I'll..."

Brett burst into a gut clutching laugh. "Fuck off Miv, you know I won't fall for that shit. I'm not Lucas, I can keep it in my pants."

Miviana's expression changed to fury.

Brett turned to Alice, brown eyes hard but wary. He scraped a palm over his military cut, the hair tight to his

skull. "You," he said, unlocking her cell. "Arthur has asked to see you."

"Oh, how lovely," Alice said, dripping sarcasm. "Remind me to complain about my accommodation." She remained on the floor, manacles lifted into the air as much as the chain would allow.

"Brett?" Miviana said, her voice hitched as if his name was a question. She banged her hand against the iron quick enough for her skin not to burn. "So?"

Brett hesitated, jaw clenched. "I know," he replied before returning his attention to Alice. "You going to be a problem?" He pointed to the runes on the floor. "You try and attack and they will break your wrists."

She nodded to show she understood.

With a click he removed the long chain, reattaching a shorter one that linked her wrists together. It gave her more movement, but not much. Her chi spiked, wild magic stirring deep inside like butterflies in her chest.

Brett looked up in alarm, his own chi stretching to feel hers, but she had already concealed what limited chi she could feel. She kept calm, not wanting him to suspect anything. She shouldn't be able to connect to her magic, not with the specialised metal flush to her skin. Yet she could, if only a little.

"Where's my brother?" she whispered when he was close. "Is he okay?"

There was a heavy pause. "You ready?" he asked instead, tugging on the chain.

"Sure," she said, following him like an obedient puppy. "It doesn't look like I have any other plans."

CHAPTER
TWENTY-SIX

Alice winced when she trod on a loose stone, the multiple corridors a labyrinth as Brett guided her with a tug of the chain. Torches lined the walls, yet they were unused as they walked the dark with a small light.

"Don't antagonise him," Brett whispered a warning as he opened up the oversized double doors into a bright hall. A table was in the centre, large enough it could easily sit ten or more but only four chairs were placed. A man sat at the top of the table, eyes piercing as he watched Alice enter like a viper ready to strike.

Spheres floated high into the ceiling, lighting up the whole room. There were no windows, just the door Alice entered through. Tapestries decorated the stone walls, bursts of colours that made no sense from a distance and plush carpets softened her steps beneath her bare feet.

A large feast was presented, a whole turkey, potatoes, vegetables, fruits, desserts and the largest gravy boat she had ever seen. Expensive white plates were placed with four piece cutlery setting in gold, as well as candles that remained unlit, but clearly used. Not one part of the food

had been touched, nor the wine that sat perched precariously on the edge.

Alice couldn't help the rumble of her stomach at the sight, especially when she hadn't eaten anything in close to forty-eight hours.

"Miss Draco," the man greeted, standing up from his chair as Alice was forced into hers. An ornate sword decorated the wall behind him, too large for a normal man to wield comfortably. "Welcome to The Knights table."

Alice couldn't help her comment. "It's not round."

The man's features tightened, his gaze flickering behind. "Brett, if you could grab our second guest while I explain to Miss Draco about the situation."

The presence at her back left immediately, leaving her with the man who watched her with a dangerous curiosity. He sat back down, chestnut hair neatly brushed to touch the nape of his neck. Gold embroidered his dinner coat, matching the large sun pendant and chain that draped around his neck.

A little girl dressed in a periwinkle dress sat in the furthest corner, playing with what looked like a dolls house. She sang, the lyrics soft and delicate as they carried across the large hall, oblivious to everything else. Alice couldn't help but stare, feeling a lure that she couldn't explain. The little girl turned, pale, blind eyes searching, settling on Alice. An intense cold settled in her gut, something she couldn't quite explain as she examined the dark circles on the young girls sunken cheeks, like bruises.

A plate shattered, causing Alice to flinch. She fought the compulsion to approach the child, instead forcing her attention back to Arthur.

"Listen to me when I'm talking to you," he seethed, adjusting his stiff collar.

Alice licked her dry lips, wrists heavy beneath the table. "I'm all ears."

"I'm Arthur, descendant of the one, true king."

Alice shrugged, trying to keep her mouth shut.

The little girl continued to sing, the music haunting.

"I'm sure you're aware that it's my duty to remove the Elementals from this realm, as was my father's duty, and his father's before him and so on." Arthur kept eye contact as his hand disappeared into a pocket. Alice heard the whispers, the voices before she saw her seal. Arthur threw it across the wood, her chair falling backwards as she scrambled to get away, not wanting to touch it. She landed into a roll, but the chain caught and yanked her back, ripping the skin around her wrists further.

Arthur chuckled, walking down the table to pick up her seal, holding it up to the light. "How convenient you had this on you, as well as your sword." He enclosed the seal in his palm. "You took your time to find it. Tell me, where was it in the end?"

Alice tried to move, her arm trapped by the chain.

"You're unique, Miss Draco. You were separated from your seal at an early age, therefore you have not been influenced by it, poisoned by it. Arguably that has put you at an advantage." He tilted his head. "What's it like to be destined to destroy the world?"

Alice gritted her teeth. "Fuck off."

Arthur sat at the edge of the table, looking down at her on the floor with a smirk.

"Daddy?" the little girl called, ballet slippers making no noise as she confidently made her way over. "Who is she?"

Arthur reached over to his daughter's long, brown hair, pushing it back from her face. "This, Ciara, is Miss Draco."

The little girl immediately looked down, even though

her eyes were sightless. The pale irises looked broken, fractured. "Hello," she said quietly. "I'm Ciara Avem."

"Avem?" Alice's magic coiled tight, reacting to the proximity of Ciara.

"Is she like me, daddy?" Ciara placed her hand on the table, the food closest to her immediately beginning to rot.

"She is my precious, she's exactly like you." He stroked her one last time, his hand covered in a few strands of hair when he pulled back. "Now daddy has some work to do, can you go play in your room?"

Ciara blinked, nodding her head. She wandered off, humming another song beneath her breath.

Alice watched her go. "Your daughter is Famine."

Arthur kneeled, his hand gripping her chin. "She inherited the curse from her mother." He released his fingers, turning to brush dust from his knees. "Which is why I needed another Elemental, needed you, but you took too long to find it."

"What do you mean took too long?"

Hands gripped her arms, lifting her up as if she weighed nothing.

"Ah, it looks like our other guest has joined us." Arthur smiled, nodding to someone at her back. "Place her at the table," he demanded.

She was pushed back into her chair, the chain locking underneath the table. Alice froze, unable to turn as the hands pressed down on her shoulders, arms keeping her head facing forward.

"As you can see when she's anxious she decays food in her proximity. I wonder, as you're War, if those around you are combative? Or has the distance with your seal restrained that effect?"

"I don't know much about being War," she said.

"You wouldn't know because you've been separated from your seal. How, I do not know because we have tried with Ciara, but every time we separated them she became sick, wasting away until she was barely bones." He returned to his place at the head of the table. "The seal was designed to mute the Elementals powers, or to 'quieten the voices' as my daughter likes to say. It's part of your very essence, just as the curse is. To remove it was to remove part of your soul. So how could you have lived most of your life not even knowing where it was?"

The hands on her shoulders gripped tighter, causing her to hiss in pain. "I don't know." Alice hadn't even known it existed until recently. "You said yourself, the seals were created to mute..."

"They were created to *try* and mute the destructive force of the Elementals magic. Over time those seals have been passed from generation to generation, deteriorating until they barely hold the power."

Alice licked her dry lips. "You said I took too long?"

Arthur stared, a few moments passing before he answered. "I was going to break your seal," he said quietly. "I wanted to see what would happen when an Elemental ascended, and then experiment with how to stop them. Maybe I still will."

"Why do you assume the power is evil?" she asked. "Who says your daughter will grow to become Famine and not embrace her power for good?"

Arthur laughed. "You really know nothing, it's pathetic."

Find the others.

Destroy them.

Break me.

Arthur smirked. "You can hear it? Can't you?"

Alice struggled against the hands that gripped her.

"Your power is pure destruction. It's destined that The Elementals combined will bring down the veil, whether you want it to or not. You are merely a puppet of fate."

"Fate can go fuck itself." Alice kicked off the table, forcing her weight back. Her head connected to the person behind her, hard enough the hands released her.

"Leave her!" Arthur snapped as Alice managed to keep the chair from falling, panting hard. "Join us."

Alice turned, heart sinking as Kyle took a seat at the table, eyes blank and completely bled to red. His breathing was laboured, and the wings at his back dragged against the floor, a forgotten heavy weight. Fresh cuts marked his bare chest, his shoulders whipped until his skin tore. It was Kyle who she had heard be tortured, it was Kyle who had taken the punishment without a sound.

"Kyle?!" she called, climbing to her feet. "What have you done to him?" she asked Arthur when Kyle remained quiet, unblinking.

"Now this was just a happy coincidence." Arthur reached for another grape. "I planned on your torture to break your spirit, but your brother was having none of it. So I asked my Knight to stop with the whip, and in return Kyle gave up his summoning name to me."

"WHAT? NO!" she screamed, pulling at the chains. Blood scented the air, mingling with the food that continued to rot.

Kyle's nostrils flared, but he remained unmoving.

"Zakuroth, as your summoner you are bound by your name," Arthur smirked. "Stand before me."

Kyle turned his head, the chair scraping as he moved beside Arthur.

"KYLE," Alice screamed, pulling harder on the chain and manacles, even as her wrists protested. "FIGHT IT!"

Arthur reached for the large decorative sword, pulling the white ball off the edge of the pommel. He held it in his left hand, the orb beating in his palm. "Zakuroth, also known as Kyle Skye, you are enrolled into one-hundred years of service within The Knights. You are under oath, and contract to carry out the tasks handed to you by your leader, with honour. You will protect the innocent; slay the corrupt and defend the realm."

Kyle stood silently. The fingers of his hand twitching.

"STOP!" Alice cried. "PLEASE DON'T DO THIS TO HIM! YOU HAVE ME!"

Arthur held out his right palm across Kyle's heart, the orb in his other hand beating faster. "You are now mine."

Alice screamed, her chi igniting in a blast that burned through the chair beneath her. It blasted the food on the table, incinerating it in seconds.

Both Arthur and Kyle were thrown back.

Alice stood panting, wild magic tingling her fingertips, testing the manacles.

"GUARDS!" Arthur shouted, climbing to his knees.

Kyle groaned, shaking his head. A brand had been burned into his chest, just above his heart. He blinked, mouth turned into a snarl. He turned to attack Arthur when he collapsed to his knees, hands gripping his head and blood rushing out of his ears.

The door burst open and four Knights ran in covered in weapons. Chester got to her first, knocking her against the table with an arm against the back of her neck.

"You are now under oath to The Knights, and within these walls you cannot harm another under the same oath," Arthur explained as Kyle snarled. "Your brand will

warn you when there is a job, and if you refuse, the pain will remind you of the vow you took today."

"Kyle!" Alice cried. "Get out of here!"

Kyle stared, eyes between green and red as he fought the compulsion. She knew he wanted to save her, but right then he didn't have an option.

"GO!"

Kyle drifted out.

"SOMEONE CALL HIM BACK!" Arthur screamed, pointing to anyone who would listen. He stormed around the table, kicking out Alice's legs until she was on her knees before him. "Chester," he said in an eerily calm voice. "Take her back to her cell, and make sure the manacles are working."

Chester chuckled. "Guess it's my time to play."

CHAPTER
TWENTY-SEVEN

Alice hit the cold stone, hands slapping down to stop her fall.

Red washed over them as the wards ignited.

"You broke my nose," Chester said in an icy tone, locking her cell door behind him.

Alice snarled as she was yanked up, arms twisted so the chain linking her wrists was pulled tight against her throat.

Blue.

"The great War," he whispered against her ear as she struggled for breath. "Is nothing but a pathetic, weak woman." He released her, her lungs screaming for air.

She called her chi, and the wards flared into light around her. The manacles squeezed, the blue-black metal warming against her raw flesh. Her chi stuttered, trying to figure a way around the cuffs that restricted her magic.

Green.

Chester laughed, a savage, almost excitable look in his eyes. He lifted a heavy boot and kicked her, knocking her into the table hard enough it toppled over.

"You're tragic," Alice coughed, climbing to her hands and knees. "You have to use spells and chains." She rolled out of the way of another kick, moving to hide behind the thick table. "What? Are you afraid of being beaten by a *woman*?"

Yellow.

"You really think you can beat me either way?"

Alice shifted further behind the wood. "Oh, I know I can."

Purple.

The wards turned off, leaving the cell in complete darkness.

"Let's play."

Alice calmed her breath, straining to hear any movement. Pulling the chain taut she held it between her palms, and waited.

A footstep to her left, heavy boots crunching. He pulled at her ankle, yanking her across the stone, but she was ready. As soon as he released her she kicked up with both her feet, using the chain to hook behind his neck. Throwing herself backwards she rolled them, using the momentum to carry her over while he crashed into the side of the table.

Tinkerbell appeared in a burst, allowing some light. Alice stared at it, eyes burning as it glowed, dancing around her head.

What the fuck?

"How did you do that?" Chester snarled. "YOU CAN'T DO THAT!"

The table shot across the cell, missing Alice by an inch as Tinkerbell sparkled. Her chi was still restricted, so how the fuck could a ball of arcane appear? Or was it not as constrained as she thought?

"ARMA!" she called with all her strength, her necklace

long gone but she began to feel the shield manifest around her, but too slowly.

A fist connected to her chest, then another, blood fragrant at the back of her throat as the third connected to her jaw. Alice held up her arms, defending the blows as wild magic sparked down her arms.

Chester staggered back, eyes wide as lightning shot out, separating the chain between her wrists.

"VENTILABIS!" Alice pushed back, flames roaring from her palms. Chester screamed, hands covering his face as her magic melted the skin from his skull. Alice punched out, connecting to his windpipe, his scream cutting off. "Fuck you," she spat.

Chester dropped to his knees, sagging to the floor. Motionless.

Alice panted, her chest tight, making it hard to draw in breaths. Her hands shook, arms heavy as she carefully rested against the cool wall.

"Hello?" a little voice called out. "Are you there?"

Alice froze, a draft teasing her ankles.

"I know you are, I can feel you," the little girl whispered. The breeze climbed up, cold across her flesh. "Are you okay?" With a click the cell door opened, and Ciara stood surrounded in darkness. Alice lifted Tinkerbell to the ceiling, quickly remembering that Ciara was blind.

"Hello," Alice croaked. "Hi," she said again, clearing her throat. "How did you get in here?" She flicked a quick look in the cell opposite, but Miv was no longer there, her cell door ajar.

Ciara dropped her head, biting her lip. "I brought you bread," she said instead, holding out a single slice. It was covered in mould.

Alice accepted it, moving slowly as not to startle her.

The scent of decay floated along with the breeze, coming from Ciara. "Thank you."

Ciara looked up, turning her head as if she were looking around the cell. "Why are you down here?" she asked with a child-like innocence. "Are you bad? Am I bad?" she whispered the last part.

"Oh, no baby," Alice said, hesitantly reaching over to touch her hand. "Of course we're not bad." Her skin was cold, and purple in tone. "Far from it."

"But you're like me?" She pushed out her bottom lip.

"I am, and we're really special." Alice stroked a thumb across the back of her hand, ignoring the flesh that sagged at her delicate touch. Ciara's thin hair had been recently brushed, pulled into a pony-tail high on her head. "I inherited my specialness from my mother, just like you."

Something glinted around Ciara's neck, a crystal wrapped in gold wire and... Alice swallowed bile, recognising Ciara's own hair attached to the pendent. She wasn't sure what it was, but from Ciara's appearance added with the scent of decay she could give it an educated guess.

Ciara tried to smile, the skin at the edges of her mouth cracking open. Her spare hand lifted to her lips, but there was no blood on her fingertips, just a grey substance that oozed out the wound like slime. "Oh," she cried, face scrunching up. "Why does it hurt so much?"

"It's okay, it's okay." Alice wiped at the grey around her mouth.

"There's something wrong with me," she whispered the statement. "But being near you makes me feel better."

Alice felt it too. Her magic recognised her in a way she didn't understand. "Why do you say something is wrong with you?"

Ciara trembled, making a sound as if she were choking,

blood dripping from her eyes like tears. "It hurts," she cried. "Why does it hurt?"

"What hurts?"

"Everything!" she screamed, the tears coming thick and fast. "Daddy said it wouldn't hurt, that it was supposed to help me. But everything hurts. Why does it hurt?" She hiccupped, reaching blindly until her cold palm touched Alice's face. "Can you help me make it stop? Make the pain go away?"

Alice felt her own eyes burn. Arthur hadn't known what to do with his daughter, and so he stopped her becoming Famine the only way he knew how. "Oh, baby, it's okay." Alice barely stopped herself from wrapping her arms around the child, not knowing whether her skin could take the contact. "I think I should talk to your daddy, can you take me?"

Ciara wiped at her face with her arm, the sleeve covered in a mixture of red and grey. "He's not been the same since I broke his special coin. But it was only a little, just a crack."

"It's okay," Alice soothed. This time she didn't stop herself from pulling Ciara into her arms, settling her face carefully onto her shoulder. "It's okay, it was an accident." She knew what Ciara meant by coin, that she had cracked her seal. Did that mean she had inherited her Elemental power? Or did her father stop her before that happened?

Ciara pulled back, blinking. "I didn't mean it," she hiccupped once again. "He was so angry. Is that why he hurt me?"

Alice stood up, squinting into the hallway as Tinkerbell floated down to guide them. "You're not bad, I promise." Her stomach dropped, knowing her own father did exactly the same thing when she was a child.

Ciara patted along her arm until she crushed their

palms together. "He doesn't believe me when I say I no longer hear the voices, but he still won't help me." New tears dripped down her petite, but hollow face. "Please, it hurts. Make it stop."

CHAPTER TWENTY-EIGHT

Ciara stood outside a door, hand hesitantly lifted to the wood.

Alice watched, pulse beating beneath the manacles as her magic burned her fingertips. Her limbs were heavy, exhaustion taking its toll as her chest continued to ache.

"Daddy?" Ciara knocked. "Daddy, it hurts." She pushed it open, the heavy door creaking as an office appeared. Arthur sat at his desk, a large fireplace blazing at his back.

"Honey," he began, looking at his papers. "You're not due another..." He looked up. "Honey," he said carefully. "Can you leave us?"

"No, daddy," she shook her head, hair falling to the floor. "It hurts!"

"Ciara," he snapped, fury apparent in every line of his body. "Excuse us, now."

Ciara sobbed, shuffling back into Alice.

"It's okay, baby," she soothed. "Let me speak to your daddy, it won't hurt for much longer, I'll make it stop."

Fight them.

End them.

Alice ignored her seal.

"You promise?" Ciara reached up, searching for her face so she could feel her nod, fingertips tracing her features.

Arthur stared, jaw rigid until Ciara had closed the door behind her. "I would ask where Chester is, but I feel the I know the answer."

Alice flicked her wrist, and the fireplace at his back turned blue.

"Those manacles work, so how exactly are you evoking your chi?" he said, eerily calm as he slowly placed his chair beneath the desk, standing behind it. "They stop Ciara and every other magic wielder here, so how?"

"How could you do that?" she asked. "Your own daughter?"

"A father will do anything for his children, just like your own..."

"No!" she snapped, the flames at his back growing along with her anger. "My father taught me to fight at a young age because he knew how my magic was unpredictable. My father read me to sleep to stop my nightmares when I was a child. My father sacrificed his own life to save me. The man who gave me up to be tortured was just a sperm donor who lived not knowing what it was like to have a family."

"Do you think I had any choice?" he lashed out with an acerbic edge. "She had broken her seal. She's destined..."

"Destined my arse. I'm tired of people telling me what I will do, what Ciara will do if and when we embrace the power."

"The scribes..."

"Meaningless words. There is no such thing as destiny or fate. We all create our own paths in life, and yes, some

choose the dark but that isn't influenced by fate." She stepped forward. "You were afraid."

"No."

"You were afraid and rather than face your daughter's strength, you murdered your own child."

"NO!" Arthur pulled out a sword from beneath his desk, plain and made of a reflective silver. It looked to be all one piece, the pommel blending identically into the blade.

"How are you keeping her here?" Flames coated her palms, bleeding up her arms. "That sort of magic always has a consequence. Whether she has to absorb others or eat from the deceased, there is always something. So tell me, how are you forcing her soul to remain in a decomposing body? Why are you forcing your daughter, your child to endure that pain and torture?"

Arthur looked down the length of his sword. "So many people get it wrong, you know?" he whispered.

Alice couldn't help her laugh. "Who really is the monster here, Arthur?"

He ignored her. "People still believe that the great sword Excalibur was the one found in the stone, and made King Arthur who he was." He moved around the table. "But they're wrong, it was Caliburn who the true king found in that stone, and it was Caliburn that broke when he defended the realm."

He lifted the sword, power thrumming.

Wild magic drummed inside her, bewitched by the weapon. She could feel its age, an ancient Fae artefact.

"And so the Lady of the Lake blessed King Arthur with Excalibur. And it will be with Excalibur that I destroy you."

He lifted the sword, and charged.

"Acri ignisiam!" Alice held out her hand... warmth opening from within her chest.

A familiar weight settled into her palm. She lifted it with all her strength, runes shimmering down her blade as it connected with Excalibur. Light appeared between the weapons, forcing them both back.

"HOW?" Arthur screamed, lifting his sword once more.

Lightning shot through her flames. She could feel Peyton through their familiar connection, his power coating her blade, strengthening it.

Fight him.

Destroy him.

Kill them all.

Whispers coaxed her, urging her.

It was the one time she would listen.

Alice moved her sword into a more comfortable position in her hand. Her grip was wet, a mixture of sweat and blood that weakened her swing. She moved fast into a reflexive attack that staggered Arthur back with its aggression. Exhaustion beat heavily against her, her arms beginning to shake once more as she used both hands to hold her blade still.

"Your life-force will keep my daughter alive."

"I wouldn't call that alive."

Decay tickled her nose, and Alice didn't have to turn to know who had entered. She was grateful that Ciara was blind, whether by birth or by her father. She didn't deserve to see what was next.

"I'm sorry," she said, speaking to the little girl dressed in periwinkle blue.

Arthur froze, his attention on his daughter. "CIARA!" He tried to block her swing, the blow forcing him off balance. Alice had already turned with his movement, slicing across with a scream. Her sword tore through flesh and bone like

butter, but it wasn't deep enough as Ciara knocked into her, almost cutting herself.

"DADDY!"

Alice immediately dropped her sword as Ciara sobbed, little fists gripping her shirt. She didn't want to hurt her.

"DADDY! IT HURTS!"

Excalibur clattered to the floor as Arthur clutched his stomach, blood leaking from between his fingertips. He scrambled towards his desk, hand disappearing into a drawer.

Fight him.

Destroy him.

Kill them all.

Alice kept her arms up, her blue flames continuing to burn as Ciara turned into her stomach, burying her face. She felt wetness soaking into what was left of her shirt.

"This ends now." Arthur produced her seal, slamming it down onto the desk.

DESTROY HIM.

"Wait, no!" Alice reached forward, grabbing Excalibur from where it fell.

Arthur lifted a paper weight.

"NO!" She threw the sword, using as much strength as she could as flame surrounded the reflective silver, helping it in flight. It was surprisingly light, and shot across the room with perfect trajectory before it sliced into Arthur's chest, forcing him back and impaling onto the wall behind.

He stood there for a moment, gasping as the paperweight dropped from his hand. He fell at the same time as Ciara, sagging until the blade sliced him in half and he crumpled to the ground.

"Hey," Alice collapsed with the little girl, wrapping her arms around her tiny shoulders. "Hey, it's okay." Alice

couldn't control the tears that burned down her cheeks. "The pain will be over soon."

Ciara couldn't hear her as she was already gone, her lifeforce connected to her father. Grey slime erupted from her eye sockets, nostrils and mouth, coating her skin as it shrank, away to reveal muscle and then bone. And yet Alice held her, rocking her as if the little motion could give her comfort.

"HANDS UP!"

Alice blinked away the tears. She carefully settled Ciara onto the ground, tucking her periwinkle dress around her. Keeping her movements slow, deliberate, she stood.

Brett stood by the open door, eyes flicking to Alice, then to Arthur who was a flash of red at the back, and then he looked down at Ciara, who was slowly turning to dust, her dress almost empty.

"Bloody hell," he muttered, turning his gun towards the wall just as the rest of the Knights smashed through the doors.

"What the fuck happened here?" one of them asked. "Is that...?"

Miviana pushed through the group of ten or so. "Looks like we have a new leader."

Alice swayed, blinking heavily. "I'm sorry, what?"

"Those are the rules," another of the Knights said, a woman with short red spikes. "It's why Arthur never left the tunnels. He was worried one of us would stab him in the back."

"I don't want this job," Alice said.

"Good." Miviana looked towards the Knights, then back again. "Then I ask for leadership."

"This is bullshit."

"I want to be leader."

"Who says you're capable, Miv?"

The Knights muttered between themselves.

Brett shook his head, crossing his arms across his chest. "I vote Miviana."

"WHAT?"

"WHAT?"

"ARE YOU KIDDING ME?"

Alice ignored them, turning to Miv. "What of my brother?"

She shook her head. "If he's bound, there is nothing we can do. He has to fulfil his contract, but I will bring back integrity and honour amongst the guild." She turned to the others. "We will be protectors of the innocents once more."

Half the Knights cheered, the other half looked aggravated.

Miv stepped over Arthur after a cautionary glance, pulling Excalibur out the wall with one large tug. Alice wasn't going to argue. If the Fae wanted their artefact back, they would have to get it themselves.

"And what of the Horseman?" a familiar woman asked, Chester's handler. She shot Alice a sharp glare. "We exist because of her."

"We exist because of War, because of Pestilence, Death and Famine." Miv looked down to the dress with a sad smile. "Miss Draco is not War, at least not yet."

"Then we should..."

Miv thrust Excalibur into the ground, the sound sharp. "And until then she is a friend of The Knights."

Alice's attention settled on her seal on the desk.

Fight them.

Destroy them all.

"Looks like this is yours. Keep it safe." Miv wrapped it in paper, sealing it with wax. "Ciara changed when she

cracked hers, the voices persuading her to do terrible things. I hope if yours breaks, you are strong enough to withstand it."

~

Alice hobbled down the busy road, ignoring all the cars that beeped at her to get out of the way. Rain thundered down, soaking her clothes to the point they clung to her like a second skin. Still, she paused at the entrance to the 24/7 motorway café, lifting her face to the rain as it washed through her loose hair, cleaning her of the muck and dust. It was cold, freezing. Yet she stood there for what seemed like hours.

"Hey?" a voice called out. "Do you need help?"

Alice smiled, keeping her eyes closed for a few seconds more before she moved towards the entrance.

The café was warm, with only a few tables occupied. The waitress held the door open, mouth agape as Alice made her way inside. Her clothes were torn, her wounds open and weeping. The manacles were still heavy on her wrists, the chain broken and limp between them.

"Are you okay?" she asked. "Do you need me to call someone?"

Alice hesitated. "May I use your phone, please?" she replied, even her voice hurting. She hadn't looked in the mirror, not even in the reflection of the glass but she knew there would be bruises around her throat.

The waitress scrambled behind the counter, grabbing her mobile from her coat pocket. "Please, take your time. I'll grab you something warm while you wait."

"Thank you." Alice sat down at the furthest table, her back against the brick wall. There was a window to her

side, but she made sure she faced forward. The other customers turned to stare, but quickly returned to their meal when Alice unsheathed her sword, setting it on the bench beside her.

"Here," the waitress placed a hot mug of tea down on the table, adding milk and sugar beside it. "On the house. Just let me know if you're peckish and I'll get the chef to make you up a full English breakfast."

Alice smiled again, hoping it reassured her. Waiting until the waitress had stepped away she dialled the number she had memorised.

"Storm," came the quick reply. *"Who is this?"*

Alice just listened, lips trembling.

"Hello? Anybody there?"

"Riley..."

"Alice? Is that you? Where have you... what happened..." The connection muffled, Riley barking orders in the background. *"KACE, GET THAT BLOODY COMPUTER OF YOURS IN HERE!"*

"Riley, erm, I'm sorry..."

"Hey, hey, sweetheart. It's okay, just stay on the line. Kace is tracking the number you're calling from as we speak. Are you safe?"

Alice closed her eyes, gripping the phone so tight it creaked in her ear. She nodded, then laughed to herself knowing he couldn't see the gesture. "Yeah, I'm safe." She pulled the tea closer, welcoming the hot steam against her face. "Riley, I'm so sorry..."

"Hey, listen to me, okay sweetheart? There's nothing to be sorry about. We'll figure this out." Some more muffling before he returned to the receiver. *"I know where you are, you're a few hours out. Stay tight. I'm coming."*

CHAPTER TWENTY-NINE

Alice looked through the kitchen window, the kettle boiling beside her.

"Are you sure you're ready?" Sam asked, his arms crossed as he sat on the kitchen counter, watching her. "I think you should wait a while longer."

Alice immediately clutched at her seal draped around her neck. She had kept the chain long, hiding it beneath her shirt. She wasn't sure where to keep it, and until she found somewhere safe, she would keep it close.

The voices were still there, whispering, urging her to break it, but they were drowned beneath the wild magic that still flowed along her chi.

They were loudest when she was alone.

Sam touched her shoulder, making her jump. "Can you hear them?"

Alice immediately dropped the seal, hiding it beneath her shirt once more. "It's fine," she lied, pouring the boiling water into four mugs. "I'm fine."

Sam stroked across her cheek, giving her a sad smile.

She pushed one of the mugs towards him.

"You coming outside?"

"Yeah," he said, hesitating. "I'll be out in a minute, I just have to finish packing something."

"Okay." Alice left him in the kitchen, the sun warm against her skin as she carried the three remaining mugs into the garden. She settled them on the table, smiling at Elduin who glared from his perch on the fence, arms crossed like a petulant child.

"Are you sure you're feeling up for this?" Peyton asked, sitting cross-legged on the grass in her garden.

Alice rolled her eyes. "Shouldn't I ask you the same question?" Apparently she had forced their connection open, almost killing him as she used his wild magic to overpower the manacles. She had accidently drained him of his chi, exposing his aura to attacks. He looked paler than usual, with dark circles beneath his eyes.

Elduin growled from the fence, swinging his legs so Poe could play with his shadow beneath.

Peyton shot him a warning in their own tongue, but even that didn't improve the elf's mood. Not that she blamed him.

It had only been a week, and she had been up and walking around before Peyton. She would have new scars, and her wrists were still red raw, but she was lucky nothing had broken.

"Let's get this over with," he grumbled.

"Arma!" Her shield burst into life around them both, the molecule thin film strong and sure, even without the assistance of her crystal. The misty green, blue and specks of gold floated around the circle, blocking out the sun and wind.

Reaching for a mirror she balanced it on her knees, asking Peyton to do the same.

"Don't break it," Sam said from the side.

Alice turned her body, scowling through the shield as Sam lounged in a chair. His legs were bare, draped over the side and free of any marks or scars. She knew he hurt deep down, his friend Ash still remaining in hospital, unresponsive.

"Shut up! That was one time!"

"Wait," Peyton interrupted. "What? What will happen if the mirror breaks?"

Sam laughed, but without his usual animation. Elduin watched with curiosity, confusion creasing his brow.

"Look," she said. "Everything will be fine."

Peyton sighed. "Talk me through this again."

"I had the idea when I was with White Dawn. Rex had explained to me that the pack gets strength and power from each other, and the Alpha regulates the flow. Together they help each other control their animals' instincts."

"Yes, but neither of you are shifters," Sam reminded them, taking his seat beside the untouched teas. "So what has this got to do with Peyton being your familiar?"

"Well... erm." She hadn't really thought it through. "Look, we have no other ideas and nothing else seems to work. Packs do have magic, it's just different to both of ours. I'm hoping that if we bring in a second familiar the connection will be more..." She made a stretched gesture with her hands. "Spread."

"And you chose this small creature whose tongue doesn't fit in its mouth?" Elduin asked. "Daeizan Raeron this is..."

"Enough, Elduin," Peyton snapped. "Alice, let's see if your plan does anything."

Alice held her hand over the mirror, concentrating on pushing her aura down onto her palm. The mirror acted as

a catalyst, protecting everything in case of a leak. Peyton had his own mirror. She didn't want to find out what would happen if she gave him some of her aura by mistake.

Could a familiar connections go both ways?

She didn't want to find out.

Pins and needles over her elbow, flowing down her right arm into her palm. Before her aura hit the mirror she reached back, dropping the circle around them.

"Psst, psst, psst," she called her cat. "Poe, come here boy."

"Meow!" Poe purred, scratching his side against the fence. "Meow!"

"Go over there you foul beast." Elduin kicked out his leg, trying to encourage Poe to move. "Over there... what is wrong with this thing?"

Sam hissed, causing Poe to growl in return. He wandered over to Alice, staring at her with his two coloured eyes, tongue caught outside his mouth. When he was close enough she scruffed him, rubbing her face against his as she settled him to sit on the mirror on her lap. Carefully she pushed the rest of her aura out, coating his fur as much as she could. He purred, reaching out to lick the tip of her nose.

The mirror cracked, and she dropped them both before a shard could cut Poe.

"Is it done?" Peyton carefully placed his own mirror on the grass. "Use some magic."

Alice called her chi, allowing some wild magic to intertwine. When Peyton nodded, she called more.

Peyton smiled. "I feel it, but it's an echo of before."

Poe casually licked at his paw, seemingly unaffected.

"How can I still use the wild magic?" She felt it, like

sparkles against the flames of her chi. "I just assumed as our connection weakened, so would the wild magic."

"It was wild magic that originally created the first witches, and you're the closest to those ancestors. It makes sense that you're able to harness what you stole, making it your own."

"Stole?" Alice snorted. "I'm taking this as a win!" Alice pumped her fist in the air, hissing out in pain as her ribs protested. She chuckled, groaning as she opened her third eye, searching for Poe.

A gasp escaped her mouth.

A thin, gold thread connected to Poe, moving along with him as he made his way back to Elduin. Alice reached for it, the thread evaporating as soon as her hand passed through, reforming once nothing obstructed.

"What is..."

"Alice, that looks like a pack." Sam appeared beside her. "How can you see..."

The gold thread connected Poe to Alice, disappearing into her chest. Another thread was woven around Peyton, and another around Sam.

A darker thread, red in colour connected Peyton to Elduin.

"Sam, what is this?"

"Alice, this is pack magic. They're the threads of life, only strong dominants can see them." Sam reached over to the thread that connected them, his finger passing through. "I guess when we were younger we sort of made our own pack, just me and you. Everyone, regardless of Breed, connects to one another though the threads of life."

"Sam, they're beautiful." She called her chi, watching the threads connected to both Poe and Peyton shimmer.

"I can't see anything." Peyton frowned. "Will this harm us in any way?"

Sam shook his head. "No, we're not really a pack. But it shows there is some spiritual link between us all." He shrugged.

Alice called her chi once more, wild magic lighting up the threads before she closed her third eye.

"Alice," Peyton said, slight worry to his tone. "Do you feel that?"

"What?" Alice concentrated, able to feel both Peyton and Poe through the familiar link. It was like before, a warmth as if she stood beside a hearth. But it wasn't as overwhelming, more like a trickle.

"I can't close it." He frowned with concentration.

"Does that mean anything?"

Poe meowed, followed by a sneeze. A bolt of lightning shot out of his nose, hitting the fence before dispersing. Everyone remained silent, watching Poe for any reaction.

"Meow!" he purred, curling up to sunbathe on the grass.

Elduin frowned. "What's going on? Does the creature with fluffy mittens usually do that?"

"I don't even know where to start." Peyton pinched his nose. "Come on, let's go and leave them to deal with the cat."

"Wait," Alice interrupted. "What about..."

Peyton shook his head. "I can't feel you unless I really concentrate. Whatever spell you have done has subdued the connection, for now at least. Unless you plan on trying to absorb me again, I think we're okay."

Sam smirked. "Come on, I'll show you both out."

Alice waited, raising her face to the sun for a moment.

"Hey, Alice!" Sam called from within the house. "What are you doing with..." His words were muffled.

"Sam, I can't hear you," she said as she made her way inside.

"I said, what are you doing with..." His words were lost once again.

"SAM!" she laughed, moving into the living room covered in cardboard boxes. "I said I can't hear you!" They had a few weeks before they had to leave, but they had decided to get a head start in packing. Sam had been in charge in finding them a new home, and has so far kept his choice secret. She trusted him, but from his mischievous twinkle she shouldn't.

"I said, what are you doing with your spooky book?" He gestured to the leather-bound grimoire that recently moved to live on the coffee table. Her parents somehow subdued the influence of her seal for years, and she hoped her mother had written it down somewhere.

"I'll pack them when I'm ready." She closed it, the grimoire growling at her touch, pages moving as if to cut her.

A glint to her left. Alice reached over a box, finding a small gold token with the sigil of a jawless skull.

"Oh shit!" Sam said when he noticed. "Sorry about that, I found it ages ago in your jewellery box and used it for a stage show. I was supposed to return it."

Alice turned the token, studying the etchings around the edge. "A show?"

"Yeah," Sam said. "I was a sexy pirate!"

The laugh that erupted lasted for minutes, her stomach aching by the time she had finished. The idea that Sam had used the token as a stage prop for his stripping Pirate show tickled her.

Sam grabbed the token, rolling it between his fingers.

"Do you know what," she said when the laughter died down and Sam had placed the token back in the carboard box. "I hate this house, I'm glad we're moving."

"Baby girl..."

"I think we should leave Frederick a welcome gift, don't you?"

Sam grinned, rushing into the kitchen and returning with a paint can and brush. "You ready?" he asked as he opened the lid to the dark blue, almost black paint.

"Thank the goddess for your love of D.I.Y." Alice dipped her brush, stepping over to write 'FUCK YOU!' in large letters across the living room wall.

Sam stayed back, hand clutching his chin as he watched her paint as if he was in an art gallery. "Now that is perfection," he said, putting on a fake posh accent. "The colour, the composition, the simplicity is just..." he dramatically made a kissing sound. "Gorgeous darling. A masterpiece."

Alice laughed, handing over the brush so Sam could express himself too. She hated the house. She hated the memories that were no longer happy, her biological father ruining it. Her first thoughts were no longer the times when she laughed as a child, her brother playing hide and seek or her mother baking cookies. No, she only saw the nightmares of Jackson shouting. Jackson shutting himself away after an argument with his wife, or the daemon Jackson summoned to take her.

No, she hated the house. And she hated him.

"Kyle would have enjoyed this," she whispered.

Sam paused, dropping the paint brush. "Yeah, he never understood why we lived here."

"Hmmm." Alice found herself sitting on the floor, legs crossed. The wall was a mess of profanities and crudely

drawn pictures. Paint fumes tickled her nose as Sam settled beside her.

"Have you spoken to him lately?" Sam asked, nudging her shoulder. He brushed a hair away from her face, and from the wetness she knew he had left a streak of blue.

Dread once told her Kyle would return home when he was ready. It was sound advice. Her brother needed time to understand the events with The Knights, and when he was ready she would be there to help him. "He's an adult."

"Yeah, but he's an adult with issues."

Alice turned her head. "Aren't we all?"

Sam chuckled. "Touché." He rested his head against her. "I think Elduin and Peyton are madly in love and should mate and adopt five-hundred little elf babies."

"Five-hundred, huh?"

"Yep," he chirped, stroking Poe who decided to sit between them for attention. "Just like you and Riley."

Alice remained silent, watching the paint dry.

"Come on baby girl, talk to me." He nudged her again. "It's been over a week and you haven't mentioned him. What happened when he picked you up?"

Alice pursed her lips.

Nothing had happened, because she had never felt so complete than when he stepped into the café, drenched from the rain. She had launched herself at him, locking her arms around his neck as if she would never let go. But she couldn't have him.

"He hurts himself when he's with me," she finally said, voice cracking. "I can't do that to him."

"Love can hurt, baby girl."

"It's not the same."

"Is it not?" He climbed up, hands on his hips. "All I'm

hearing is one excuse why you shouldn't be together. Not all the reasons why you should."

"I don't want to be the thing that destroys him." She couldn't.

"Then find a way around it."

Alice wrapped her arms around her knees. Poe head-butted her hand, purring when she scratched behind his ears. "Find a way around it," she murmured.

But what if there was no way around it?

CHAPTER THIRTY

Alice got out the car before she lost the nerve. She had a key, but she still lifted a fist to knock on the door three times.

"Please be in," she whispered, nervously dancing from one foot to the left. "Shit."

What if he was at work? What if he didn't want to speak to her? Riley had driven across the country to get her when she called, and in return she told him she needed time to herself.

"I'm such an arsehole!"

She knocked again, louder.

The door swung open, and Riley stood there dressed in casual jeans and a tight black t-shirt, and her very carefully prepared speech about how she was an idiot and could he forgive her vanished.

"Alice?"

"I love you," she blurted, panic rising. "I'm sorry, we need to talk and figure us out..."

His lips swallowed the rest, her arms immediately wrapping around his neck as he lifted her into his embrace.

"Say it again," he growled.

"Riley, I..." A moan, his lips crushing hers once again. She pulled him towards her, savouring the rough embrace that she craved. "Stop it!" she laughed, pulling back.

"Alice Skye, I have loved you from the first time we met."

"The first time we met you tied me to a chair," she narrowed her eyes. "In my underwear."

"Exactly," he grinned. "You sat there making jokes as if you were in complete control of the situation. You, Alice Skye are the strongest woman I have ever met, and I'm in love with you."

Alice dropped her head, resting it against his chest. "Riley, we need to figure out your beast..."

"I know sweetheart, we'll figure it out." He stroked her hair, fingers tangled in the length. "Together."

Alice tilted her head, looking up at him. "You ever think we just weren't meant to be?"

Riley smiled, just a deliciously slow curve of his lip. "Never."

* * *

She stared at the pathetic Fallen that was chained, his head low as blood blinded him. It dripped to the floor, the earth greedily soaking it up.

The second seal had broken, revealing more of her memories, but with it went Famine. She didn't have time to wait for another Air to be born, no, not when she was so close.

"I've heard of you," the Fallen coughed, blood splattering his dark skin. "I know what you're after."

"Do you now," she purred, kneeling in the dirt to touch his face. She smirked at his flinch, the once strong celestrial nothing but a whimpering shell.

She remembered the Fallen, also remembered the celestrials that were once a thorn in her side. They caused trouble, hunting her when she was on Earth Side before... before... she couldn't remember.

But she knew it was a celestrial that betrayed her, who had helped someone of her blood bind her, punish her. But why was she punished? Why was she hunted?

Pestilence stood to the side, his leg lifting up to kick the

Fallen to the ground, his boot adding pressure to his head a second later. Nether rats scuttled around him, bigger than those found on Earth Side with smoke floating between their exposed ribs. They chattered to one another, waiting with patience for their master to command them.

They would carry diseases to those above, and messages for those below.

"I need to open a stronger portal, and your blood will allow me to do that." She nodded to Pestilence who pressed down with his boot.

"No, no, wait!" he wheezed. "Please, dark elf!"

Pestilence yanked the Fallen up by his throat, only releasing enough pressure for him to speak.

"Dark elf?" she asked, touching the tips of her pointy ears.

Yes, that was what she was, an elf. But why dark?

A memory echoed, but it was cast in shadow.

She needed another seal.

"I can help," the Fallen licked his lips, eyes darting. "I can help you find another Horseman."

"Bullshit," Pestilence growled.

"Wait," she said, lifting a hand. "How can you find another Horseman?"

"My mother."

Pestilence tightened his grip.

"She lives in Aetherna," the Fallen wheezed, eyes bulging. "She can find out where Death resides."

"Death?" Pestilence released his hand, the Fallen crashing to the earth.

"How can you find Death?" she asked. "They are yet to connect to their seal."

"My mother was a watcher, she can help."

She smiled, a laugh building up her throat. She guessed it

wouldn't be long at all, because once she knew where Death was, it was only War they had to trap.

And she already knew who War was.

Then she would be complete.

And the veil will fall.

EPILOGUE

Valentina tapped her long nails on the side of the chair, watching her fellow councilmen carefully as they took their own seats in the circle. She paid extra attention to Frederick, whose nervous pulse was a siren to her constant hunger.

"Mon ami, are you well?" she asked him with a dangerous smile. He stood on behalf of both the witches and mages on The Council, supposedly the strongest of them all. Yet, she knew he had been weakened recently with the betrayal of one of his pet black witches.

Xavier sniggered, jumping up to crouch on his chair with bare feet. "Yes Fred, are you well?"

Frederick flushed, jaw clenched as he looked away. It had been Xavier who had taken down the black witch, and from the mark across his left eye it looked like he didn't come out of it unscathed.

Valentina smirked, knowing the tiger would have thought it a trophy.

Xavier was one of the only councilmembers who met

her stare dead on, the others but a fleeting glance. She would have been impressed if she knew it wasn't because he thought of himself higher than her.

"Valentina, I've heard you're having problems back in Paris," he purred, pointedly showing his teeth.

But he seemed to have forgotten, she also had fangs. "Is that what you've heard?" she laughed, sipping from her red-tainted glass.

"What is the meaning of this meeting?" Bartholomew asked as he took his own seat. "The message was very vague."

"Did you not–"

"– call this meeting?" Quention finished for his sister, Liliannia. "We were told–"

"– that we were required here in person." The twin faeries occupied the last seat on behalf of all Fae, with Liliannia sitting in the seat, and Quention sitting on the armrest.

Xavier chuckled, resting back in his chair. "I too received a message."

Frederick frowned, tugging at his velvet lapels. "I didn't call this meeting."

Valentina pursed her lips disapprovingly. "Then who?"

"That would be me," a voice called.

A man appeared, a silhouette against the door. Behind him he dragged a large hellhound. He lifted the beast, throwing it into the centre of The Council with a heavy squelch. Valentina felt the warm spray of the blood on her face, but her attention remained on the tall celestrian with wings of copper.

Frederick jumped from his seat, looking down at the corpse in disgust. "Who are you?"

The angel stretched his wings, the span as large as the room, large enough to carry such a heavy weight through the skies. With a click they disappeared into his back.

"My name is Cassiel, and I'm here because the first seal has broken, and a horseman has arisen."

Valentina gripped the arm of the chair, her nails cutting through the hard wood.

"I've heard rumours," Frederick said when no one else spoke. "We should have done what I wanted with Alice, now there's a chance the prophecy may come to light," he muttered, returning to his seat.

"It doesn't work with just one," Liliannia snapped, Quention remaining silent beside her. "It requires a minimum of two to barely scratch the surface of the veil."

"My Guardians have reported an increase of Shadow-Veyn across Russia and eastern Europe," Bart added. "And increased activity in Daemon possessions."

"Someone is agitating those imprisoned below," Quention turned his lilac eyes to the celestrial. "What can you tell us–"

"– about this?" Liliannia finished.

Xavier scraped his claws down the chair, leaving deep marks. "Tell me more about the below."

Cassiel smiled, dark eyebrow raised. "The Nether was created by the Fae in penance, but maintained by a powerful heart, a Fallen. It is he who is stirring up trouble, organising an army."

"How do you know of this?" Valentina asked.

Cassiel ignored the question. "There are strong Fae imprisoned, as well as some Fallen and creatures like the one I have gifted you." He kicked at the hellhound.

Valentina carefully stepped down from her seat, not

caring that her dress mopped up the blood from the dog. "Monsieur, why are you here?" She stepped up to him, having to tilt her head. "Celestrians have no interest in politique."

Cassiel looked down at her with disinterest. "I believe a change is due, don't you agree?" He turned to address the group. "The Wild Hunt is coming, and you're going to need my help to stop it."

https://www.amazon.com/gp/product/B08V85B86L

VEIL'S FALL
CHAPTER ONE

Why was she nervous?

She had beaten Daemons, a corrupt Archdruid, hell-hounds and trials by The Council, and not once had she been nervous.

Riley gripped her hand tighter, almost as if he sensed her hesitation.

"I don't trust you," Alice whispered as they walked side by side, towering lights glittering around them. It was a beautiful summer night, the sun setting in the distance to give the sky a pink hue that softened the hardened city of glass and steel that she called home.

Riley's chuckle made her shiver, anticipation overtaking the butterflies that twisted her stomach.

He was definitely up to something, she thought, a smile tugging her lips. It had been a while since she had seen him, her eyes taking in his profile appreciatively. The Guardians had been busier than usual, meaning their dates had consisted of hurried phone calls late at night.

She understood, her work picking up also, keeping her just as busy. However, the fact it was the first time she had

seen him physically in a couple weeks meant nothing considering her instincts were screaming that there was something he was keeping from her.

"Seriously," she said louder, tugging his hand for him to stop. "What is up with you?"

"Maybe I'm just enjoying spending some time with you?" he replied, wiggling his eyebrows. "Maybe I'm just enjoying spending some time with you, alone."

Alice's smile began to hurt. "We're not exactly alone." Someone walked past, nudging them gently before they moved to the edge of the pavement.

It only emphasised her point.

Alone time didn't come easy, not when their lives were so active. With the increased Shadow-Veyn sightings and portals across the world, Alice knew they were running out of time.

She was running out of time.

Her hand crept up to the small seal draped around her throat, the hollow coin cold against her palm. The voices were silent, but she never knew for how long. Riley noticed her anxious move, his own coming up to wrap around hers in a comfort she welcomed.

His fingers continued moving up to cup her jaw, his chi stretching to cause electrical sensations across her own. She sighed when his lips touched hers, the kiss deliciously slow before developing into something more. She had to concentrate to stop the moan from escaping when he moved to kiss down her neck, his teeth biting down gently on the sensitive place in the crook of her shoulder.

"Stop it," she growled, her voice deepening. "You're distracting me."

His next kiss was rough, his hands hooking under her thighs to pull her closer to his height. "Is it working?"

"Riley!"

"Come on," he laughed, setting her back down on her feet. "Let's go grab a drink from Blood Bar, I need to finish up some paperwork anyway."

It was definitely a distraction, but one she would embrace until their demanding lives split them apart once again.

The walk was only short before they were at the bar, the velvet rope outside suspiciously void of the usual crowd.

"Do you have weapons on you?" Riley paused, watching her from the corner of his eye.

Alice's anxiety spiked. "Riley?" she said more sternly than before. "What have you done?"

Riley's eyes dropped down to her thighs, laughter dancing behind his irises as he tried to spot the hidden weapons he knew she had. "Do you trust me?" He pushed at the door.

The nerves heightened, stomach twisting. "What have you...?"

"SURPRISE!"

"SURPRISE!"

"SURPRISE!"

It was only Riley's hands centred on her waist that stopped her from going for the knives she had strapped to her thighs.

"Bloody hell!" She was grateful that her control was good enough to not instinctively burn the place down.

"Happy birthday, sweetheart," he whispered into her ear.

"I'm going to kill you," she hissed back, her heart a rabbit in her chest.

Sam grinned from the bar, his height towering over everyone as he walked the length of it, much to the annoy-

ance of the bartender. Alistair, Brady, Michelle, Jones, Elduin and Peyton were just a few of her friends that held up their drinks. As well as her old Paladin colleagues, Rose and Bee.

The tall tables had been placed around the dance floor with little candles on mirrored glass. The stage was empty except a single microphone, a banner stating *'HAPPY BIRTHDAY'* draped across the front.

"A party?" She was engulfed in hugs and greetings. "You closed the bar for me?" she whispered to Riley, who smiled when she turned to face him.

His hand squeezed hers. "I know you want privacy."

And they both knew privacy was something she was giving up by being with him. She wanted to stay under the radar as much as possible, especially as she was still figuring out her powers. The paparazzi had been interested enough to make her life more difficult, but It would be much easier if the newspapers and magazines weren't watching, waiting for her to fall.

It was the reason she no longer enjoyed reading any gossip magazine.

"The party, however, was Sam's idea," he continued.

"Of course it was!" Sam chuckled as he rushed her, crushing her into a bear hug that lifted her off the floor. "My baby girl deserves the best party considering the last year!"

Alice waited for him to release her before stepping back into Riley's waiting arms. "Sam, my birthday was a few weeks ago."

"Aye, It's why it's called a *'surprise'* party," he replied, rolling his eyes before moving back towards the bar. "Who wants shots?!"

"Don't worry," Riley murmured into her hair, "he'll be fine."

Maybe, she thought to herself, knowing he was still in pain from losing his friend. Sam was used to loss, but that didn't mean it didn't affect him in ways his flamboyant personality disguised. Ash had survived his ordeal, but their relationship hadn't.

So if Sam wanted to throw her a surprise birthday party several weeks late, then so be it.

"Thank you for letting Sam have the party here," she said, examining the tissue paper stars hanging from the ceiling. "And I'm really sorry for undoubtedly the amount of glitter he's used."

A kiss to her bare shoulder. "Next year we're going away for the weekend. Just you and me."

Alice turned in his embrace, noticing the liquid silver in his eyes.

"Seriously though," she said, placing her palm over his heart, "good luck cleaning up all the glitter."

"Hmmm." A kiss to her bare palm. "Maybe we can go somewhere hot..."

"You'll be finding those sparkly bastards in your crevasses for weeks."

He brushed his thumb across her bottom lip. "I love you."

Three simple words tightened her chest. She initiated the kiss this time, keeping it soft as she showed him exactly what she felt.

The microphone gave off a high-pitched whine.

Tap. Tap. Tap.

"If you would please excuse the disgusting public display of affection over there from the birthday girl," Sam chuckled. "I would like to start the karaoke!"

"Oh, us!" Michelle squeaked from her table, hand raised. "We'll go first!"

"Wait, we?" Brady grumbled, his deep tone carrying across the room with little effort.

Sam handed over the microphone, smirking as Brady begrudgingly joined his wife on stage. From the glazed eyes she had clearly had a few drinks, and Alice didn't blame her considering it was the first time she had seen Michelle without their gorgeous baby.

"I need to speak to the Guardians." Riley nodded to Xander who stood in the corner, arms crossed and pale eyes scanning the crowd. The room looked empty compared to a normal night, so he stood out in the dark shadows even more so. When Riley turned back to her, his eyes hardened.

"Ma petite sorcière, I hope you don't mind my intrusion," a familiar voice said from behind.

Alice froze, lips pursed. "D?" She hadn't heard him sneak up on her, but then again, he was a vampire. "What are you doing here?"

"How damaged is my door?" Riley asked, annoyance husking his tone.

Danton looked between them, dark eyes in skin as pale as snow. He looked horrifying, his usual humanity he wore like a mask gone. "Pardon, but I need to speak to you urgently."

Riley kissed her palm once more, never taking his eyes off Danton. "I'll just be over there," he whispered, moving towards Xander who had already began in their direction.

"What do you want D?" She gestured for him to move to the side, waiting until both Riley and Xander were out of ear shot before continuing. "Why have you gate-crashed my party?"

"I have no way of contacting you since you moved, and you haven't replied to my calls."

She studied his lean face, his skin pulled tight across his skull with deep bruises beneath his eyes. "You look like shit. What's happened?"

Danton tightened his smile. "I'm here to warn you that Matteo has been spotted in the city."

"Matteo?" she frowned, thinking back. "The Italian that shot you?"

"Oui." His attention slipped behind her. Just then Rose took to the stage, her voice only marginally better than Michelle's. Alice turned too, watching one of her oldest Paladin friends take the mic as if she did it regularly. She looked cute in her short skirt and heels, brown hair tied up in a high ponytail that swung around her shoulders as she swayed along to her the music. Her eyes scanned the crowd, enjoying the cheers before they settled on Danton. Her panther immediately appeared in her irises, her voice taking on a husky growl as she continued singing without pause.

Alice returned her attention to her former friend. "Why would it matter that Matteo's in the city?" When he continued to stare behind her she waved her hand. "D?"

"It was not intentional," came his reply, even though he still faced the stage, body rigid. "But he may remember you from the townhouse. I just wanted to warn you to be careful." When his eyes finally met hers they were darker, his pupils dilated. "Hopefully he will pay you no consideration considering you are nothing in the world of immortals."

Charming, she thought dryly. "Thanks for the warning." She had no interest in dealing with vampire politics.

"It's the least I owe you."

Applause erupted as Rose finished her song. Alice

expected her to march over and confront D, but instead she headed for the bar, her back purposely turned towards them. Alice wasn't sure if D was disappointed or relieved.

"You should speak to her, you know." She had no idea what had happened between them, but they had been partners at S.I. for three years before Danton disappeared back to France, back to his Mistress.

When Danton replied, his voice was heavy with emotion. "There are reasons I push people away. Reasons I choose to have five women in my bed rather than one. It's safer... for all those involved."

"You think she can't handle her own?" Rose was one of the strongest women she knew.

Danton shook his head. "Un jour j'espère que nous pourrons redevenir amis."

Alice rolled her eyes. "English, D!"

Danton bowed, the movement elegant as a small smile tipped his lips. "Apologise to Riley for the door, s'il te plaît." He left as fast as he appeared, giving one last look towards the bar, and his old partner.

(CHAPTER BREAK)

Alice smiled over her cocktail at Michelle, who was being carried off on Brady's shoulder, drunk. After several hours, too many poorly sang songs and half the bar drained dry, people were starting to filter home. Sam, who had a few drinks of his own, was belting out a ballad as hard as he could, his words slightly slurred while Jones provided back-up.

Peyton sat beside her, agitated with his hand curled around a beer, the drink barely touched as he watched Elduin attempt to juggle glasses with the bartender.

"You look jealous," Alice stated, hiding her smirk behind her drink.

Peyton slanted his eyes in her direction. "Don't be so ludicrous." He flicked at his silver hair, tugging it back to reveal his pointy ear, the tip pink. "Should we be concerned about that?" he gestured to Axel, who cradled a bottle of whiskey like a lifeline.

"How many has he had?"

"I've counted five," Peyton replied gruffly.

"Drinks?"

"Bottles."

Her eyebrows raised, but she knew Peyton was deflecting. "You want to talk about it?"

"Drinking that much is impressive." He took a sip of his own beer, the same beer he had been drinking all night. Alice hadn't had much more, the cocktail she cradled only her second. "Makes us look like light weights."

She was a light weight when it came to alcohol. But that wasn't something she was going to admit.

Peyton smirked as if he knew, which was possible knowing him especially when their familiar connection flared with a comforting warmth. Peyton seemed to know what she was feeling, even at a distance, so the increased awareness was something Alice was still trying to learn. So far all his emotions felt the same. Which wasn't all that surprising considering she thought he had the emotional depth of a plastic doll. Just a plastic doll who seemed to be very interested in his commander. Not many people could say they had their own commanders, but he was the Dark Fae Prince after all. A Dark Fae Prince who casually worked as a Detective Constable for the notorious Spook Squad.

"Why are you giggling?"

Alice blinked, the bubbles on her tongue popping. It

only proved she was indeed a light weight. "Just thinking about Spook Squad," she said, which was only a partial lie. There seemed to always be enough cases to keep Spook Squad busy, enough so that the team had expanded into various locations across the British Isles and talks about more in Europe. It was definitely a step in the right direction for Breed.

"This is supposed to be your birthday party, you shouldn't be thinking about work."

"Said the elf that doesn't even celebrate birthdays."

Peyton shrugged. "Why would I count?"

"You're just old."

A glass dropped from a height, but Elduin caught it with little effort. Peyton sat, shoulders tight with ears that continued to glow.

"Peyton..."

"Kyra's here," he grunted, turning.

"Kyra?"

Alice automatically spun on her stool, watching as Kyra walked in dressed in black leather, eyes scanning the large room until they settled at the bar.

"I invited her," Peyton explained. "You need more friends."

Alice shoved him. "Excuse me?" She actually liked Kyra, the witch interesting with a dark sense of humour. She had a compassion that was unexpected in a magic user trained in blood. "I have friends."

"You need ones that aren't tied to you as a familiar."

"You're a dick, you know that right?"

"I'm sorry I'm late," Kyra said, tugging her long dark braid, bound so tight Alice wondered if she would have wild curls. "I was caught at the mortuary."

"Mortuary?" Alice asked as Kyra took the stool to her left. "Why were you there so late?"

"A member of Dr Anderson's team asked me to attend," Kyra said with a frown, "they're having... problems with some of the recently deceased."

"Problems?"

Kyra bit her bottom lip, a crease appearing between her brows. "Actually, is there anywhere we can speak privately?" She leaned forward as Sam started another song, even louder than before. "I would like both of you to give me your opinion on it."

"Sure," Alice said as she pushed her cocktail away. "Riley's office is sound proof. Follow me."

Sam's less than desired singing voice dampened when they started up the stairs, the corridor leading to the glass office dim. Lifting her fist she knocked against the heavy door. Riley answered, his features hardened with Xander equally annoyed over his shoulder.

"I'm sorry..."

"You okay sweetheart?" Riley asked, noticing Kyra. "We've just finished. You need the office?" He stepped to the side, allowing them to enter. The office was lit only by the glass wall that looked down onto the bar. It bathed the desk in the centre of the room in a soft light, but kept shadows in the corners. Alice looked down through the one way mirror, a smile tipping her lips at the sight of Sam, Alistair and Jones all singing into the single microphone. She couldn't hear the song, or even the vibration of the beat, but from their puffed cheeks they were giving it their all.

"Xander, we will give them the room," Riley said as both Kyra and Peyton joined her.

Xander grunted, arms crossed. "You should be wary of dark witches."

"Oh?" Kyra tensed, shoulders tight. "What specifically should you be wary about?" Her voice was quiet, but there was steel behind the calm.

Xander moved closer, his wrap around glasses hiding his expression. The snarl he wore softened, but he gave no reply. After a few moments passed a flush brightened the bronzed brown of Kyra's skin.

Riley cleared his throat, and Xander growled.

"Xee?"

Xander's snarl returned, but he left without hesitation.

When Kyra continued to stare at the closed door Alice stepped forward. "You wanted to show us something?"

"Oh." Kyra frowned, pulling out her phone. "I need you to take a look at this." She held out her arm, revealing a photograph on the screen.

There were eight bodies, all lined up one by one and covered by identical matching sheets. White. Clinical.

What a surprise, Alice thought as Peyton looked with crossed brows. *White sheets.* She had visited the morgue enough times in her lifetime to understand the reason hospitals used white, but the absence of colour always tightened her chest.

"What's out of the ordinary?" Peyton asked.

Kyra flicked to the next picture, which showed Dr Anderson standing beside the furthest left gurney, the white sheet in her hand.

"What the fuck..." Alice blinked, trying to understand what she was seeing. The sheet had revealed the head and upper torso of a male, and he was opaque. "Can I see that?" Kyra handed over her phone for Alice to flip through the next few images herself.

The deceased looked human, but Alice could just make out scratch marks on the metal table beneath his chest. It wasn't as if his skin was opaque, it was everything.

It was Peyton who broke the stunned silence, his voice deeper when he spoke. "How long has he been like this?"

"Just over twenty-four hours."

"And his cause of death?"

"Dr Anderson hasn't determined that yet," Kyra replied, holding her hand out for the phone. "They were registered as human, but I suspect they're Fae."

Alice remained silent, watching Peyton as he gave a subtle nod. Fae didn't usually decompose like humans and other Breed, they broke down at a much faster rate and returned to the earth.

"There are seven others?" he asked, mouth tight.

Kyra clicked through the images. "This is Number Eight, and she's been with them the longest, closer to sixty-two hours."

They could barely make out the female, her body completely transparent.

"Could you see anything through your third eye?" Alice asked.

"No, that's why I wanted both your opinions. I've never heard of anything like this."

"They're being absorbed." Peyton shook his head, jaw clenched. "They're being absorbed for their power. It's a fate worse than death, outlawed by both courts." He turned away.

"Who could have done this?" Alice asked.

Peyton hesitated. "I don't know. Where were they found? Was there any jewellery?"

Kyra tugged on her braid. "I'm not sure, I wasn't given that information. Is that important?"

Peyton grunted, moving to stand over by the one-way mirrored wall. He stared down into the bar, arms crossed. He was asking if there was evidence of what court they belonged to, if either. Two courts, the Light Fae of the Seelie Court and the Dark Fae of the Unseelie Court. Light usually adorned emeralds while dark would wear ruby.

Alice wasn't sure what it meant to be part of either court, of what they had to do with the eight disappearing corpses. But it looked like something dire was happening, because she was confident she just felt felt fear pass through the Dark Prince.

VEIL'S FALL
CHAPTER TWO

"I see you've already begun decorating," Riley laughed when he pulled up outside her new place. "Looks... festive."

"You know the deal with the new landlord," she muttered, staring at the faerie lights Sam had strung from the roof to the tall, yet to be cut hedges.

The little lights twinkled amongst the stars, giving the worn down building a magical glow. Sam had decided not to return to Club X, not with the animosity amongst the wolves. So when he saw an abandoned train station advertised in the paper, he negotiated a price with the owners that if he renovated it, they would get half rent. It gave him a passion project to help him take his mind off the past, while also sorting out a place for them both to stay after being evicted from her family home.

Sam snored loudly, as if even in his sleep he had to comment. He was draped across the back seat of Riley's car, arm thrown dramatically over his eyes while his mouth lay wide open. Alice couldn't tell you the model, but it was a dark blue and purred silently down the tight streets. Her

new home was on the outskirts of the city, where the buildings got smaller and the views became greener. It was further from her work, but being able to be closer to nature while still seeing, and being part of the city was a great compromise.

The small train station had been deserted for close to ten years, the train line retiring to be replaced with faster, more up to date tracks only a few miles up the road. The tracks that weren't ripped up or built over were hidden beneath bushes and overgrown grass in their new garden.

"Come on," Riley whispered as he carefully manoeuvred Sam onto his shoulder. "Let's get you to bed."

Sam groaned as he was lifted, but otherwise remained asleep.

The large wooden door creaked open when Alice unlocked it, the inside cold compared to the warmth of outside. The lights flickered to life, whining before they settled into a steady hum. It illuminated the room, revealing the scratched, worn wooden flooring to the bare brick of the walls.

Their sofa and tv were set up in the space to the right, the left full of boxes yet to unpack and decorating supplies that they planned to turn into her office. Directly behind their living room was a semi-modern kitchen that looked out into what would have been the platform. There was a wall that separated the kitchen to the main room, but that was the first thing Sam had knocked down. The bathroom jutted out, breaking up the soon-to-be study and the back creating an open-plan 'L' shape. Squatters years before had turned the two bathrooms into one, saving Sam the job. It awkwardly had two toilets and two sinks, while a bath had been placed in the centre where the wall would have been.

"Where's his room?" Riley asked, adjusting Sam who was moaning in his sleep.

Alice walked him through to the kitchen, pointing out the spiral metal staircase that went to the platform above their heads. It used to be the old managers office, which was around half the size of the whole floorplan, but with railings looking down into the living room and office. Alice, on the other hand, had the small room right at the back beside the kitchen. It was the old ticket office, including the glass partition which she immediately covered with thick curtains. The only bonus for having the smaller bedroom was that she had the storage room attached, which Sam had the bright idea to turn into a walk in wardrobe. It was great except Alice didn't have that many clothes.

The kettle had already boiled, and Alice poured two cups of tea before Riley remerged.

"He propose to you again?" Alice asked, keeping her voice low. At Riley's smirk she laughed, muffling the sound with her hand. Sam had a tendency to propose his undying love to the closest person when he'd had a few drinks. Which always amused her considering he had repeatedly stated he was not a one-person guy, and would never be tied down to something as "mundane" as mating.

"Is there a reason your cat is suddenly white? I distinctly remember him being black."

Alice sipped her cup of tea, embracing the warmth in her palms. "It's non-toxic paint," she explained. Her cat, and other familiar was far too interested in the water-based paint Sam was using on the walls of his bedroom. She had caught him several times trying to climb into a pot, or licking the freshly coated walls. She was just grateful that it was a specialised paint and would cause him no harm.

Riley approached, taking the mug from her hands and placing it beside his own, untouched cup. "How did you enjoy your surprise party?" he whispered, his breath intimate against her skin.

"I learnt a lot of my friends are tone deaf." Including herself, but she knew that already. "You should have told me about the party."

"What part of 'surprise' don't you understand, sweetheart?" he chuckled, lip curved in a way that made her flush with anticipation. "Besides, you can't be mad at me. I didn't plan it, that was all on your roommate."

Alice rolled her eyes. "It was fun, and also explains why Sam has been weird all week." On her actual birthday they watched an action movie together over at his place. What was supposed to be just them quickly turned into a group as the other six guardians joined. She couldn't remember any of the film, she was too distracted with them all bickering between themselves regarding the unrealistic fight scenes. A quick call and Sam had joined them, bringing with him a cheap supermarket birthday cake which was eaten before Alice even got a look in.

There was no fuss. No overbearing attention.

It was perfect.

"Your grimoire is out." Riley gestured to the thick leather book that was left open on the kitchen counter. "What were you searching for?" His voice deepened, his eyes settling on her lips even though she knew she had his full attention.

"That bloody thing," she sighed. "Useless piece of crap."

It was her mothers, the grimoire aggressive, hissing as if it knew it was being spoken about. She had more than one mark across her fingers from when it would randomly change the page, slicing her with a papercut.

"You're searching for the spell your mother used." He said, matter of factly.

Alice clutched the seal draped between her breasts, the surface cold as usual. Whispers hissed, indistinguishable before she dropped it, allowing it to settle once again hidden beneath her shirt. Her crystal, on the other hand, was warm against the hollow of her throat, comforting.

Riley moved forward, hooking his hands beneath her legs until he had her sat on the edge of the counter, his body positioned between her thighs.

"She somehow muted the seals aura of effect. Why can't I?" Alice had her spells and hand written recipes. Yet the one thing she needed wasn't there. What exactly did her mother have to do that she felt she couldn't write it down? What did she have to sacrifice?

Riley placed a finger beneath her chin, pushing gently until she met the liquid silver of his eyes. If she didn't figure out the seal soon...

She would never allow herself to turn into War, to embrace the power that whispered to her in the dead of the night. A power that scared those who understood it more than herself.

She knew she didn't have long.

And deep down, he knew that too.

"Kiss me."

Riley's lips touched hers before the words even finished, his tongue like silk as she savoured his strength and warmth beneath her palms. She pulled him impossibly closer before she angled her neck so he could easier claim the kiss.

A loud bang, directly above them.

"Fuck sake, you sound like horny teenagers!" Sam

shouted, his voice easily carrying over the open-air bannister down to the bottom floor.

"Go to sleep!" Riley growled, ignoring him as he nipped at the sensitive flesh between her throat and shoulder.

Sam banged again. "Poe is blushing with all that moaning! You have a perfectly nice bedroom, why are you shagging in the kitchen?"

Alice laughed, tugging at Riley's hair as she slipped off the counter. "You should go, Xander mentioned you were going out tonight."

Riley sighed, stepping back. "We still haven't figured out why there's a sudden increase in activity." He tilted his head, hair brushing down to cover his eyes. "Get some sleep, it's been a busy night."

Alice smiled, hoping the exhaustion that she felt didn't show. She hadn't slept properly in weeks, if not longer, and as she waved him out the door she knew she wouldn't be going to bed, not straight away. Not when she had work to do herself. Answers to find.

The sky was still dark, which meant she had a few hours left until dawn. A few hours before she had to pretend that everything was okay, and that the voices weren't howling at her. Pressuring her.

If there was one thing she had learnt from her mother's grimoire was that old magic evolved over time, changing in ways not many people understood. Her seal was once a gift to help with her ancestors powers, to mute the Elemental's magic until the bearer decided whether to accept or not. A choice.

But now the seal was an hour glass, and one crack could overwhelm it until she had no choice.

Find the others.

Ride together.

Become one.

The grimoire snarled when she picked it up, the leather undulating beneath her fingertips as she made her way into her bedroom. She left the door open, the sound of Sam snoring heavily something she could use to help drown out the whispers.

Poe jumped up only seconds later, his large eyes watching her with curiosity as he settled himself into his favourite position on her pillow. He had white flecks across his dark fur as well as an entirely white nose. She scratched him behind his ears, their familiar connection strengthening the closer they were. He seemed to find security in it, his purr loud.

"Meow." He settled his head in his paws, bright pink tongue stuck to the outside of his mouth.

Sitting cross-legged on her duvet, with her cat watching her through slit eyes she opened the grimoire for what must have be the thousandth time. She was missing something, there had to be a spell or recipe she could use. The grimoire turned a page, forcing her to start again. It growled when she pinned it open, but calmed down once she began to stroke her fingers down the edge slowly. Each time it opened, the pages had rearranged or moved. It created so many combinations that even though she had read it so many times before, it was like it was the first time.

There must be something here, she thought, *anything.* She just had to figure it out.

So no, she couldn't sleep, not until she figured out how to contain, or even control the power that was a pendulum hanging over her head. She needed to take control of her own fate.

Loving *Veil's Fall*? Order your copy today!

https://www.amazon.com/gp/product/B09791CXMR

THE ALICE SKYE SERIES

Witch's Sorrow

Druid's Storm

Rogue's Mercy

Elemental's Curse

Knight's War

Veil's Fall

About the Author

Taylor Aston White loves to explore mythology and European faerie tales to create her own, modern magic world. She collects crystals, house plants and dark lipstick, and has two young children who like to 'help' with her writing by slamming their hands across the keyboard.

After working several uncreative jobs, and one super creative one, she decided to become a full-time author and now spends the majority of her time between her children, and writing the weird and wonderful stories that pop into her head.

Made in United States
North Haven, CT
27 January 2024

48003430R00189